Enfie

GW00341892

Lunbrick			
7|18			
10|9			

Please remember that this item will attract overdue charges if not returned by the latest date stamped above. You may renew it in person, by telephone or by post quoting the bar code number and your library card number, or online at http://libraries.enfield.gov.uk.

www.enfield.gov.uk

THANKS TO...

Linda Patrick, Sharon Reid (design), Jacqui Howchin of Waterstones,
Lorna Cracknell and Elizabeth Mackie

Publisher address: 484 Oundle Road, Peterborough, UK PE2 7DF
neil.patrick1@ntlworld.com

ISBN 978-0-9576083-4-4

Also by Neil Patrick...

The Healing Hut (ISBN 978-0-9576083-0-6)
Just Dying To Tell (ISBN978-0-9576083-2-0)

Hey There (biography – out of print)

1

Seven weeks had passed since the poisoning. But for Gus, the shock of it all didn't ease. In fact, on his walk this morning he'd accepted that he would never get over it. There simply wasn't enough healing time.

Gus liked to think that his little treks to the top of Haig Bank – taken daily now – were helping him cope but he knew that it would take more than fresh air and exercise.

He stopped to take a breather, well short of the pines at the top of the rise. His heart had begun to thump alarmingly as he tramped through the ferns that clothed the hillside.

Gus leaned on his stick for support but rocked slightly in the wind, like an ancient tree with rotten roots. Today he had found his limit.

The dogs were a hundred yards ahead now, rampaging wildly through the gorse, over the hill brow and into the copse, way up above the village. He so envied their manic energy.

Gus felt damp warmth on his back, beneath his oiled jacket. He had to face it; walks were almost joyless now. It was not so much that old age seemed suddenly to be catching up with him; it was because Olly was no longer around.

There had been terrible consequences of the business at *Zac's*. Untypically for such a giving man, he felt an almost childish resentment that it had robbed him of the company of someone special.

Autumn was on its last legs. Winter was gaining pace. Gus watched the ragged clouds being bowled along the skyline by a biting, relentless wind that had made this morning's outing something of a fitness test. Then he gazed down to the buff church tower, and the cluster of homes made of the same honeyed stone.

The anger was rising in him again. Just as the walks were different now, so was his view of his fellow men. He would never feel the same about the folks he lived alongside, the people down there.

Neighbours. So-called friends. He had always rubbed along with them, making allowances, giving and taking. But now he couldn't help despising their insularity.

He scanned the neat row of age-mellowed cottages, each fronted by autumn foliage; splashes of scarlet, yellow, purple, fading green. The wind was loosening the last of the leaves and scattering them like thrown rose petals.

There they all are, he said to himself; out of the wind, snug and safe beneath their thatched roofs; walled up against change. They'll be content now that Olly has been vanquished but they'll be missing the notoriety that for weeks had added zest to their mundane lives.

He was proud that he had broken from the pack and followed his instincts; that he'd stuck with Olly when things turned bad. But there would be a price. Gus knew that occasionally, in the snug at The Plough, or in the bowls club bar, beer would stir the sleeping rancour.

Fraternisation in the *Zac's* affair would certainly be raked over, by bigots like the Pyggs, in the huddles of the worthies outside church. They were like that round here.

◇ ◇ ◇ ◇ ◇

Gus felt revived. He was glad to be back on the downward slope. His step quickened and his mood brightened a little. He was cheered up by looking back to good times, back to spring.

He remembered Olly's delight when, one morning, as they turned into the trees to get out of the rain, they had come across some wild garlic beneath a hedge. Gus had known that within minutes Olly would have ten ideas of how to use it on the menu at *Zac's*.

That's what Gus loved about walking with Olly; he provided the excuse to dip into a lifelong knowledge of all things natural and share it with someone who was interested. It was almost like the old days, on the field trips.

On the way home one day, Gus had shown Olly where Good King Henry grew. They'd also gathered sorrel – Olly planned a puree. During another walk, Gus pointed out some comfrey and Olly said he'd try the leaves as fritters. He never mentioned comfrey again, so Gus concluded that it had not passed Olly's taste test.

Gus had been surprised how many mushrooms Olly recognised in the wild – oysters, chanterelles, ceps. Not surprising – he'd worked in Italy, all over. But it was obvious that he was used to getting them delivered.

On one trip he had brought a knife with him and Gus had intervened, to show him how fungi had to be eased from the ground with a gentle twist. He remembered Olly's impish glee when he had led him to the old paddock carpeted with field mushrooms. It was as if they had come across a hoard of gold.

On the next walk, Olly carried a small punnet. He looked faintly ridiculous, this burly man, carrying on one finger the sort of dainty basket a toddler might use in an Easter egg hunt. Such fun. Always fun.

When the weather had turned unexpectedly moist and warm, Gus – encouraged by Olly's interest – had taken him on an educational forage. They had found three Penny Buns and Olly had held them in his cupped hands all the way down the hill, fearing that they would be crushed in his pockets.

That evening, Gus had imagined Olly over the stove at *Zac's*, lovingly creating something – a pasta dish perhaps, or rich mushroom tartlets. Yes, tartlets. He imagined the mushrooms sliced and arranged symmetrically on a creamy bed, atop crisp pastry that would turn instantly into buttery crumb. The taste would be of wildness and damp leaf mould.

But of course the joy of those recollections had been blighted forever by what had happened, and how their walks had somehow been implicated in it all.

Sometimes lately, when Gus woke after a nap he wondered for a moment whether what had happened was in fact some silly dream, amazed that several lives could have been changed forever in a single afternoon. At other times he woke in a troubled state, knowing he had been involved – in a tenuous way – in something so dramatic, something that was national news.

Poor, brilliant, unlucky Olly. How he'd loved to walk here, down this hill. He would unwind, take big gulps of air, rabbit on loosely and freely. His worries seemed to tumble out of him, carried away on breezes, washed away by the rain.

Gus was nearly at the low dry-stone wall. He lowered himself on a flat stone and sat with the dogs at his feet, and when he glanced down to the cottages it set him thinking once more of the bad feeling there had been.

Try as he might, he could never find a plausible reason for all the local opposition. They had fought against *Zac's* in the planning committee. They had forecast problems over cooking smells. They'd predicted chaos over parking.

When they failed, they mocked his food. Because *Zac's* had actually served fish raw! *Raw!* Unforgivable. Not only that, Olly served *sea urchins*, and *octopus* even, and cheap, unpleasant bits of animals, sweetbreads and things, that folks now found disgusting.

Gus remembered how, in the spring, he had shown Olly "bread and cheese," the new hawthorn shoots eaten for generations by country children. Olly had nibbled on it thoughtfully – and

6

integrated it into a green salad. Word got out that it had been mentioned on the menu and Olly had been stung by a snide whisper from someone in the post office queue.

Gus had begun to feel stiff and cold after his rest. The weather had made his eyes run. He was sure the wind was to blame. He was not one for shedding tears.

He called the dogs and they froze at the sound of his voice and then hurtled towards him. Their coppery coats trembled in the wind and their ears flapped as they lifted their long legs, like high-kicking dancers, breasting through the tall grass bordering the path. Then they snuffled behind Gus who was still deep in thought, oblivious of the wind now.

He so missed Olly. He liked his role as Olly's unofficial mentor. In a way Olly was the son he never had. But of course as well as missing Olly, he missed the food – and so did Brenda.

Their pensions did not allow for more than monthly visits but the four-week wait sharpened the appetite. It was well worth the wait. Since *Zac's* shut, their bank balance was a little healthier but they felt they were very much poorer. Gourmet grub on the doorstep; it had always felt a little bit too good to be true.

Brenda was forever talking about the meals they'd had. "Gus – remember that Sicilian rabbit dish I had? Mmm – that lovely gravy!" Brenda would say, and Gus always replied, "*Sauce*, love."

She had almost fainted with rapture when Olly created a spun-sugar star with a B in the centre, and sent it out laid atop a *clafoutis*, at the end of her 65th birthday dinner.

He'd come out to wish her happy birthday, put his arm around her and said: "As it's your special day, here's a trade secret. Give the cherries a nice, long bath in kirsch. A pinch of pepper goes into the batter, and a *teeny* bit of nutmeg."

Gus was now on the gentle downward slope leading to the main street. He could just see *Zac's*, on the corner opposite the church. He put leads on the dogs and they led him on to the road and towards home.

There was a van and workmen outside *Zac's*, and as he approached Gus could see that they were taking down the restaurant sign, the individual, gilded letters that had caused such a fuss with the planning people.

They looked so much bigger close up, and so chic. Gold-painted plaster, Gus guessed, and damned expensive.

One workman was sliding the Z into the back of the van while his mate, on a ladder, prised the other letters from the stone wall above the door. For a second, Gus wondered whether to ask if he could buy the Z. It would be a shining memento, in the corner of the garden.

The workmen stepped aside to make way for him and the dogs. One man was holding the golden apostrophe.

Gus asked: "What are we getting instead of the restaurant?"

The man holding the apostrophe looked guarded. Then a smile spread across his face.

"Not really at liberty to say, mate. Sorry. But if you think fleeces and country clobber you won't be far wrong. And if you think Chinese you won't be far wong!" He looked for appreciation of his little joke but it had gone over Gus's head.

So, a boring shop filled with racks of clothes. But the Chinese? Gus wanted to go back and say "Pull the other one, sunshine" but it wasn't worth the bother.

As he walked, Gus's mind switched to launch night at *Zac's*, that taster event, after they had converted the place from a penny bank built in Victorian times.

He had been struck by Ella's nervous but warm welcome. Lovely, loyal, long-suffering Ella. Every bit of her was beautifully rounded and smooth. She was what he thought of as a *comely* girl, rather than a beautiful one. Such flawless skin. She was so talented too; the restaurant design was hers.

She was quite small, just up to Olly's shoulder. Gus liked the way she clasped herself when she laughed, as if she might burst, perhaps a nervous, self-protecting gesture? Gus told Brenda that

Ella looked as if she needed a good cuddle and if ever she needed one, he would jolly well volunteer. Brenda said simply that Ella's kindness shone out of her.

He loved Ella's menus, on virginal cream paper, her delicate hand-written descriptions in purple ink, on the Chef's Specials card. Brenda still had a copy of the menu from that birthday meal. She had thought of framing it.

He recalled Ella and the girls, on that preview night, threading their way through the restaurant, handing out oyster cromskies, and little plates of crisp squid decorated with chilli, cut as fine as hair, and flutes of champagne – the first glass complementary.

Gus's first sight of Olly had been that night, through the glass dividing the dining area from the kitchen. He was imposing, with the chest of a wrestler, the round head of a rugby hooker. His hair was the colour of sand under the hot lights.

He was at the stove and momentarily had been hidden by a curtain of flame flaring from the pan he was shaking. When he reappeared he had caught Gus's eye, raised his tongs in welcome and had made a comical face of mock-horror, pretending he'd just been in terrible danger, and then laughed uproariously. Pure Olly...

The face had reflected excitement, optimism, fun, the pleasure of a dream fulfilled. What a contrast with the torture he had seen going on in Olly that day, when the details of the tragedy began to unfold.

◇ ◇ ◇ ◇ ◇

Glancing down the side of the restaurant now, he could see part of the vegetable garden Olly had been so proud of. The path was overhung with a jungle of artichoke leaves but he could make out yellowing pea vines, rotting tomatoes and great fat leeks. Late raspberries bejewelled the other path side, the canes bowed by the weight of the fruit. What treats Olly would have created from them.

Gus could smell lunch, and yet he was still 20 yards from

home. It was liver-and-onions day and normally he'd be hungrily impatient for Brenda to dish out. Not today.

He unleashed the dogs and they settled contentedly on the hearthrug in front of the dead fire.

It was good to be out of the wind. He was tired, too tired to share with Brenda the keen sense of loss he was feeling today, to explain again.

Brenda was right; he had begun to sound like a stuck record. He spared her his outpourings but the irritation continued to burn like indigestion. He took off his oiled jacket, and went off to wash his hands.

It had all been so unjust. The slanderous portrayal of Olly as a gun-toting madman, towards the end, had been unforgivable. The poisoning was different. Of course it was. The fuss over that was more understandable. But it was never a *crime* – not in a million years, and the police agreed even if the locals didn't.

A sudden shout from the kitchen intruded into his introspection.

"Gus! *Served!*"

He could smell the onions. He'd always said that apart from bacon frying (*good* bacon), and the glorious garlicky whiff that hit you when Brenda lifted the lid off one of her lemony chicken casseroles, the aroma of frying onions was the most appetizing smell imaginable.

But yet again today, for a reason he well understood, Gus found he had absolutely no appetite.

2

The girl in the sky-blue cotton dress and sensible sandals was tired of summer. It was sweltering. It had been like this for days.

Her thick pile of hair, pale brown topped by bleached blonde skeins, felt heavy. Her calves prickled where the sun had burned her skin, turning it pink.

Roasting hot. Friends away. And so quiet. *And* having to keep an eye on Olly.

"Summer sucks," she said to herself.

There was a strange stillness in the garden that the girl found disturbing. The world was soundless. She couldn't have explained it but somehow the searing early afternoon sun and boredom seemed inextricably linked. There was something dream-like about these afternoons.

Since late morning it had been too hot to do anything but loaf around, watching insects busy in the flowerbeds. It was stuffy inside the house, her bedroom hot, the lounge airless and dark behind the curtain pulled half over the window to repel the glare of the sun.

The girl's burnished cheeks felt tender to the touch. She lay face down on the crisp, brown lawn. She opened her book but didn't have the energy or inclination to read.

She laid the book on the crown of her head and then lowered a cheek on to the back of her hands. The book gave some protection against the oppressive bombardment from the sun but not much.

The girl had no idea where Olly had disappeared to, the garage probably. It was cool in there. Dad had been a bit panicky in the morning; he was out in the car getting seat belts fitted (he said everybody had to have them from today). With the car gone, there was room for Olly to delve and discover.

They had fought after Dad left. She had told Olly, maybe *too* sternly, that he ought to put more sun lotion on; she had used her mum's bossy tone of voice and Olly had rebelled with a hysterical outburst.

Suddenly he had come at her – red-faced, teeth bared, near to tears. Tilly had held him off, at arm's length, and let him vent his anger. His arms flailed harmlessly. Neither had been injured in the skirmish although it left both of them hot and bothered.

She could tolerate a bit of grappling and hair pulling from a brother who was not big enough to be dangerous but at nearly thirteen, she found these dust-ups so undignified.

As the temporary custodian of the house while Mum worked for the afternoon, she knew she should stir herself and check on Olly, in case he had cut a finger off, or opened a bottle of some lethal liquid. He was an inquisitive boy.

She knew she wouldn't find him sulking. Olly never sulked. Never bore grudges.

Opening the kitchen door leading to the garage, she peered in and said: "Want some squash Ol?" sweetly, as if the scuffle had never happened.

Olly was on his knees in the corner of the garage, sorting through toys. He looked up and said brightly: "Oh. Please, Till."

That was Olly, she said to herself. Meek and lovely just minutes after his furious outburst. All forgotten, all forgiven. It occurred to Tilly that he had insight into his tantrums but no means of controlling them.

Girls at school moaned endlessly about their brothers, and although Tilly joined in, complaining that he would always deliberately make a row so she couldn't hear her Duran Duran, she adored him.

Tilly brought glasses of squash and sat on a box as Olly examined each toy, lifting them in turn from the plastic chest destined for a charity shop. She looked at him fondly.

"Sorry. It's all got to go, Ol. It's my old stuff. Some of it goes back yonks."

He pulled from the bottom of the pile a tin toy cooker. It was pink and bore the name Chad Valley. He became engrossed. He worked the sturdy oven door that clicked as it opened and closed. There were metal hotplates and knobs.

"*That* cost an absolute bomb," Tilly said.

Olly remembered that two miniature metal pans had come with the cooker. Once Tilly had gone outside, he rummaged around and found them.

An idea had come to him but it involved matches and candles, so he would have to entice his sister into supervising. He felt sure that, as she had been so unreasonably bossy earlier, she would agree. Tilly often found herself giving in to Olly whose charm seemed to grow more potent by the day.

Within minutes they were in a corner of the garden where the neighbours couldn't see them, and she was watching over Olly as he slipped night-light candles into the cooker oven. She allowed him to light them.

Beside him, on a plate, he had arranged cubes of red cheese and bits of sliced bread. Once the candles were lit, he slipped the cheese into the toy pans and put them on the hotplate. He could feel the heat coming up from the oven. He watched eagerly.

The cheese began to melt and then to bubble fiercely. He slid the little tin pans off the heat to study the melted cheese and its oily coating. Then he returned them to the hotplate until the cheese became bubbly discs.

He speared each with a stick to lift them out in turn, and worked them on to the pieces of bread. The discs had turned crisp.

"Try it, Til," he said, and proudly handed his sister the morsel of bread topped with the fried cheese.

"Gorgeous!" said Tilly, swallowing. "No, really, Ol. Absolutely delish!"

Olly had devoured his bread and was nodding in agreement. He had been fascinated by the way bits of cheese had mutated. They were like cheesy crisps.

"Not a word to mum," Tilly warned.

When Tilly had snuffed out the candles and the cooker had cooled, she told Olly to take it back to the garage. He obeyed but stood on the workbench and reached up to hide the cooker and candles behind paint cans.

He was hatching a plan to smuggle out one of mum's proper pans and fry an egg, when no one was around. He wanted to see whether he could work out how to get frilly crisp bits round the edge. He liked the frilly bits.

Putting the cooker away, Olly wondered also how fried slices of banana would taste. He would heat up some sugar because he knew toffee was made that way. He'd seen Grandma pour it into trays.

On Mother's Day he'd done a surprise breakfast on a tray, and for a moment had been a hero. He basked in the praise. He was learning that you could show love by giving people nice food you'd prepared. It was no trouble, in fact it was fun, and it made you feel really good to see their faces.

There were loads of blackcurrants in the garden. What about blackcurrants and sugar heated up...?

It was like science, only much less boring. Maybe, he thought, he could make amazing new discoveries about different foods. He needed a notebook to record his experiments. He would keep it all to himself. Later he would find a really safe and secret place for the cooker; it was *his* cooker now.

Just imagine, Olly said to himself, Tilly was actually going to *give it away* – a cooker that actually *cooked things*. Sisters!

3

During that summer when Tilly let me have her old toy cooker, there were four truly unforgettable moments, even more dramatic than my discovery that cooking was actually exciting. Five, actually, if you count the exciting arrival of the new Transformers.

First, my big sister turned out not to be my sister after all. Then my father fell dead in front of us. Not bad for starters.

Then my mother, who had never used even the mildest bad language in our hearing, was revealed to have the mouth of a fishwife. And I discovered that culinary miracle, the Wimpy Bender.

I seem to remember that the most affecting of these big new experiences was not the news about Tilly, not even Dad's hasty exit, not even the Wimpy Bender epiphany. It was mum's filthy language. It taught me that adults were not what they seemed to be, quite a chilling truth to stumble on at nine years of age.

Chronologically, though, the first of these big special moments, that summer, was the Tilly revelation.

One night, after I'd shouted my "Goodnights" and settled down with *The Witches*, Dad came up and sat on my bed, offering to read to me. This was a rare treat and I wondered what had prompted the offer.

I sat propped up against the bedhead and listened. He read fluently and grippingly, putting on different voices for the characters. But then he stopped mid-chapter.

"Hell, Ol, is this actually for *kids*? This Dahl bloke really must get a kick out of scaring nippers. Doesn't this stuff give you the heebie-jeebies?" he laughed and then said, "He kills off the parents before he even gets *started*! Charming."

I said that it was only a story, that probably there were many real people and real things that were scarier. I wondered whether what Dad was about to broach with me was going to be one of those scary things.

The last chat of this sort had involved the sudden passing of Aunty Tina's husband Uncle Gavin, about whom I didn't really have any feelings, and so had to remember to act sad for a while. This time, I was given a hint, but then had to wait for the full news release overnight. It all seemed more mysterious than frightening.

Evidently, Dad and Mum and Tilly would have to go somewhere "official" next day. Aunty Tina would look after me for the morning. There would be a treat afterwards. We would go to the Wimpy in the town centre and I could have a Bender Brunch, the circular sausage, with fried egg and chips – and me and Tilly could each have a Brown Derby (doughnut, ice cream, chocolate sauce, nuts. Yum.).

Mum would tolerate Wimpy because they gave you food on plates with cutlery, and their Shanty Burger didn't disagree with her as much as a meat burger once had.

We had been to the Wimpy to celebrate a few weeks before, when Dad received some money he had been expecting – A legacy? An insurance payout? – and had bought the car. On that evening, I had decided that the Wimpy was what heaven might be like.

The Bender did it. This was not sausage, not as I'd known it. I learned it was a frankfurter, and it had been slashed along one side, so it resembled a pinkish car tyre. By a stroke of what I regarded as genius, it perfectly encircled half a grilled tomato.

But, what was the price to me of the free lunch, what was it compensation for?

Quite simply, acceptance that Tilly had been *adopted*, that morning. The "official" business had been the rigmarole of Dad having to accept her as his own, and Tilly legally taking his surname.

I would have accepted all this without the softener of a meal. I knew that Tilly would always be the same old Til but obviously I wasn't saying no to a Bender Brunch and Brown Derby.

Before we set off, Dad explained it all – in official-sounding detail – and I even let Tilly kiss me to show that everything was fine by me.

All this parentage business explained why I had reddish hair and was a chunky build and why Tilly was tall and elegant and had a heavy mop of brown hair with a few blondish bits on top.

Mum had Tilly before she met Dad. After they'd married they believed that they couldn't have kids of their own. Then I came along.

It seemed to explain why Tilly seemed to be so favoured – not that she didn't deserve every crumb of love that came her way. She had settled in years before me and she'd been a bond, I suppose, showing Mum that Dad loved her enough to take on her child, and entitling Dad to make her feel eternally grateful.

Anyway, the dreadful truth, kept under shrouds for years, was finally out – and I was totally underwhelmed by it all.

When Dad told me about my surprise entrance he felt it necessary to joke – "Mum and me were like this...(he held up his hands in horror)...Oh no! A *baby!* Eek! Just when we'd got new carpets throughout, just when we thought it was safe to get rid of Tilly's old pushchair..."

I didn't think at the time, of course, but I've wondered since whether behind the amateur dramatics was a bit of truth.

"So...God gave us a little bonus," said Dad, no doubt trying to make me feel I hadn't been a total blight on their lives.

There was lots of religious stuff at the school I went to –

old-fashioned Church of England – but, young as I was, I was sceptical about everything that I was told.

For instance, I couldn't work out why, instead of unsettling people's lives by dropping children on them, the Good Lord didn't sort out more urgent things, like stopping my best pal Alistair from getting leukemia.

In my childish naivety I didn't think He was on the ball at all. He wasn't perfect. Of course He wasn't. I was living proof – one of His little oversights.

◇ ◇ ◇ ◇ ◇

The night before Dad died, I was sitting on the settee with my new Jetfire and my Bumblebees, and my G1 Targetmaster Scoop, laid out on the cushion. Tilly (now my half-sister but still the same Tilly) had plonked her girl-woman self on Dad's lap as he watched golf on TV. She was being giddy.

"See! Still not too big to sit on pop's lap!" she giggled.

Dad had protested, in a squeaky voice, shouting for heavy lifting gear to be brought. Mum shouted through to tell them not to knock anything over.

Next day, Dad took time off from work to come to the sports day. He and Mum had watched Tilly win the high jump and javelin at the senior sports in the morning, and then, at the junior sports, had witnessed me shamefully lose the second-year novelty event.

This involved dressing up in oversize trousers, crawling at speed, trying to hula-hoop, then running backwards, while being laughed at by two or three hundred of your peers, and striving not to cry over the humiliation of it all.

I came next to last. People have always said how strong I looked, how stocky, but they never explained how I could move my limbs in synchrony. Athletically, I was a ninny.

After my disgrace – and after Tilly had grabbed me and said "Ol, that was hilarious. *Wicked!*" with her usual kindness – I sat in the shade of a track-side tree, allowing the heat of my shame to evaporate and to become part of family lore.

Then I went over to join Mum and Dad and Tilly relaxing on a blanket in the sun. Our involvement over, we surrounded ourselves with the stuff we would take home now we were breaking up for summer. But it was not over.

When runners for the 70-yard Dads' Dash were requested to come to the starting line, Dad was up and off without encouragement, tearing off his tie, throwing down his jacket.

"Are you *sure*, Gerald?" Mum called to him. He appeared not to hear, or chose not to. Tilly and me nudged each other as we watched him at the start line take off his shoes, and share a joke with Mr Blake.

There was to be a standing start but Dad, looking across to see that we were watching, crouched down into a sprint crouch, joking with the other dads – an ill-assorted bunch in various stages of unfitness. There were too many runners for the width of the track so they formed a pack, playfully jostling each other for position, and then holding themselves stiff awaiting Mr Blake's whistle.

We couldn't believe how fast Dad set off. I had never seen him run, this rather sallow, slow-moving man nearing middle age. In the last photos of him his temples are whitening, his waist has begun to spread. I had never ever expected him to be able to *run*, let alone sprint.

Our Dad, whose only gestures to physicality was a Sunday morning bike ride for a newspaper and to mow the lawn, was moving like a train. He had his head up, his chest out and his arms were pumping like pistons.

To our delight and surprise he finished second. The winner shook hands with him and then they almost hugged each other, gasping and laughing.

Dad came back to us at the track side, carrying his shoes and looking delighted with himself. He was still a little out of breath and had begun to sweat. Mum said only "Goodness me, Gerald," but we were more generous in our congratulations.

"My hero!" said Tilly slapping her hand onto Dad's shoulder as he sat down.

"That was absolutely ace, Dad," I said.

"I used to run. Didn't I ever tell you, Ol?"

◇ ◇ ◇ ◇ ◇

We reached the car park and threw our bags into the car boot. Dad was at the driver's door, holding my plaster sculpture of a fish leaping out of the water, the best thing I'd ever done in art.

I'd had trouble getting the wire armature through the tail so it wouldn't be seen but, with Miss Harbon's help, finally I had done it and got a beautiful arching curve, matching the fish on the label I'd taken from one of mum's tins of salmon.

I was pleased with the way I'd splashed thin blue paint over it, with deliberate carelessness, to give the impression of water, delighted that I'd left it fresh and not too finished.

Dad was waiting until Mum got in so she could nurse the sculpture. His other hand was on top of the car door.

I remember every one of the last words we uttered as a complete family, before Dad began to sway and lose a brief battle to stay upright. He had looked over the roof of the car and chuckled. He said to Tilly: "You know, if you've got it, gal, you *never* really lose it..."

Tilly said: "No, *really* Dad. You were great. At least you didn't show us up!"

I was beside Tilly, ready to get into the back seat, but wasn't tall enough to see over the car but I shouted over "Yea, Dad. You were brill."

At that moment I heard Mum shout "Gerald! *Careful!* Watch Olly's *fish!*"

In seconds, Dad lay dying with his head against the front tyre of his beloved Vauxhall Astra ("Bought it new" he would say, proudly).

I've often thought of the irony of Dad being struck down as

soon as the words "You never lose it" had left his lips. I see it as an omnipotent correction; it was Dad being put in his place, perhaps a little heavy handedly, from Upstairs.

Mum started to make weird noises of distress, and I saw boys running, scattering, looking for other adults. Tilly put her arm around me. She was silent. She just held me tight and led me away a few yards and pointed my face towards the school.

Her darling father was dead or dying ten yards behind us, and her instinct was to shield *me*, to prevent the ghastly scene being imprinted on *my* memory. When I looked up at her for reassurance, tears were running down her face but she was keeping it expressionless, trying not to look horrified. For me.

What was going through Tilly's mind – Tilly the favoured one, the adored one, the near-woman who only the night before had larked around with dad as if she was a small child again?

I heard Mr Blake talking breathlessly, having run from the starting area, or the tea tent. Then I heard from behind the car the terrible rhythmic pumping of Dad's chest, Mr Blake's heavy breathing. I felt Tilly at my back, taking me away from the sound, a sound that, once heard, would never be forgotten.

As well as pity for my father, I felt fear. But most of all, I felt embarrassment over the scene we were making, in full view of pupils and parents. We were being shown up after all.

Clumps of boys, kids I knew well, stood around solemnly staring our way, before parents gathered them and took them away. A doctor, father of a boy in my class, ran from his car carrying a black box.

How absolutely *embarrassing* that your father, near-hero of the Dads' Dash, is now sprawled on the ground next to his car, with his shirt undone, and his mouth open! How humiliating that your mum, in her cheerful, yellow summer dress, is on her knees, swaying and keening and pleading, her noise bringing more onlookers to the scene.

And there, for all to see, is your big sister *babying* you! Holding your head and twisting you away from what you're desperate to see.

Mr Blake was taking the keys to the car from mum, who was being helped into another car. Then he came to us and said that he would drive us home. He clasped my shoulder as he steered me to the car.

"Best if only Mum goes to the hospital. They'll want everyone out of the way while they do their best for him, you know," he said, his eyes flitting round the dashboard as he familiarised himself with the car controls. "Your Mum says to go next door till she's back."

Then he drove off slowly, and I heard the crunch of my fish sculpture being run over.

That night, Tilly came to my room crying softly, and got into bed with me.

"Aunty Tina's here," she sniffled, "and Mum will be home soon. It might be all right. The hospital might, just might have saved him, you know Olly."

Tilly being around always made me want to appear brave. I remember saying: "No, he's dead Til. It's OK. Don't worry, I know he's dead and it's all right." But what I said set Tilly off crying twice as hard.

We heard the front door close then Mum and Aunty Tina wailing in unison.

"Let's leave them a bit and then go down Ol," Tilly said, and I was only too happy to agree, to stay away from the drama, with Tilly looking after me. We moved to the top of the stairs and sat in the dark, her arm round me, my arm round her.

I knew Tilly was fearful of having Dad's death confirmed, even though the noise from downstairs had told us as much. That unearthly whining. It frightened me to think of adults being helpless, of them losing charge of themselves.

But there was to be another grave embarrassment, completing my day of awakening, a day of understanding that grown-ups could be wiped out without warning, and that they had a secret, extremely naughty side, one that they kept from children.

This was the day that I learned that my unimpeachable, slightly prissy mother was capable of uttering filthy words. Words that I had to pretend I had never heard; words that you could not even mention objectively in the family, by way of discussion as to their relative vileness.

Aunty Tina was trying to calm Mum down, saying it would be all right, in direct contradiction of the truth. She was fussing. Mum was furiously rejecting the offer of tea.

"And, no! I don't want a bloody paracetamol, Tina! What good will *they* do?"

(Bloody! First time she's ever said that!)

We heard Tina crying, and saying that she felt so helpless... "You should eat something, Denise. Let me do you a sandwich..."

Then came that moment of rude awakening. Mum started quietly, but her voice rose in a roof-lifting crescendo...

"Tina! For the last fucking time...." *(The F word!)*

"I don't want a bloody sandwich. And I don't want a sodding tablet. I don't want another cup of bleeding *tea*. I... just... want... my... fucking *Gerald back!*"

They carried on crying for a while and then I heard Mum say, between sobs: "Sorry, Tina. Sorry. I can't believe it was me saying that." Then: "I ought to be up with those poor kids. To tell them."

On top of all the discoveries of the day, there was an extra one: That Mum really wasn't a great Mum. She had hardly thought of us since Dad had hit the deck. Tilly had done the mum bit for me.

We started to move off the bed to go down and face everything, and as we did so we heard Mum say: "He's never been ill, not really. Ate apples. Didn't smoke. Only drank at the weekends. Always used healthy margarine...."

(Her voice turned into a wail. I knew there was yet another F-word coming)

"...and *this, this* is the fucking reward we get..."

4

The first time I met the bloke I'm supposed to have wanted dead (i.e. my best friend) was when I was looking for a flat and a bit of kitchen work for beer money.

I was a student about to start an English degree, a would-be writer, treading the first step on the career ladder. I had not the slightest doubt that I'd climb sure-footedly to the topmost rung. From there I would see myself at a sunny table, in a billowing cotton shirt and straw hat, beside a twinkling sea, penning yet another quite brilliant novel.

Meanwhile, I had to find a room in one of several identical rows of depressing, grey-fronted houses that looked as though they had begun to crumble before the fall of the Empire.

I'd clocked three places where there was a room to rent, and I'd taken a train into the city one muggy, late-summer afternoon. I'd left it late, having been preoccupied with getting together a wad of cash by working every available shift in a pizza place near home.

When I rang the bell at the first Rhodesia Terrace address, a knocked-about little place in the shadow of a tower block, I heard voices inside. The shouts were in what sounded like broken French.

The door was opened – with some difficulty – and there, before me, was a swarthy lad, maybe a shade older than me. His face was at groin height. My first thought – an amputee. And *so* young. My second – oh, shit. Disabled. My third: Careful, Olly;

24

you could be roped in here as a carer...

I remember the chap looking up at me. His face was a mixture of mischief and delight in my discomfort. I spotted that there were well-muscled legs behind the knees.

"*Sorry* – I was expecting a girl..." he said, with a big, white smile, as if that explained things.

I could hear raucous laughter, blurred by drink, from somewhere deep in the house.

"It's just that today we've had this French thing going, a jokey thing – Toulouse Lautrec Day...We're having to stay like this until the stroke of six tonight. For a bet. " He looked up inquiringly, to check whether I shared his sense of the ridiculous.

I did. I laughed. He laughed.

"*Bien! Entrez*, Monsieur!" he said, ushering me in.

I remember being struck by the blackness of this bloke's hair; short, black curls that you might find on a labrador's back. That, and his enormous smile – and his confidence. Also, there was precision in his speech, a fineness in his features.

"I'm taking it that you're the Oliver who rang?"

"*Oui*," I said. His grin returned.

"*Je suiz Zac.*"

We'd hardly exchanged a word but there was already in the air a sense of rapport, friendship even. I stooped and we shook hands.

It turned out that with that "*Oui*," I was enlisting for a cavalcade of merriment and mayhem lasting a couple of years, and leading to an enduring entanglement with Zac, and with a woman who was to be a leading player in the disaster that lay in wait for me, years in the future.

◇ ◇ ◇ ◇ ◇

The place was a slum, littered with mounds of newspapers, sweet wrappers, teetering piles of books, a scattering of CDs. Cables ran perilously across carpets.

Zac stomped on his knees to a corner of the room and cleared a mountain of textbooks and lads' magazines from a tattered deckchair and indicated with a thumb that I should sit.

"*Café?*" Zac asked.

I remember that there was a really rank smell – of stale beer, sour cigarette smoke, feet, garlic, and of sweet, damp biscuits. I could hear a strange clumping as I waited for Zac to return, and as I lowered the magazine I'd been leafing through, I saw in the doorway two men of about my age, both on their knees, both unsmiling.

One was a beanpole with heavy-rimmed glasses too big for his narrow head, and over-large ears. The other – gingery, squat, pug-faced – resembled what I imagined a leprechaun to look like. They could have been bit-players in a drama about Bedlam.

The pair were swaying slightly, and panting from the effort of walking on their knees. Their dull eyes and gaping mouths showed that they were sozzled.

They looked at me as if I was something exotic in a zoo cage.

"*Pardonez-moi,*" said one, the tall one in the glasses, adding a belch. Then they turned laboriously, like parts of a pantomime horse, and shuffled to the kitchen.

I could hear the leprechaun talking to Zac.

"Zac. Zac...listen! *Hilarious!* I was just going say ..." he wheezed, suffocating with suppressed laughter, "I was going to say to him... 'See you shortly'! *Shortly!*"

This set them off into more paroxysms of laughter.

There was a lull and then the pop and hiss of beer cans being opened.

I could hear one of the two say, very seriously: "*Quelle fun, mon brave!*" Again, someone belched, theatrically this time, and the leprechaun, I think it was, said something like: "*Oui. Je nearly pissed mes pantalons.*"

When Zac shuffled back he was carrying a stained and chipped mug of black coffee. I recall that he apologised for not having milk, saying that it "appeared inexplicably to have turned into cheese," as if this transformation had been miraculous.

I was to find that Zac had great gaps in his knowledge of the world. He had been bought a good education but there had been no tutorials on the consequences of leaving milk hanging around for a month.

The kneeling pair had returned to the door. They were now holding beer cans and looking at me again with focus that did not seem to be quite reaching far enough.

"Right..." Zac began. "It's the front bedroom that's free. Teeny bit cramped but enough room to swing a cat. Next to the toilet, a boon for the indolent and the inebriated. Just twenty quid a month dearer than the Crow's Nest, which is probably taken. A girl has rung asking me to save it until she can view."

"View." I loved the fancy estate agent's parlance. By the look of it there was not much to view anywhere at Zac's place unless you were an environmental health officer.

Zac came across as so open and informal. Carefree. As it turned out he wasn't any of these things, but at that stage in our lives there was no doubt about the earnestness of his quest for sheer, unrestrained hedonism. The calculating side lay well hidden for years.

"Those two will be moving out this weekend," Zac said, nodding towards the kneeling pair. He spoke as if they weren't there and in a sense they weren't. The beanpole had a lean. He was passing out in slow motion.

"Both medics," he said ruefully. "Unbelievably, Seamus, the gingery one, is specialising in brains. A reason to keep healthy, Olly ..."

The leprechaun looked distant, and seemed to be struggling to get his mouth to work. Finally he shouted: "Yes, Zac's going *to lose* us! Geddit?" He slapped the skinny man hard enough on the back to make his glasses jump and to bring him back to consciousness. "Get it? Going *Toulouse* us!"

Zac muttered, in a measured, tired way: "Seamus. *Voulez vous do moi a favour and fuck off?"* He then began to explain to me about the girl who had rung earlier.

"Think she must be skint. She was so very careful to get it straight about the rent and what's included. Anyway, the Crow's Nest would have been no good for you. It's tiny, under the slope of the roof. If she's a whopper we'll have to grease her to get her in..."

Zac explained that normally those living at the house would vote on whether a newcomer was accepted.

"As the madamoiselle is not here, I hereby give you my deciding vote. I'm sure we'll get along without killing each other," he said.

Those words coming back to me now, after all that has happened, seem disturbingly prophetic.

◇ ◇ ◇ ◇ ◇

It turned out that my room *was* indeed big enough to swing a cat, albeit one that had been dismembered and packed in a freezer bag. Or a kitten with a very hard skull.

The single piece of furniture was a wardrobe, the sort my grandparents had bought just after the war. It was jammed tightly against the bed which was made of tubular steel and which had the sort of wee-stained mattress you might find on a child's cot.

I worked out that it was only possible to get into bed by pushing my buttocks back, and edging along the wall and then falling forward.

A patch of grey sky was visible through the little square window above the bed adding to the feeling that you were in prison. But no prisoner would have tolerated this claustrophobic cell – the fire danger, the poor sleeping conditions, the noise, the daylight nuisance, denial of walking space....

But for me it was ideal.

Well, it was absolutely dirt cheap, and it was all I needed in order to fulfil my ambition, which was to spend a little bit of time unpicking great literature, enough for my BA, and a great deal of time as drunk as the ginger leprechaun.

I was ready to party. Eager to explore all that extra-curricular student life had to offer. To wash away A-level strains, and motherly pressures applied with a paining love. To flush a mawkish sixth-form romance out of my system.

I had chosen well. Here was the pit of oblivion I'd fall into each night, a spot where, when funds allowed, I could drift into untroubled sleep, reeking of lager, kebab, or curry, or weed, or all four.

5

The first time I saw Ella was that afternoon, the day I met Zac.

I was about to leave the house after agreeing to take the room. I'd just asked Zac who the landlord was, and he'd said: "Me. Or, rather, my dad. He's a property geek. You give me the rent. I pass it on."

Zac was still on his knees but leaning heavily against the settee, having found a tiny island of space.

He said he was in the second year of a business degree and was telling me about his ambitions when the doorbell rang. Zac started to shuffle on his knees into the hall but I said that I would go.

I opened the door and there was Ella. Either she had over-dressed for what was a very humid afternoon, or she'd been rushing. She had a round face and her cheeks were red and slightly damp. Her skin was immaculate, like the bloom on a perfectly ripe grape. I thought: She looks like the milkmaid in kids' books.

Homely was the word I'd have used later to describe her, and we were soon to see how different she was from those we were to mix with. Wild girls. Neurotic girls. Girls you would never take home.

Ella was also much younger than the girls who would come to shindigs in our flea-bitten abode. In fact, she was a very young nineteen, and nervy. I sensed she had gone through the mill, and my instinct was right.

As I moved to let her in, she shook her head and freed her hair of unremarkable brown – nut-brown to be generous – but which, that day, was enlivened with a slash of luminescent green.

Years later, she had herself forgotten what she had worn that day, and if our meeting ever came up in the conversation, with the infuriating self-deprecation that she never overcame, she would say: "Whatever it was, I'm sure I looked a mess in it."

She didn't look a mess. Well, she did in the conventional sense; nothing really matched. The white shirt, unbuttoned to reveal a glimpse of breast, or maybe simply to cool off, showed off her pink wholesomeness.

Over this she wore a greenish cotton top. The raggy cuffs, and scuffed shoes, spoke of Ella's poverty, as did the rara skirt of flimsy, faded stuff. Ella was short and plumpish and, to me, the skirt seemed to exaggerate her broad hips. The quirkiness of the clothes would be explained soon after. She was starting an arts foundation course.

"Zac?" she said. "I'm Ella. Is the room still free? Hope I'm not too late..." I said that I was not Zac but that he was in.

I moved to the door, which was ajar, to usher her in but didn't open it fully until I had warned her what to expect. She dragged her wheeled case forward, and put down an instrument case.

"Zac's in there. Don't be alarmed. You'll find him on his knees." She took a second to assimilate this statement.

"Is he proposing to someone? Is it *decent* in there?" she said with a dirty, deep-throated laugh that I would grow to love.

"It's..." I began. "It's Toulouse Lautrec Day. *Only* in there. Nowhere else."

She looked bemused and laughed again to give herself time to weigh things up.

I pushed the door fully open and could see Zac, on his knees, beaming, the black eyes and that big row of teeth shining in the darkness of the hall.

"Ah, Zac!" Ella said.

"*C'est moi,*" he said.

"I was expecting a taller man," she said, closing the door. They laughed in unison.

Obviously she had forgotten me within a second of meeting Zac; she hadn't even said goodbye and I felt a bit needled. But what on earth had I got to feel prickly about? I didn't even know the woman.

◇ ◇ ◇ ◇ ◇

Looking back, I guess as a group we were quite retro in our approach to student life. We liked to think of ourselves as university throwbacks, drawing on the rebellion of sit-ins, marches, and anarchy when it caused splenic outbursts in vice-chancellors' offices throughout Britain.

In this we were special. We knew no students who were as dissolute, as consciously messy, as artfully unbridled, or as savage as we contrived to be (it was "savage" with a soft centre, savage-lite).

At its most frenzied peak, our antics could escalate into petty vandalism, such as dustbin races, to wailing like wolves in the dark streets on the way back from the pub. Once we tested the boundary of delinquency by carrying a discarded mattress with us from near the pub all the way to Rhodesia Terrace, where we flung it over someone's wall.

In short, we were pitiful, and it is only years later that I can look back and see just how feeble we were. Zac was especially pitiful, I think; he was a bit older, and his outrageousness became painfully laboured towards the end of our stay at Rhodesia Terrace.

But at the start, Zac and me were ringleaders, determined not just to experience life but to devour it, whatever the cost to our health.

"They're all so bloody *earnest* on my course. So horribly *focused*," Zac had protested, contemptuously, at the same time somehow stealthily fitting in enough study to keep up with the testing schedule towards his Master's in business studies. He had been taught to achieve. Hard cash had been invested in his brain cells and I could tell that he would not dare to let his parents down.

We might be brutish. But, I decided, we need not eat like animals. I quickly became resident cook, on the strength of the paupers' *coq-au-vin* I made soon after we'd all settled in.

Twenty "manager's special" chicken drumsticks bubbled in the oven while we enjoyed a long, Sunday lunchtime lager session and as wintry darkness fell they were chomped down eagerly between orgiastic cries of "Oh, shit man! This is so fucking *good*. Oh *man!*"

Zac had no interest in food but he thought it wise to encourage me. He would sometimes say "Olly, this really *is* the dogs' bollocks!" and I would inevitably reply: "No, it's beef, actually, Zac. We have *standards*, dear boy."

We had many tired jokes of that sort but recycling them was not wearying for us. We laughed more back then than at any time in our lives. Ella would laugh too but would cut off if we were being especially cruel.

Once, I was roped in to cook a celebration dinner to mark Zac's dumping of a very intense dental student who had sunk her horsey fangs into him, and wouldn't let go.

This well-shod filly would call for Zac in her S-reg car bringing a brief flash of glitz to Rhodesia Terrace but would never come in. Zac would joke that it was because she knew too much about infection, from her training.

"She promised to take me away from all this..." he said, one day, casting a wafty hand out over the assorted junk filling the room, after dumping her for the third and final time.

"But how could I...leave...you all?" he said, faking tears with nice thespian timing. Zac had played Lady Bracknell in a school production, and Ophelia, and could do convincing impressions.

I could see that Ella was in thrall but not wanting to show it; also, she felt for the girl being chucked. Ella, having known pain, was a girl who felt for everybody.

For this meal, which Zac called a Piss-Off Party (we always had to name our domestic thrashes) I made a huge cottage pie for us all, in a bashed-about enamel basin, to go with the main "event" – litre boxes of the cheapest, roughest, red wine.

Gradually, I began to see my duty was to prevent malnutrition among my flatmates. For the most part we alternated tinned stuff and takeaways with generous servings of an all-purpose broth.

This soup was ludicrously cheap. A couple of ham hocks, a few leeks, carrots. It was left blipping away for hours on the encrusted, carbonised stove top in an old jam pan I'd bought at the market. I would throw in a handful of barley to bulk it up.

It was slurped down, day and night. It served as pre-drinks stomach-liner (it was as salty as hell), and hangover elixir. If you were lovesick or in shock over exam results it was as comforting as a mother's bosom. When Ella was down in the dumps, or more skint than normal, she would also find solace in the reviving gloop.

There was another staple – fried bread. Zac had never tasted it (too plebian for the dining room of his posh school) until I once did a few slices, and then he was hooked. A blackened frying pan containing two centimetres of solidified grey grease – rendered from a few weeks' worth of bacon bits – lay next to the soup.

Cooking became my ticket to popularity. I loved it when people ate my stuff as if they were famished, when drunken, late night callers said "Oh *man!*" when they tasted it.

I liked being that man, the provider. My passion for food and the payment I received in praise was still there long after my love of writing was blunted by having to read what was prescribed for me.

I was convinced that cooking, not teaching or writing, would make me. And it did. And just as surely, eventually it caused me to crash and burn.

6

If I'd pushed ahead with my studies, and become a writer, and penned a memoir about my days in Rhodesia Terrace, I'd have gone for the extended seafaring metaphor.

Well, it certainly had been a voyage of discovery. There'd been squalls, mutinous mutterings about Captain Zac, a lot of yo-ho-ho, and, if not copious amounts of grog, a sea of lager and a lake of the cheapest wine.

Our voyage was a callow substitute for what, I'm told, proper sailors once knew as rum, bum and concertina.

We'd survived two years cooped up below decks, so to speak. Through my ministrations, there had been no scurvy, and the mice had been manageable, but nerves were becoming shredded and, with a girl on board, some stirrings of sexual tension.

But land was in sight. As we scanned the far horizon we could each make out the place where, in a week or two, we would dock. It was a place called Responsibility, in an even bigger place called The Future.

I would sally forth without a degree. The uni and I had agreed to part amicably – irreconcilable differences, as they say in the divorce courts. In short, they wanted some work out of me but I'd developed a ravenous appetite for cooking.

It had been a memorable trip, and I suspect we would all miss the emotional sustenance we had given each other.

Ella was the innocent at the centre of the growing twitchiness, up there in the oppressively small Crow's Nest, perched on the end of her little teen-size bed, plucking her mandolin, seemingly oblivious to petty and unspoken rivalries between Zac and me.

With my writer's pen still uncapped, and another metaphor at the ready, I would say I saw her as a captive bird, an image that grew truer on the few occasions she managed a tinkling run of the right notes on that mandolin, a perfect fragment of melody that cascaded down the stairs from her gloomy cubicle. Wasn't there a song..."She's only a bird in a gilded cage..."?

But as we grew used to the idea we would soon be saying goodbye to each other, a new shipmate came aboard for the final leg of our journey.

Richard was large, rather slow and introverted. There was a childish vulnerability about him. We knew him to be grotesquely clever.

To accommodate him for the last months of our tenancy, Zac had sacrificed what he called his "upstairs study" but which was in fact a virtual recycling depot. He blitzed this dump and rented it out, ostensibly in the interest of helping out a homeless soul but in reality because it would be another nice little earner.

One night, while we drank cider and our new housemate worked upstairs on deep mathematical conundrums, Zac asked us to suggest what creature Richard most resembled.

Ella made a protective noise and said: "Don't be so bloody cruel, you two! Leave the poor man alone."

"Giant sloth," I said, "he's the Greater London Giant Sloth," and immediately felt ashamed, more so when Ella glared at me. Zac somehow had a knack of making me less pleasant than I wanted to be.

"No, there's something prehistoric about him..." Zac said. "I think that maybe he's a living relative of some large-brained dinosaur that died off because its head was too big."

Ella flared. "And *you*? Did you get the teeth from an ancestral horse?" she said then, fixing him with a burning look: "Zac – I've noticed something. You seem happiest when you're making somebody uncomfortable. Were you a bully at that fancy school they sent you off to?"

Zac hooted with laughter but I noticed that neither his facial expression, nor his eyes, quite matched his attempt at lightheartedness. Ella could be formidable.

Zac had been sent away to school, and had once said, quite seriously, that school had become his home. He also once confessed, over the dregs of our pints when we were swaying drunk: "Tell you what Ol, you really have to learn to grow up fast when you're sent off at eight or nine. It makes you less scared of things when you do grow up, I suppose, but I sometimes wonder what it does inside. It's all right them saying: We wanted the best for you...."

Richard had been adopted by Ella. She loved the tranquillity around him, and his languid way of cruising along, his head (well, his brain at least) somewhere in the stars, the subject of his studies.

She was guardian and carer, doing his washing and reminding him to eat. She would constantly check his trouser fly.

"Oops, sorry – left the bomb bay doors open!" he would say, blushing and retreating in his lumbering way. Occasionally, Ella would walk past him and say in a robotic voice from the side of her mouth: "Calling Richard. Bomb bay alert."

Ella would tend to swoop on him as he left the house, and wipe shaving foam from behind his ears, tut-tutting like a fussy mother. When he left sniffling, she would tuck paper hankies into his pocket.

She was a compassionate presence in a house where the piss-taking could be pitiless; she was a reminder of the decency we had left behind. She was savagely self-protective when, in her phrase, we "went too far." We loved her.

Of course, I had no claim on Ella, and had never made a serious effort to win her over. It would have been all so public. We were forever scrutinising each other – me watching her, her watching Zac being amusing; Zac catching me out being tender with her for brief moments.

These tiny caring gestures from me amounted to a squeeze of her toes as she stretched out beside me watching TV. A mug of morning tea left at the foot of the stairs up to the Crow's Nest. A couple of paracetamol – nothing that churned up the group dynamics.

When Ella wanted to show affection, she would call me "Ginge." No one would say I was truly *ginger* but when she said it, I didn't care. It was what a teasing pal would say, or a sister, like Tilly.

It would have been difficult back then to try to win Ella for myself. She was jointly owned. But sometimes I wanted to rush in regardless.

I sensed Zac was suppressing a similar urge although his attitude to women was ambiguous. Perhaps he disliked women, held them in contempt, or was afraid of them. But I could see that he respected Ella. She had the power to bring out his generous side and the frankness to tell him when he was being hard-hearted.

For me, the most testing moments, as we tiptoed round each

other, were when Ella and Zac played chess. It looked so much like love-play once they really got into it, with all that staring into each other's eyes, the interlocking of minds (that in my head might as well have been limbs). The silences and the verbal taunts.

The best moments were when we were out of the house, doing an evening shift together at the bistro, me behind the counter and at the range, Ella waitressing. It almost felt like a date night.

We were a partnership, us against the world (of customers, that is). Sometimes we would make surreptitious eye contact if someone amusingly strange came in. Ridiculous, but the secrecy of it felt so good, just me and Ella being in on the joke.

There were good opportunities for me to show off, well out of Zac's shadow, beyond the range of his wit and inventiveness.

Once, when Ella was picking up meals, and a pompous-looking customer called out over the servery: "Chef! What, exactly, is *in* your Fisherman's Pie?"

I replied: "Oh, *real* fishermen, sir. Locally sourced. Organic. But we find some customers don't like the eyes…"

I laughed, to show him that I was joshing. He didn't reciprocate. He scowled. I knew, and he knew, and Ella knew, that I was saying: *Fish*, you stupid windbag. *Fish* – that's what's in the fucking Fisherman's Pie. I knew that Ella was impressed.

Ironically, around that time, several girls who I had no interest in impressing were impressed by me – or maybe by my cool indifference to them. I played along. Only Lakshmi, a breathtaking Guyanan girl, threw me off kilter.

She was in my year, and was universally loved for her sweetness, and also loved – and hated – for her exquisite beauty. No, *beauty* isn't enough: she was a dream, and what was excruciating was that she didn't seem to know it. Grace and modesty personified.

On a night off, I had proudly taken Lakshmi to the bistro where I did shifts (a third off for staff!) and the following week

I arranged for her to visit me in the hovel when Zac was away, Richard was working late, and Ella had been out looking for freelance work to service her overdraft.

Lakshmi arrived with a basket of Guyanese food, stuff with lovely names like moi-moi and coo-coo, and was sheathed in a dress that captured the pristine colours of the Caribbean... banana yellow, chilli red, plantain green. Set against that was skin the colour of chestnuts.

Yes, picture that, and then add eyes like wet, black glass and inky hair that looked as if it had been polished. Then add silver pendant earrings swinging beneath exquisitely sculpted ears, above the concave pockets of her perfect shoulders.

Lakshmi had brought for me a faded, slightly battered booklet as a belated birthday present – *A Useful Guide To British Food For Those Migrating From Overseas*. It was printed in the early Fifties and the text began..."*There are no British restaurants abroad and so you must read in advance about native British food and customs...*"

The booklet explained that in England, "soldiers" could mean toast dipped into egg, as well as an invading army; that bangers didn't necessarily explode ("*but beware, they will probably contain pork*"), and that no toads were used in the making of toad-in-the-hole.

Having handed over the booklet with a peck on the cheek, Lakshmi took it back immediately, and searched for a particular page, her daddy longlegs fingers nipping the pages.

"Just listen to this Olly. It will *kill* you...

'*In Great Britain, you will find that Dinner follows High Tea and is another common name for Supper, but sometimes also refers to Lunch...*'

She threw her head back, and heaved with laughter. "It's a wonder my poor grandparents didn't starve to death here, from not knowing when they could eat!"

I heard the ill-fitting front door being shoulder-charged open. We were on the settee together. Before us were trays covered with foil and plastic containers and bits of uneaten food. We were enjoying the last of the wine.

Ella looked surprised, then embarrassed as she walked in on us, carrying her portfolio.

"Oh, sorry!" she said. "Won't interrupt!" and turned toward the stairs.

"No, wait a sec, Ella! This is Lakshmi. Lakshmi – Ella, my housemate."

Housemate? Why not friend, comforter, shared companion? Was I playing Ella down?

Lakshmi smiled charmingly and said: "There might be a little food here if you're hungry Ella...and we've a drop of wine left. You're welcome."

"I've eaten, thanks," she said, although I knew she wouldn't have. I couldn't work out what was in the look she gave to Lakshmi then but it was deep and weighty, possibly inquiring. It was one of those looks that, I guess, only a woman might have been able to decipher.

When Lakshmi had gone for her bus, I sat and leafed through the booklet she had given me. In the front, I found an inscription she had written. It said:

HAPPY BIRTHDAY!

My very old ajee (grandmother to you) sang a song...

Cookie, yu na see nobody pass ya?
Well, one a me dumplin' gone –
me pretty likkle dumplin' gone

PS I know that if you do decide to become a chef, everyone will want to pinch your dumplings!

Love, Lakshmi X

As I bundled up and binned the remnants of the meal, Ella came down in her dressing gown, pale and drawn, the brown hair flat and wet, wearing huge woolly bedsocks, carrying her mug.

"All right, El?" I asked. "Did it go OK today?"

"Fine," she said flatly. Then "Sorry to barge in on your...is it a tryst they call it...? Nice meal?"

"Different. Guyanese stuff. Interesting. Some of it would have been better hot. She was planning to heat some of it up but then saw the cooker."

"She's the one from your year, the one everyone raves about?"

"Yea," I said: "Don't you think that she's a bit special?"

Ella paused. Was she about to kick away the pedestal from under Lakshmi's brown, bony, perfect feet, those chocolate confections of toes, lit by those lapis lazuli toe rings?

"*Special?*" she said, with a dismissive emission of air, almost a snort. "Special?" She shook her head resignedly.

"Put it this way, Ol, nobody, *nobody* should be allowed to look like that. No mortal should have been given a bloody neck like that, or a figure like that, or a smile like that. And no one who looks like that should be *nice* as well. It's unjust."

Good, generous, self-critical Ella. I felt relief.

"She must be universally hated by the girls on your course. Actually, I'd like to be able to hate her myself."

"Yes," I said, "and she's *so* self-deprecating. She always says 'Oh I'm just the usual Guyanese mix.'"

I picked up the booklet and said: "Look, El, she gave me this hilarious old booklet about English eating habits...she's written an inscription..."

But Ella was turning to the stairs with her mug of water.

"Really nice of her. But can I look at it tomorrow, Ol? I'm dog tired now. Goodnight."

7

We all moved out of Rhodesia Terrace on the same day as each other. I say it was *day* but it was early evening before we'd dragged our sorry chattels down to the hall and, in what turned out to be a staggered exit, had each stepped into the darkening new world of separateness.

I was the last to nudge the stubborn front door shut with my shoulder. And as I did, what struck me as odd was that we hadn't said goodbye to each other, not properly. We had crept away stealthily, avoiding each other.

There had been ample opportunity at the party the night before to make our fond farewells. We'd been drunk enough. But there were no maudlin, slobbery last embraces. Not a tear; not a manly handshake.

Ella had already taken her clothes, her paintings and her mandolin to the house she was to share with three girls, in nearby Tanganyika Road. She had come back to Zac's for the party crowing that her room there was *so absolutely enormous* she could *actually walk round her bed.* I was so pleased to think of her enjoying space, the captive bird being able to spread her wings.

Early in the morning next day, Richard had headed off with his bags and suitcases for his new digs he was sharing with some foreign science students. Zac had slept on, long and deeply, into the afternoon. I heard him stirring but when I came back from my walk to buy a jar of coffee, his stuff and his car had gone.

I felt hurt. That really was no way to say goodbye. Month after month we'd shared space, food and drink, farts, music, jokes, domestic disasters, and (very occasionally) had been as emotionally frank as it felt safe to be. Now we were saying goodbye by not saying it. Perhaps splitting up was simply too painful to confront. We had become some sort of a family.

I remember that when I'd dragged myself down, around midday, propped up against a mug, was a note. It said:

"Key, Zac. Speak soon.

Love Ella XXX".

Three kisses for him. No note for me. Perhaps because Tilly had become a friend of Ella's, and because I would be staying with my sister in Edgware while I waited for a place on the cookery course, she knew we were unlikely to lose touch. So there was no need for a message. But there was.

My head thumped with last night's music. I needed more coffee. I palmed a space through the sink full of food-encrusted crockery to fill the kettle. Zac had said that the house was going to be cleaned and fumigated before a family moved in. I was ashamed that we were leaving such chaos for fellow human beings to deal with.

I took my coffee to my room, edged round the bed and leaned against the wardrobe. Suddenly I felt very, very sober, but the depression that is the cost of an alcohol high was settling over me like rain clouds. I was finally confronting the parting with Ella.

We'd set everything up to have a ball last night but a strange hysteria pervaded the high jinks. I felt sure somehow that things would turn sour and my instinct was right. Misunderstandings littering the party. Jokes went too far, much too far. In the small hours Zac had about him the emotional coldness that revealed itself through drink.

I knew that the shindig wouldn't have lived up to his expectations. He planned for it to be much more than a farewell piss-up. He'd wanted this, The Last Supper as he called it, to be ultra special.

Maybe he was finding our break-up especially difficult – he had planned things so carefully.

His invitation – only to selected guests – said *"bring a bottle but don't bring Judas, or I'll be cross."* He'd dug out bedsheets so that he could come downstairs, with apparent spontaneity, as Jesus. He had decided that everyone would pose for a Last Supper video, which would be circulated as a memento.

He would be in the middle of the line-up and he wanted Ella to be Mary Magdalene.

"I'll say something like 'Meet the wife,'" Zac had said with a laugh. "And while it's being filmed I'm going to do this really obvious switch with a glass of water and a glass of plonk. Crap conjuring. You know. Tommy Cooper stuff."

As hosts, we were laying on Middle Eastern bread and wine, in keeping with Zac's Biblical theme. I'd found a reasonably clean chunk of paving in the garden which I planned to heat in the oven, so that my flatbreads would balloon up, and taste authentic.

For me the party had started nervily; Ella was bringing somebody. He was a charismatic character, evidently, a computer graphics whizz from her design course. As I put out bowls of olives and hummus, I grew curious as to how he might look, and anxious about how they might be together.

He was the first to arrive, carrying a six-pack of cheap, weak beer and a timid look. I was delighted to note that the oft-mentioned young guru was neither good-looking, nor imposing, nor even interesting – clearly Ella regarded him as simply someone to hang around with.

Jason was skinny and wore green-frame glasses and a T-shirt bearing a huge logo saying WHY? in luminous orange; Ella would like that bit of artiness. But as I said to Zac, as we sorted the wine and I put my flagstone in the oven, obviously he was all T-shirt and glasses.

"A lightweight," Zac said. "Just watch him flake out."

Zac's prediction – that Jason would have a low capacity for, and poor tolerance of, alcohol – proved correct. He was talking nonsense by the time the main phalanx of guests charged through the front door like wildebeest. They had already imbibed heavily.

Sitting stiff-backed at the edge of the settee was Richard. He had tried to escape the party but Zac had pretended to be insulted by the very idea and so he had obeyed. He was clutching a glass of something fruit-based and looking lost, or deep in some intellectual struggle; you never could tell with Richard.

Ella ruffled his hair and sat with him, trying in vain to be heard over the din. She would miss Richard, and worry about him, I knew that. And she knew that he would miss her, in a Richard kind of way.

Zac came from the kitchen and kissed and fondled a crop-headed girl who was doing her best to stay inside a sparkly red dress. It had a ridiculously high hemline. So this was Jade...

She tugged the hem down constantly, and I was amused to see that each time she struggled for modesty at thigh level, her breasts teetered forward on the cliff edge of her bodice and threatened to make a break for freedom.

For half an hour Zac and this juddering woman thrashed around to a relentless hard rock beat, Zac nodding mechanically, with his eyes shut and his knees locked, her shifting and dipping in the sparkly dress, her long earrings lashing her cheeks.

Finally, Zac shouted over the cacophony for me to come and meet her. Jade's face glistened with sweat. Vodka had robbed her of what was left of her modesty and she flopped on to the settee panting, indifferent now about her expanses of wanton bareness. Richard, knees together, edged his bottom away perhaps to avoid any risk of contact.

Zac sat on the floor in front of her. She draped a leg over his shoulder and he played with a bare foot. I sat beside him with Richard at my back. I noticed Zac quaffing, rather than sipping, wine. He looked to be on one of his self-wrecking missions.

Clearly he was indeed dreading the separation, and, on top, the prospect of joining his father and having to buckle down to business.

"So you're the great Olly..." Jade shouted. Was that sarcasm or boozy friendliness in her tone?

"And you're.... sorry, Zac did tell me but I've forgotten!" I yelled back. "I know it's something precious..." I cupped my ear for a reply. Her eyelids resembled half-raised window blinds and her big red fleshy mouth was lolling open.

"Jade..." she said, eventually. "Not precious.....*semi*-precious."

"No, you *are* precious," said Zac in a baby voice, kissing a big toe. He was being ironic but Jade would not have picked that up drunk or sober.

Women came to Zac willingly; no insincere verbal foreplay was ever necessary. He offered a winning combination – shining teeth, the Latin hair, a confidence that in some would be seen as cockiness, and, behind the dishevelled façade, intimations of wealth... the diver's watch, the prestigious label inside the heavily-pilled sweater.

Yet some of our friends regarded Zac as a bit of a conundrum, or even a fraud. Everyone knew he came from money, and had a future assured in the property business but he seemed to thrive on subsidence living, on fried bread breakfasts, on being one of us. Was it pretence?

At any rate, to some extent he was playing at it, and it irked even those who were fond of him. But in a sense he couldn't win. If he was generous, and he could be touchingly kind (he'd helped Ella out of a couple of financial scrapes), he was in danger of appearing condescending.

I remember seeing Ella in the far corner of the room gazing fixedly at our little group, while Jason passed time by reading the notes taken from Zac's pile of CDs. I think she was trying to lip-read. I wanted her to join us, to spend time with her on this last night but Jade was a deterrent.

"Precious. And green. G r e e n!" Jade said, trying to put on a scary voice. "*Green...* for jealousy and envy..." She was looking at me challengingly, her scarlet talons raised, waiting for me to engage in some rat-arsed wrangle.

Perhaps sensing confrontation, Zac looked up over his shoulder and – as if Richard had just materialised at that moment – exclaimed, as a diversion: "Richard!"

"Zac," said Richard, in his customary flat monotone.

"Having a ball? Getting into the zone? Really rocking?"

"Yes. It's nice. But I have to be up early, remember," he shouted.

"Richard, this is Jade, who is named after a rare and precious stone. Jade – may I present Richard, our resident genius." Richard huffed and puffed in protest but Zac rambled on.

"We won't have it Richard! We all know you can do *really* hard sums and understand time and space and things."

I noticed that Ella was now on her own, eyes shut, swaying gently from side to side to the music. I guessed that Jason had gone off to be sick. I waved her over and she sat on the floor beside me.

"Ella! *Ella!*" Zac yelled, as if he had not known that she had been in the room for what had been hours. "This is Jade. Named after an *exquisite* precious stone. Ella. Our lady who *does*. Keeps us sorted, lives in the Crow's Nest."

"You're pissed Zac," said Ella coolly. "Don't go all unlikeable on me."

Jade was staring at Ella; her eyes searching but not registering any response to what she saw. Ella looked back with what was part contempt, part pity. The only sound now was the thumping music.

Jade seized the moment to yell: "Most people call me Foxy. I'm Jade Fox see. So I get Foxy. I like Foxy. It really suits me."

Really? Ella thought. She threw a withering look Jade's way and then said: "People like us with short names like Ella, Olly and Zac don't get nicknames."

Zac didn't seem to hear. He was constructing an amusing monologue in his head. At last he drained his glass and said: "It's good if nicknames describe people or tell some story about them. Say I was choosing a nickname for Richard here, I'd go for...well prehistoric. Exotic prehistoric," he paused appearing to wonder whether his words rhymed.

His eyes were beginning to go. Jade reached into her bag and poured vodka from it into his empty glass. After a pause he declared: "He's a big boy. And he's a Richard." He held up his glass and shouted: "I decree that from henceforth he shall be known as... Biggus Dickus..."

Ella smiled sympathetically at Richard while Zac, warming to his theme, looked into his glass, wondered where the vodka had come from, and said: " You know, I fancy that once, millennia ago, entire herds, absolute squillions of Biggi Dicki squelched their way through what is now the Thames Estuary."

Zac was starting on one of his drunken verbal rambles and I knew, from previous experience, to expect casualties. He droned on, like a lethargic lecturer.

"I can hear you, you know, Zac" said Richard unnecessarily from a mere yard away. "He's making it up, Jade."

There was the crash of a bottle breaking in the kitchen and then a cheer as a big, bare-chested guest finished the last of the half pint of vinegar he had been challenged to drink.

"Zac, I wanna know...." Jade said with a slur. "I wanna know is he *really* called Biggus because of what I'm thinking...? You know..." Jade said, giggling, trying to sound coquettish.

"Jade! You brazen hussy! No, he's just big and he's a Dick. A dick in the Richard sense, that is," he said touching Richard's shoulder as an apology.

"Zac, you really are a cruel shit sometimes," said Ella, in an even voice. She went to the kitchen to find a drink. She was scowling when she came back.

After a moment's silence, Jade let out a long whinny, at whatever was in her lolling head.

Zac put out his arm and gathered the reluctant Richard to him. "We think that it's in the Dickus area that the problem lies, and that it's why the Dicki are dying off. It's time this one got a girlfriend, a lady Biggi – isn't it Biggus? But maybe he's already busy in that department..."

"Had no complaints so far," Richard said without conviction, breaking away. This was something that he'd heard people say sometimes, when the opposite sex was mentioned.

Jade leaned back, cackled once more, and then tucked a cushion under her head and wriggled to get comfortable. Her breasts fell about like ten-pin balls, nudging each other, then losing momentum and settling side by side.

"It'd be *very* interesting to know exactly how many complaints *you've* had, Zac..." Ella said. I was horrified to think that she might have some intimate knowledge of Zac. It was as if she wanted to inflict private humiliation that only the two of them could appreciate.

I couldn't shake off the sudden emotional chill I had at Ella's taunt, a feeling that would return many times in future years....

Did Ella know something from personal experience? Could they have...? Did they want to but hadn't...? Had he actually tried with her and not mentioned it to me?

Then I remembered with a stab of jealousy that when Ella came to join us, as she had carried her stuff to the Crow's Nest that day, he had watched her climb the stairs, and said: "*Mmm...* Peachy!"

8

That morning, after re-reading the little note from Ella to Zac, I placed my keys alongside hers, and gathered the last of my things, ready to set off for Edgware. Tilly's place would be so comfortable after Rhodesia Terrace, I knew that, but my heart was heavy.

I thought of Ella, settling in with new people, walking round her bed for the hell of it, juggling what money she had, picking out plaintive chords from her mandolin, and going back and forth to Milton Keynes to see to her chronically ailing – and endlessly demanding – mum.

I thought of the day I'd taken the bus with her, to see her mother, and to satisfy my curiosity about Milton Keynes. In one sense, the trip had been depressing, in another it was gratifying: I knew Ella so much better by the end of the day. I liked her more, and knew I could do without Milton Keynes.

Ella's mother – emaciated, and strangely mauve – seemed intent on dragging Ella down, ensuring that she returned to London burdened with guilt.

Ella took me upstairs to her old bedroom – laughingly calling it "the studio." Two walls were covered with pinned-up scraps of paper, samples of cloth, images snipped from magazines. It was as if an entire team of artists had run a brainstorming session and left behind their collective embryonic concepts.

But the centre of one of the walls had been left uncluttered.

In the space was a black-and-white photograph of a gawky young soldier, cigarette in mouth, leaning on the barrel of a large gun. Beneath it was a faded colour photo of the man many years later, sitting in front of a Christmas dinner. He had Ella's full lips and the slightly crossed front teeth. Dad.

A third wall was covered with Ella's paintings. The treatment varied but there was a recurring theme and a single motif – a small, round-headed figure set in varying densities of darkness. Each figure had a wedge taken out of the upturned head, as if it were an open mouth.

Also, in each picture there was a suggestion of a moon and it was easy to imagine that the figure was baying, or shouting in protest, crying perhaps, or singing. I mentioned this to Ella and she said: "You get it, Ol. Just add your own sound."

The figure I saw as Ella, and the imaginary sound I heard, was of Ella protesting. I felt deep empathy for her. She was making her way out of barrenness and poverty, unsupported, carried on the magic carpet of her imagination. If she stopped believing that the carpet existed, she would have plunged down to earth.

Ella's mother met us at the bottom of the stairs, breathing heavily and supported by a walking frame.

"You need to get that lot cleared some time Ella. You'll only be faced with it afterwards if you don't," she said. Afterwards.

That evening, when we got off the bus to wend our way back to Rhodesia Terrace, we called at a pub, and then at another, and another, and at each our companionship seemed to deepen.

"A nightcap. A very last nightcap. My round," I said when we were within a few hundred yards of the house but Ella was walking unsteadily and the idea evaporated as we talked.

We had said goodnight as she got her mug of water to carry to bed. She said a very sincere "Thanks for today Ol" and swayed towards the steep stairs to the Crow's Nest. She was bound to fall.

Ella had announced a firm rule about her living area. That it was sacrosanct. *Hers.* That it could never be visited whether or not she was around. But I took her elbows, steering her up, and then I stepped in. There was no space to skirt the bed. She fell on it and then I followed.

We lay in the soundless dark for a time and then she said: "You can hold me a bit if you want Ol."

So I did. Just held her, for maybe ten minutes, until she was asleep.

That was my moment, our moment. Now she had gone, without a word, taken off with just a vague belief that some day we'd be back in touch, probably via Tilly. "Probably" seemed perilously close to not at all.

As I gathered my carrier bags and reached for my rucksack, I found a card with my name on it, wedged into the top. I opened it. There was a caricature on the front of me in a chef's toque, grinning and standing in front of a huge steaming pan, holding up a soup ladle.

Inside, Ella's message, said:

"THANKS FOR EVERYTHING, GINGE. PLEASE DON'T DISAPPEAR!" Then *"Lots of love. Ella XXXX."*

Lots of love. Four kisses. *Four.* I liked that. Kiss, kiss, kiss...*kiss.* But if Ella had added that extra one for luck, it didn't work. For me or for her.

9

In the lecture room at the culinary school, Monika pressed a button and projected a diagrammatic image of the human tongue.

This was the start of the talk she did in the early weeks of every course. It was down in the syllabus as *Taste, the Only Judge*.

Most students at the school would have preferred to be working with food, not talking about it. The lectures could be over-scientific, and Monika could be quite intense. But then some course members (among them the more posh and pampered) found they neither understood the science, nor knew how to cook.

The Culinary School course was no sinecure. Monika trained students as if they were soldiers. To test what they had learned she set up four-course dinners that the students had to prepare against the clock.

The battlefield was the stove. The skirmishes could involve scalding fat, vicious knives, flames from hissing pans. There were casualties. Some of what Olly thought of as the "ski-chalet girls" fell away in shock when disembowelling a rabbit, or felt faint digging into the dead man's fingers of a boiled crab.

They had all volunteered to suffer the torrid heat and the barked orders in a battle that was never really won. There was always more to learn even if you took in Monika's lecture on fatty acids, macrobiotics, flavonoids, stuff at a microscopic level.

Most students – some coming unenthusiastically to cookery after failing on academic courses – lounged, checked the time, examined their nails, and from time to time looked intently at Monika, feigning interest.

Monika was no fool. She believed that to be an artist in food, a virtuoso, you had first to learn the chemistry of food. She was contracted to pass on what she knew; it was a matter of personal choice whether anyone chose to listen.

But Olly listened – keenly. It was invaluable, in his view, if you were serious about cooking, all part of what he thought of as a lifelong apprenticeship. He knew that having the theory would eventually strengthen his perception of himself as a true professional, a *chef*, a huge step up from the "cook" he had once been.

Monika was pencil-thin, blue-eyed, famously straw-blonde, but grey at the temples now, though still readily recognisable from the picture in the recipe book Olly had bought when his vocation revealed itself.

He noticed, when she came near, that ageing had given her a faint, whitish moustache, and many fine lines dissecting the even tan of her face. He was sorry for Monika and supportive of her, holding a smile for long spells to show that at least *he* was paying attention and soaking up her knowledge.

Monika had long ago attained the status of food guru. She had achieved all there was to achieve in cuisine by the time she had reached forty. That was what he had paid for, gone into debt for. To learn from the best. Olly justified the cost by likening the course to lessons from a football superstar.

Yes, he felt for Monika. He was touched by her valiant efforts to drop in a little joke here and there, leavening her tutorials. She delivered the carefully constructed quips formally, and therefore unfunnily (*"You say that too many cooks spoil the broth but I think you have too many cooks here who spoil everything!"*).

She would dispense epigrams, hoping that they would be

recalled and found to be true once the students went out to begin their careers.

"Frying..." she would say, "deep-frying, should be a process of which the diner is unaware. It is your secret. It should not be detectable on the plate. It should be as if food has been crisped by fairies."

This would prompt a grouse about English fish and chips that she referred to as fat and carbohydrate, made edible by the hidden presence of fish and the acid effect of vinegar – *"It is only good to save you from perishing when you are enduring the British seaside."*

"So..." Monika began, pointing a finger at the illustration, showing the diagrammatic tongue with outlined patches ranged round the edge and numbers superimposed. "So...we all know about taste buds? The many, many thousands waiting to work on the food you prepare. So. How many types of taste?"

In her crisp whites she might well have been a scientific researcher. She had an earnestness about her, the air of a seeker after truths.

When bitter, sour, salt, and sweet had, rather haltingly, been identified by the group, along with the parts of the tongue which registered each one, she said: "So, we are happy?" She left time for a response. Her piercing gaze ranged over the students. A few gave some grudging sign of agreement.

"Well, I'm not happy!" she said decisively but with a smile. "Because we are looking at a *myth*. A *lie*." At this, some heads were raised, some brains re-engaged. *All* taste buds, she said, could register all flavours to some degree. And what about umami, the taste of glutamate?

"You all believe that you know what flavours are but you don't. It is a never-ending study."

Monika declared, forcibly but amiably, that her intention was to make every student really think about *flavour*, and *texture*, and the *feel* of food in the mouth.

As a group they would find words to create an entire library of flavours – "Think of the flavour you liked about your grandmother's stew, and your mother's fruit cake, and the chemicals in your crisps. Flavours are like shades of colour in an enormous paint catalogue."

She declared: "We will make a list of what your mouth says about your food." When the course was finishing, she said, she would print out the list, have copies laminated, and at the last session hand them out, instructing each student – no doubt with kindly sternness – to pin the list up in any kitchen they worked in.

This project suited Olly, with his eager-beaver love of cooking and his writer's love of words. As the list grew each week, he felt like the despised brainy pupil forever thrusting up a hand, trying to catch teacher's eye.

Honeyed...astringent...ferrous...peppery...gamey...chalky... brackish...

Monika rewarded him with a pinched smile each time he contributed a word. He was embarrassingly keen compared to his sleepy and indifferent peers but he didn't care.

At the final tutorial, she made an appeal: "Never, ever say that you cannot be inventive, or bold. Or that it's all been done. Explore! Invent! Combine! Just look at the list you have drawn up as a reminder of the power you have to give pleasure. You have magic at your fingertips."

She wished them all good luck and as they gathered at the door, and began to leave, she called: "Remember, good cooking is ... it's what, back at home, we would call *zauberi*...like, sorcery. And love. Love for the ingredients, love for what you create with them, and love for those round your table. Enjoy!"

10

Zac and Olly and Ella might never have got together again if it had not been for Richard's love life.

Love life? No one who knew Richard would have guessed that his name, or his macho nickname, could possibly ever rub shoulders in any sentence with "love life."

Yet – out of the blue – came the news that he is to be married. It was quite a surprise for him too. His girl friend had decided his fate before he had even realised that that's what she had become.

Vi was controlling, meticulous and strong on detail. But it turned out that she had been less than careful about contraception and, in an old-fashioned way, was now keen to camouflage this oversight with a marriage service. The ceremony would solemnize the handing over of Richard (known to her as Ricky) to her firm ministrations.

Vi had allocated on the reception plan seats for ten non-family guests, and Richard had been given the freedom to ask which friends he chose to invite.

He was unaware but the pregnancy really had done wonders for his reputation. The socially inept Richard was less of a staid Dickus now and more of a Ricky in the perception of those who formed a supportive ring around him. Some now even regarded him as a bit of a dark horse.

As to the marriage, he had no strong view. He'd noticed that this was an event that tended to happen to people; nevertheless he had been startled that it had happened to him, and with such bewildering speed.

The prospect of the wedding delighted Ella ("Can't *wait* to meet the missus!" she wrote in an email to Olly, checking that he would be attending). The invitations reminded Olly of how fond they had been of Richard, and how badly they had treated him. But old habits die hard, and Zac couldn't resist making a crack, in an email to Olly, about Immaculate Conception.

It turned out that Richard and Vi, an obelisk of a girl who stood a foot taller than her squat paramour, had met a few months earlier at a gathering of Blackheath Space Watchers and then again just a week later at a Science Museum lecture on quantum field theory.

Vi took this as a sign: Astronomy meeting astrology. As Richard had not resisted her overtures, she presumed that he desired her in some way. But romantic love was just beyond his scope.

Truth be told, he found people pretty much the same. Vi was as tolerable as most, and he was growing to enjoy her supervisory attentiveness. Being organised by somebody gave him time to think.

Conception had taken place after a relaxing day out at the National Bus Collection Annual Cavalcade, held on a disused aerodrome in Lincolnshire. They were back late in London and Vi had suggested he stay the night. She waved away his protest that he had not brought his pyjamas, and that his guppies had not been fed.

In the way of seduction scenes last seen in Fifties rep, she had changed into something silky, given Richard a large vodka and, as he viewed that day's photographs of buses on his laptop, had seductively closed the lid and hauled his resisting bulk towards the bedroom, putting her index finger to her lips in the manner of a seductress.

"Hush, Ricky," she whispered. This intimate note struck fear into Richard. Vi normally spoke in a forceful monotone that was only rarely enriched by vocal subtlety.

Richard had always tended to simply go along with things in his rather clunky way but he had broken away and gone back to the armchair to check that he had put his glasses safely in the case. He was quickly reclaimed.

His face was heavy and bloated for one so young; he was bulky, round-shouldered, unkempt. In contrast, the elegance of his mathematics was legendary. His greatest quality (those lodging at Zac's agreed) was not the famed brain but his endearing lack of common sense – and his blissful ignorance of the fact that he was being made fun of.

Richard's language was numbers. He said only what it was necessary to say. What was in his mind was far too interesting for him to feel the need to venture into the big world out there. The disorder at Zac's place had not troubled him; the inside of his head was equally untidy, jumbled with half-resolved theorums.

It was generally known that Richard was already something quite special in the university maths department at a remarkably young age, but no one in the house ever knew exactly what his role was. They had asked, of course, but when he began to describe – haltingly, and in excruciating detail – what he did, they couldn't even begin to understand.

Once, they had yawned in unison to tease Richard as he was lured into talking about a new line of research in the department. They had broken into laughter when he shook his head, mystified.

"So what's funny about Zermelo-Fraenkel set theory?" he asked, his eyes widening behind his glasses.

"Nothing!" said Zac. "No, nothing," said Olly. "Absolutely *nothing*, darling Richard," Ella said, pinching his cheeks and planting a kiss on his forehead.

Ella was to insist on using the name Richard as a defensive gesture long after the party.

When Vi graciously gave Richard the chance to choose his guests, Zac and Olly and Ella, whom he had not seen since The Last Supper, were at the top of his list. The invitations heralded a long-overdue reunion. Olly was relieved that, evidently, Richard's Rhodesia Terrace experience as the atypical chicken that the rest of them pecked had not been resented in retrospect.

Ella's sporadic contact with Olly seemed to have come to a full stop, until her email, just before the wedding. Zac, who had been in touch with Ella and Olly more often, sent a message to both saying *"Both free to see BD sacrificed? Bet she's a real Bridezilla. Actually calls him RICKY!!!!"*

The wedding lit up a soggy November afternoon in a grey corner of Clapham, guests filtering into the rain-lashed old church, fancy hats and bright dresses producing splashes of colour against the grey backdrop of the day.

As he sat in a pew with his new girlfriend Jane, Olly was much more curious as to how Ella would look, than Richard was about his bride. The groom was now standing to attention in front of the altar in a slightly over-sized suit.

Olly had not seen Ella in many months, not since Tilly – who remained a friend – brought her home briefly for a bite after they'd been to the theatre. Ella had needed to hurry to catch her train back to her late mother's home in Milton Keynes.

They'd hugged as she arrived that day, and she had looked flustered. She was beautifully dressed he noted. He had taken her hand and held it rather too long. She'd said: "Bit of a change from Rhodesia Terrace..." admiring the neatness of Tilly's little living room.

There had been so much to say, and Ella was hurriedly eating between questions and answers – about work, the death of her mother, about her progress on the mandolin. She wanted to know about the course he'd taken, about cheffing in London.

They had cuddled again as she left, with Tilly, for the station. He had not wanted her to leave, and on the doorstep they crammed in more exchanges, and promises to keep in touch before Tilly looked at her watch and shouted.

He had noticed that when Ella laughed – he'd missed that deep-throated laugh –she still gathered her cardigan round her. It was a pleasing gesture of familiarity leading straight back to Rhodesia Terrace days.

When Tilly came home, she sat at the kitchen table, and said breathlessly: "Doesn't she look *well*? Ella. Love her! Such a sweetheart! Hasn't got a bean but dresses so *stylishly*…"

Olly wondered whether Tilly was fishing, and it dawned on him that his sister might have had an ulterior motive in bringing Ella back to the house. It was strange – there had been so little time before her train left.

"She's a bit less intense than Jane, although I really like Jane. Jane's a sticker. For me, Ella's got that character but she's also got more flair, more sensitivity. I was really surprised that neither you nor Zac didn't end up with her…"

◇ ◇ ◇ ◇ ◇

Richard had invited a couple of science colleagues and a leading light in the world of old buses as his wedding guests, along with Olly and Jane, Zac and his chic girlfriend Gaby, and Ella and her newish partner Joe.

They shared a pew and after whispered attempts at introducing each other failed because of the silences demanded by the service, they sat and watched as Richard and Vi were joined in what Zac described, in an aside to Olly, as unwholesome matrimony.

Olly had a surreptitious look at Joe. He was older than Ella, prosperous at a guess, and certainly smart, showing a touch of flair with a tartan tweed waistcoat the shade of a thistle flower, beneath his dark jacket. Arty, like Ella.

It was clear that Joe was smitten with Ella. He whispered to her as, heads together, they consulted the order of service and she laughed, gathering her suit jacket round her.

The rings having been exchanged, Vi stooped low and Richard shut his eyes, knowing that he was going to be kissed. As the organ struck up, he marched with his bride, in a slightly military way into the fine rain and a forest of umbrellas.

Later, upstairs in the function room of a gloomy pub, Richard rose to toast the bridesmaids. He held a sheaf of notes, crib sheets Vi had prepared, so that he said the right things in the right order.

Ella was silently rooting for Richard, who looked slightly dazed by it all. She knew that this part of the proceedings would be agony for him, and regretted that someone had not shortened the sleeves of his suit, as she would have done, or seen to the trace of dried shaving foam on his left ear lobe.

His speech was totally devoid of humour or real interest, and a humorous story he began about his clothes being confiscated by Zac while he was in the shower dissolved into a mumble. It was as if he was expecting guests to provide their own punch line.

The best man, an astrophysicist with quicksilver movements and darting black eyes, proved disarmingly witty and entertaining, having weaved information he had gleaned from Zac about the Rhodesia Terrace days into an affectionate verbal portrait.

The guests loved the tale of how Zac added small amounts of cotton wool into the toes of Richard's shoes each night, so that he began to believe that his feet had put on a late spurt of growth. They liked the idea of the genius being blind to the obvious.

The two bottles of wine – one red, one white – proved niggardly when Olly and Jane, Zac and Gaby, and Ella and Joe joined one of Richard's cousins at the table Vi had nominated for them. Twice that amount would have been needed to diffuse the tension that hung over the dry Hunter's Chicken and confetti-strewn tablecloth.

On the next nearest table, the bus enthusiast, who was

apparently deaf, was bawling at Richard's university colleagues about his latest acquisition and the logistics of moving an old bus from Kilmarnock to Lincolnshire.

Olly asked Gaby about her job. When she replied coolly that she was a corporate investor, he saw no way ahead conversationally. She did not ask, in turn, what he did for a living.

Zac, who had hugged Olly as they met at the church ("Olly mate! It's been *so* long!") now seemed equally remote. He was two seats away from Olly and had Gaby at his shoulder. He looked inhibited.

Ella, seeing that Jane was ill at ease, ventured a kindly inquiry about how she and Olly met.

"We were both working at Sevenoaks Lodge and Spa," Jane said. "Olly had got the *chef de partie* job, I was running banqueting. But you two go back absolute *years!*" said Jane. "Even before Olly did the cooking course."

"Yes. He practised on us!" Ella said brightly. "Used to do us a thick soup that hung around for days. The only thing that kept us alive!"

Jane tried to picture the younger Olly back then, and the even-younger Ella, and the intimacy of the flat.

Zac looked on, untypically reticent, as he followed proceedings, no longer the conversational adventurer teasing out tales, telling his own.

"And what about you two?" Olly asked, looking to Ella and Joe, who said: "Well, I'm in PR and we were working on a concept and we urgently needed some ideas. Ella had sent in a portfolio on the off chance so we got her in and she ended up doing the lot." He put his arm round her shoulder and squeezed.

Olly put aside his cutlery, losing interest in the meal. He looked across the table and Ella was staring at him; she had noticed his reaction.

He wondered whether it might appear greedy if he topped his

wine up again; he knew he had already had more than the rest.

"It must be difficult when you're a chef," said Robin, Richard's very normal-looking cousin, who also noticed that Olly had stopped eating. "You probably keep thinking: I could have made this much better. Or... I can tell this came from a bag."

"Yeah," said his wife, in support. "You must get *really* picky."

Zac appeared to feel the need to contribute, at last. "All I can say is that until you've tasted Olly's fried bread you haven't lived!" he said, and for a moment the table was united by a gentle burble of laughter.

Ella looked across to Olly and he met her gaze again. There was the old affection there somewhere up above the mysterious workings of whatever force it was that made strangers even of those people in the group who knew each other so well.

After the tiramisu had been eaten in near-silence, Richard and Vi arrived hand in hand, the groom being led, as if he were blind. There were handshakes and kisses and Vi gave a forceful account of honeymoon plans and domestic arrangements. Richard just smiled benignly.

As the couple circulated, an uneasy silence descended. Eyes fell on the near-empty wine bottles but no-one risked appearing ill-mannered by finishing it off, or facing the awkwardness of offering it to others, thereby showing a self-interest.

Zac looked over to where Richard and Vi had settled to talk with family members.

"Olly mate," Zac asked suddenly, "tell me honestly. Were we *really* horrible to him?"

"Well, I was. A bit. But you were worse. You really made him have it!"

"Come on man! You went along with it. You're like those after the war who said 'I was just following orders.'" He's right, Olly thought. I let him do most of the dirty work while I looked on.

Ella chipped in: "You two were as bad as each other! You never let him alone." She sounded good-humoured now. Time had taken the edge off the outrage she used to feel over their treatment of Richard.

She said: "What about that thing you did with the match when you were drunk. Testing his fight and flight response – or was it his pain threshold? And he sat there and let you! You both took advantage of his good nature. You were disgraceful!"

She sounded disapproving but amused too, in a nostalgic kind of way. She was back for a moment at Rhodesia Terrace, nagging Olly and Zac, nursemaiding Richard.

"He loved it, Ella," Zac said. "Loved it. Well, he invited us to his wedding didn't he?"

When the over-loud music struck up, there was relief among the Rhodesia Terrace trio and their partners. It was good to throw off the burden of polite conversation, just to sit.

Vi was going round the tables cajoling people, pressing them to dance. Olly tried to show goodwill by inviting Gaby on to the floor but she said with a grimace: "Can't. Heels!"

Olly danced with Jane, and Joe with Ella and as one song died and a new one started, a circle of dancers formed. Olly found himself next to Ella who was dancing in exactly the same, elementary way as she had done years ago. She was turning to him and then away, swaying to the music.

As the number finished on a blaring chord, and they moved from the dance floor, she looked at him intently and said under her breath "*Ring* me." In a second, Joe had moved towards them. He gathered Ella's hand proprietorily and led her back to the table.

11

More than three years had passed since Jane had slept with Olly on that last night. It had marked the end of their marriage, what had been a fruitful partnership, with Olly's career flourishing, and Jane taking her supporting role and finding solace in the children.

At the end, Jane delivered the fatal blow in bed, as he fought to keep awake. She had built herself up for the moment and assembled the carefully chosen phrases that she believed, unrealistically, would let them wipe out their past.

She soon realised that their life had not just been a muddle of chalk marks on a blackboard, to be rubbed out in an instant. What they had put down together would keep showing through in stubborn traces.

As result, it had been a long goodbye. Olly had been waiting, knowing it was inevitable. For once, Jane was taking charge, and he was grateful in a way. He wouldn't have known how to go about separating, especially as he felt so bad for his part in the way things had turned out.

By the time he had crept upstairs, well after midnight, anxious not to wake the children, she had lain awake for two hours, turning over restlessly.

At last Olly fell into bed in the dark room. As usual he was heavy with weariness from the restaurant shift and the drive home. Although she was turned away from him she could smell the drink and nicotine on his breath. He always stayed around after service for what he called wind-down time, to let the adrenaline ebb away.

Somehow Olly sensed that Jane was awake and whispered that in the morning he would get up to take the children to school. She knew this was another peace offering.

Most of their arguments over recent months had been on the same old theme. About Olly's career, the fact that he was so rarely at home that she might as well not have had a husband, or the children a father.

"No need. I'll see to the kids."

Weeks before, all conversation had become curt, except when either of them had needed a cathartic shout.

Of course the children had noticed.

"Kids OK?" Olly whispered.

"Yes. Fine."

"And you?"

"Nothing's changed."

"Did you see about the riots? London's gone bonkers. I got diverted. There's looting and fires. Over the shooting."

He threw off the duvet to cool off. He lay in the dark with his eyes open to avoid sleep, waiting for a reply.

Jane had gone silent so she could line up the words, like bullets in the magazine of a gun, words she was now primed to deliver.

But Olly spoke first. "Do you want to talk?"

"No. But we can't go on, Olly. You realise that?"

"No, but let's *talk*. Let's forget us. Let's think of the kids."

"The talking's over Olly. We're over. We both know it. You need to move out."

And so it was over, simple as that, apart from a rather feeble resistance from Olly – "Think hard, Jane. Think hard. Think of the kids."

"I've thought. You need to move out."

◇ ◇ ◇ ◇ ◇

All had been so serene and hopeful and so joyous at the start.

Jane just remembered Olly clowning about, and the chink of glasses on the terrace – that, and the happy sounds from the rambling pub-turned-bistro deep in the Kent countryside.

Their two years at The May Flower had been blissful, like one long, lazy summer's day. They lived above the restaurant so Olly was always within reach. She had no memory of feeling fretful, and Olly had been such good fun – a large, gentle bear to hug.

Olly had attracted a coterie of admiring customers. Once, when she was talking with staff in the beer garden, a woman eating her meal had asked whether she also worked at the restaurant. She had been so proud to say: "No. I'm chef's wife."

"You lucky woman!" the customer said. And she had felt lucky.

Zac once come to stay for a couple of days and had spent both nights in the pub, watching Olly at work.

He was no gourmet – far from it – but he could see that Olly's food was special and he felt privileged when Olly came out of the kitchen and gave him titbits to try. She could see that they had a very special bond; a kind of masculine love she supposed.

Later, the birth of the children had enriched their lives, made them think less of their own needs, and it was only when they moved to the fringe of London that the marital path became cluttered with bad stuff. There was the loneliness that came with the move so that Olly could work in the city,

She had never really integrated, so in the main, life amounted to her and the kids, being closeted in the little box of a home, or treading the featureless roads on the estate. She had lost all confidence in herself beyond the realm of home and children. She was astounded to think that she once managed a team of half a dozen feisty young women.

Olly had never really understood. He thought that Jane didn't want to bother fitting in, finding friends. When a week earlier she knew that Olly had almost accepted that they should part, she had risked revealing feelings she had kept from him.

"I worked something out Olly. You make me feel lonely."

"That's bollocks Jane. It doesn't add up. Me *being here* makes you *lonely*?"

"Right. It's like this..." she began, then took care to change tense, so that there was no room for offers of remedies.

"It was like this. When we moved I buckled down to being without you, with no proper friends near, and mum 200 miles away. I *managed*, even when I felt scared over so many little things."

Olly listened well aware that he was about to hear what he knew but hadn't faced.

"I'd nearly get on top of it all and then you'd have a day off, or just go in later, for dinners. I'd get used to you being around but as soon as you drove off again, I'd weaken."

Olly protested. "I can't do more than I'm doing...I've had to earn, I've had to keep swimming hard to stay in front of the rest in the shark pool. Cheffing is competitive."

As she lay in bed, turning this way and then that, Jane wondered whether parting from a husband was easier when there was a lover involved. She had always imagined that if the marriage ever ended, Olly being Olly, and with the attention he always attracted, there would have to be a woman at the heart of it.

Jane hadn't quite worked out how she would tell the children about the break-up. Sophie would be the problem one. She had already asked why daddy didn't like mummy any more.

Only days before, as a bedtime treat instead of a story, Sophie had asked her to play the "Daddy pictures," a recording of Olly's first appearance on regional TV.

Dylan had professed not to be interested but then settled on the beanbag to watch Olly stirring a sauce, holding up ingredients and talking engagingly on screen, as the woman presenter and two would-be cooks basked in his sparky presence.

Jane remembered the magazine article about up-and-coming chefs, and how they had called him "Jolly Olly." Although nowadays he seemed glum and worn in her presence, they were right about him. He had a happy disposition when things were OK.

She was sure that away from her, and their problems, that he came alive, especially at the stove. She could see him lifting morale and filling any kitchen with banter.

What she had decided was for the best, for him as much as for her.

"You'll survive, Olly. And you'll prosper. You'll find somebody. Maybe you have..." Jane said, inviting a confession, surprised at her composure. "You'll forget, start again but I won't."

Olly didn't reply. He had turned away and had drawn the duvet up to his ears as if to shut out everything.

No, she said to herself, Olly wouldn't be having an affair; wouldn't have the time. But if there *had* been a woman, it might have helped with tonight's mission. You could vilify a woman but not a job, and it was the job that was his mistress.

She had lost him to a vocation. Twice before, at times of crisis, he had pledged to change jobs, find something that asked less of him, something that didn't involve moving on and up all the time but that paid better.

It had been different for her. She had enjoyed her job as banqueting suite manager. All of it – the meetings with clients, the nervy run-up to big occasions and the release afterwards. But it wasn't a passion, not like Olly's cooking.

If ever she was tempted to think of herself as a blameless victim she would reflect on what she regarded as failings – her insecurity, the almost irrational fear she now experienced when Olly was away.

The anxiety had arrived with the kids. She believed that her protective instinct had somehow become over-developed. She fretted about the children when there was no need. Other mothers at the school gate seemed simply glad to get them off their hands.

She pictured the children in the school playground, fearing that they might fall. She imagined them at lunch, anxious that they might be choking on a bit of packed lunch, or picking up a lethal germ. Olly didn't know how disabling this had become, or how silly she felt about the constant expectation of something bad about to happen. She had never really explained.

Lately, money problems had made life doubly difficult. They had taken on too much, to be near London. The mortgage was crippling them and Jane wondered whether this had added to the permanent state of fearfulness she seemed to be in.

It was only during this, their last night, that she had started to explain to Olly about the nervousness she carried with her everywhere. Her voice had broken at the sadness of it all.

The indefinable sound Olly had made when she had paused, after revealing the extent of her feelings, she took to be one of pity. He had always tried to understand, once she could get him to listen – not easy when he was so tired.

His instinct at her confession had been to reach for her and hold her; he hated the idea that she'd felt so anxious all the time. But he held back and said, instead: "I'm so sorry Jane. I had absolutely no idea that it was as bad as that for you."

There was silence in the blackness and then Olly said: "You really should see somebody. Get some tablets. Some help. Have a break at your mum's. You've not been yourself for months."

"*I'm* not sick. Olly. *We're* sick... it's us, the marriage."

Olly lay in silence for a while once more, and then said: "I know. And I'm so sorry. You'll be better when I've gone."

Jane was tempted to find Olly's arm, to give it a squeeze that transmitted her regret. But having girded herself up for the decision of her life, she was not going to weaken now. Yielding to the last vestiges of love would have confirmed forever her powerlessness to change things.

They began to talk as they used to talk. Olly had been shocked and touched by her inner frailty and had held out a hand in the dark to find her face. He felt tears. She took his hand and gently pushed it back towards him.

She said, almost inaudibly: "It's as if I've been living on shifting sand. I've got to find my feet. After all, I'm a bloody adult, a mother of two for heaven's sake!"

Suddenly he felt grateful that at last it was over. He wanted to kiss Jane in gratitude for rejecting him so cleanly. Being so resolute. It can't have been easy, not for Jane.

She stopped still and silent at the sound of a small voice from the bedroom next door. It was Sophie, muttering gibberish, sleepwalking in her room. Jane was usually sleepily amused by these nocturnal moments but tonight the murmuring carried a note of distress.

As she tended to Sophie, she found Olly beside her. "Let me, tonight," he said, and carried his daughter to bed.

When he came home in the early hours, Olly rarely looked in on the sleeping children. He was afraid that they would wake. Now, as he kissed Sophie, he wished he had gone to the children every night, just to see them sleeping.

By morning Jane had begun to gather in around her a protective shell, and to practise the new, impersonal form of dialogue she had decided they needed to use.

Olly got together the things he needed for a few days' existence and kissed the children. He left with only gentle protest, and with the air of someone who was relieved finally to be doing what they both knew was inevitable.

After taking the children to school, Jane sat with her coffee at the kitchen table. Soon she would start to send texts, the first to Olly's sister, Tilly, so she would know that it had really been her decision for Olly to leave.

Tilly was a superlative sister-in-law, a neutral force for good. She would give support to them both. She had not married, never had children, yet she seemed to be so good on relationships, seeing things so sharply. Maybe the law training had helped.

Tilly knew Olly better than anybody and was devoted to him, glowing in his presence. She must have known that things were not right. Olly had probably talked with her, as he always did when big things came up.

Jane was so glad that she had Tilly to turn to. She was so reassuring when she rang for a chat. Jane had a theory that, out of kindness, Tilly often invented a pretext to phone. Watchfulness. Always, for a while after her calls, the butterflies in her tummy disappeared.

When Tilly heard that she had asked Olly to leave, she would be non-partisan, treating each of them with sympathy.

And why shouldn't we get a bit of sympathy? Jane asked herself. It really was a tragedy, only a little domestic one but it was a tragedy. And there was no one – well, not one *person* – to blame.

12

Olly was back from a vexing visit to the children. He felt that doing his familial duty was even more testing than the longest and heaviest of cooking shifts.

That was because Jane made it so.

As usual the visit had been sabotaged. She always carefully contrived to initiate conflict and, within minutes of his arrival, what had become a ritual had begun. Today it had been particularly bloody.

Jane had been speaking to Tilly and evidently Tilly had

mentioned that Ella was now waitressing at the London restaurant where Olly worked. Jane, the tough nut who had turned him out, was showing herself to be bitterly jealous.

She had always liked Ella but that was on the basis that Olly wasn't available. Now he was, just as Ella was. And here she was, a loser.

Biting words flew. It was a murderous, verbal tennis match that neither combatant could ever win. Jane was always the server, Olly the hapless receiver flapping around...

"Did you not think to mention that Ella's working with you – you know, Ella, my friend, our friend?"

"So you didn't set up the standing order? It's OK, we'll live on fresh air..."

"You can't start telling me now that you actually care about the kids...

"Don't patronise me... chef"

The to-and-fro of mutual loathing was delivered in a low dialogue, as if the rivals believed that by keeping their voices down, the children would be unaware of the warfare above their heads.

But they heard every word, and their diversionary tactic was to laugh to drown it out, the embarrassment of it, and tease each other, and play with the dog. They had never been told what children should do when grown-ups seemed about to kill each other.

Olly had looked down and noticed conflict playing in Sophie's face. She was giggling a little too hysterically, but frowning at the same time. He knew that image would stay with him. It was like his own unintended smiles that often masked his true feelings.

The children tickled and grappled. They spread Jasper on its back, so he was sprawled out like a sunbather, in their little hearthrug world.

The whispy hair on the dog's underbelly was white now and Olly suspected he had already passed a terrier's predicted lifespan. He had been an adored pup in a loving family and had grown old in the time it had taken for everything to fall apart.

Olly had brought colouring books, bags of sweets, and some chocolate cake from the restaurant sweet trolley. For a moment he felt like some kind of predator, trying to lure the children into his trust. Once again it proved too much, to compress weeks of missed family feeling into two or three hours.

Time had to be allowed for Jane's sniping, and for him to explain things slowly and reasonably, to keep his temper, to promise again that he was doing his best to wipe off his debts and to let her have more money. Time for the children to shake off the awkwardness of the reunion.

When they became relaxed enough to begin to enjoy Olly being back in their lives, he had to leave.

First, he grunted "I'm going" to Jane, who inevitably pretended to be deeply absorbed with preparations for the children's tea. Then there were the hugs with the children at the front door, the handing out of pocket money given in exchange for gifts from them.

There were always gifts. A drawing from Sophie, Olly shown as the largest member of a family of penguins with his wing around Mum penguin. School photos. A key ring for Father's Day, photocopies of school end-of-term reports, a gift list for Christmas.

Finally, after one more high-five each, there was the waving as the car pulled away, for Olly the most exquisitely painful moment of the visit.

Sophie was at the window, smiling a little too bravely, holding a soft-toy zebra. Dylan was out on his scooter, pushing his way up the slope of the tarmac to the garage, not looking round, waving over his shoulder.

Olly suddenly noticed that a tilting fence panel that had leaned for a couple of years had been righted and a new post installed. Maybe Jane's brother had popped over. But wasn't there a deodorant beside the sink, one that looked like a product for a man?

Maybe there *was* a man. If there is, Olly said to himself, his stomach twisting with outrage, the bastard will play with my kids.

He'll even swing my bloody dog on my rubber ring. This man will make them laugh and give them treats and win their hearts. He'll sit in my chair, use our loo, spot the bumpy filler round the windowsill. And he'll sleep with my wife – although at this moment that matter seemed to Olly far less distressing than the sound in his head of the children laughing at this man's jokes.

No, there won't be a man. Can't be...yet. He couldn't imagine Jane's self-protecting carapace parting far enough to let any man see what a warm and funny and generous woman there was inside. It will have been her brother staying for a day or two.

Either way, it was plain to Olly that Jane was well and truly freezing him out. The glaciation had been gradual but now he really had been left out in the cold.

Jane's strategy involved being sufficiently confrontational to prevent any emotional softening from him, or from her. A generous reading would be that she was being cruel to be kind. But when she turned to him, Olly sometimes could see that there was contempt in her face.

When they had been together, they had enjoyed family rituals, some of which Olly managed to keep alive for a time after the parting. He regarded these as emotional lifebelts the children could hang on to when they felt lost and confused, no matter that for him they sharpened the pain of parting.

There was a game involving Jasper and the rubber ring. The dog would run, slightly arthritically, to retrieve it then cling to it for dear life in a tug-o-war battle as the children squealed and the dog growled through clenched teeth.

There was the Yellow Men tea Olly had always prepared, and which Jane had sulkily allowed him to make each time when he visited. She always left out the eggs, the sliced bread, the maple syrup and the gingerbread cutter and went upstairs to read while Olly fried French toast Yellow Men until the children could eat no more.

One bitterly cold day, he had arrived and noticed that the kitchen counter was bare. When the children left the room, he asked Jane whether he could cook for the children. She replied: "I've lost the gingerbread cutter. And anyway, I've run out of eggs."

The Yellow Men were never mentioned again by Jane or by the children. He felt that something important had been taken from him. It was vindictive, but surely Jane couldn't have known how much such a little thing could hurt. Surely.

That was two months ago but it had marked another step towards communication at a robotic level.

Feelings, Olly decided, were as impermanent as the steam from his breath, condensing, disappearing. Everything that had been good and joyous was now unmentionable and every bit of warmth had been driven out.

As he drove off, Olly wondered why Dylan was not looking round to wave goodbye. Was this his way of hiding his feelings?

Had saying goodbye become too painful, or had it now become painless? Was this the first signal that he was losing the children?

As he drove, distractedly, not really aware of anything around him, Olly brooded on the dreadful possibility that Jane really had got a new man and that one day the kids might not really care whether he visited or not.

13

Ella and Olly were naked together under the duvet in the bedroom of the hotel.

They lay face to face, stupefied at finally accepting what they had felt from the moment they first met on the doorstep at Zac's house.

It had taken them eight years to own up to their feelings. Then it took just a few minutes to hold each other, once they reached the hotel room, and then a minute to get into bed together.

It could have all happened so much earlier, perhaps soon after Richard's wedding. But Olly – by then committed to Jane – didn't get in touch with Ella. He knew that if he had, he'd have become entangled.

What Ella had conveyed when she instructed "Ring" with that urgent, almost fierce look, on the dance floor, was that she herself had become enmeshed, and didn't reciprocate Joe's feelings.

Olly feared that by making contact he might become just a means of escape, the platonic friend once more, the chum, the helpmate who left hot lemon juice at the door of the Crow's Nest when Ella had flu, and talked with her into the night to ease her guilt over her mother.

Anyway, Jane was – had been – lovely, supportive, fun. But he knew that some of his love for her came from her readiness to understand him and the demands of his career. Endearingly, she would become as excited as he was about what he might achieve.

Ella had been something different, not so much a slow burner as a non-starter. But whatever seed was sown in Rhodesia Terrace turned out to be tenaciously viable. Now, fragments of unspoken fellow feeling scattered through their history as housemates, finally coalesced.

They had ignored the thumping great elephant that had towered over them in every room they had ever been in together, and it was now trumpeting their acceptance of the inevitable. The pretence was over. They were together.

They were talking in whispers now and looking at each other as if slightly astonished.

Olly laughed in an exasperated way. "Where do we begin to understand why we took so bloody *long*? Was it some sort of stubbornness?"

"We don't need to understand, Ol," Ella replied gently. "Let's just *be*."

"But remember," he said. "This isn't the first time I've got you into bed..."

"It was *on* to a bed. And you had to get me drunk first," Ella said with one of her throaty laughs. "This time I'm sober but it feels a bit like being drunk; the nice bit of being drunk..."

Olly sat up, his back against the bedhead. Ella shut her eyes as if she could better concentrate on the pure happiness she was feeling.

Finally Olly said: "I know somebody who's going to be very pleased. Tilly. She knew from the start that you were the right one but she never came out with it. Just kept banging on about what a lovely woman you were...are."

There was no reply and he wanted to say more. There was something, just the one thing, getting in the way of his sharing the pure elation that Ella was feeling.

He had to admit it – it was the niggling stuff about the parts of Ella's life she had lived out of his sight. Specifically men. It was the wrong time – in fact, as he knew, there was never a right time – but he couldn't stop himself moving towards the no go area even though he was sure that Ella would resent what she was bound to regard as unreasonable possessiveness, imposed retrospectively.

"Tilly was really thoughtful," he said, "because she never mentioned whether you were in a relationship, or who you were with. It wasn't as if I didn't ask. I hated to think of it. She just gave me health bulletins and said how you were getting along generally."

Olly put a hand on Ella's head, and stared intently to signal that there was something more he had to say.

"Just one thing. I've never, ever told you. When you first came to see Zac's place, when they were all arsing about, literally arsing about, with that Toulouse Lautrec stuff, and you went in to meet Zac, I was as jealous as hell."

Ella said playfully: "And you want me to say that I really liked the look of you? Fancied you rotten? Well, I did. In a way. You looked tough and sweet at the same time. The artist in me liked the hair."

She raised herself on an elbow and looked intently at Olly. Her breasts distracted him but his mind was in turmoil.

"And you really want to know what I thought of Zac?" she said.

"Well, yes, I suppose."

His casual reply gave no indication of how keenly he awaited the reply. Zac and he had often talked about Ella but always in an abstract way, as if they were playing each other at poker, taking care not to reveal their cards, bluffing, hiding their lust for the bounty.

"Well, he was exciting because he was so confident and entertaining, and I felt like a simple young lass coming for the first time to the big, evil city."

"Exciting? In what way? His looks do you mean? Or his posh accent?"

"Sort of dashing. As if he was a man of the world. And, as somebody who was so insecure, I suppose I latched on to him in a way. I thought – 'This bloke doesn't give a shit.'"

They lay for a moment longer, then Ella smiled and said: "Olly. Look at *your face*! It's a picture. It's *you* here, you know, not Zac!"

So it could have been Zac? That was a possible scenario that Ella could imagine? It's obviously something she had thought possible once...?

Ella looked serious. She said firmly: "Olly, we're going to have a rule. New page, new chapter, new book. Stuff will keep cropping up but let's not be bullied by the past."

Olly looked a little ashamed, knowing that he was spoiling things.

"For me it'll be like finding a path through a minefield," he said. "I can't seem to leave some things behind. It's like I'm being haunted. Even the thought of Joe, even the thought of that wimp in the green glasses, gets to me. And some bloke you went away with – Greece was it – when Tilly helped you with the passport?"

"Would that be the bloke I went to Greece with when *you* were married with two children? Come on Ol! I'm not going to talk to you about Jason or his bloody glasses. I'm not going to explain myself – ever. Or talk about Joe. It's slightly unreasonable of you to think that I should have gone to a nunnery until it finally dawned on us that this is what we both wanted?"

She turned away, suddenly deflated. The bubble of happiness had popped. One thing he had always loved about Ella was the way she stuck to what she believed, and the way she would stay and fight her corner. That spirit of resistance made him feel even more contrite.

But he persisted. He lowered his voice, striving to seem reasonable, knowing that he was being anything but.

"If you could just tell me about Zac. What you really thought of him when we were all together. Whether you ever meant more to each other than you let on..."

Ella sat up suddenly and turned angrily to shout in his face: "Are you asking what I thought of him at about the time your airhead with the whale tail was under our feet?"

"Which airhead? *Whale tail?*"

"The bloody thong one. The bubblecut one. When people like her thought it was fashionable to let everyone see their bum crack. The whimpering one we all got lumbered with for bloody weeks."

"Jude. Yeah Jude. I remember."

"I bet you do Ol! Want to tell me how things were with *her*? Or about you and the bloody jewel of the orient, Lakshmi?"

"You remember Lakshmi's *name*? I can tell you about Lakshmi. I'm happy to tell you all about Lakshmi..."

"But I don't want to *know*, Ol! That's the difference. I went on a journey after Rhodesia Terrace. I met people. You had a very *eventful* journey. Just think, all those places you've worked in. Now I've arrived, *we've* arrived." She looked as if she might cry.

"Ol, I want you, and I want what you once had with Jane. Security. Children. We won't find that back at Rhodesia Terrace, or anywhere else in the past. It's *here*..." she said, raising herself up, next to him, against the bedhead.

Olly looked pained. "Even when I was with Jane I'd think of you sometimes and get really upset that you were probably with somebody, even if you might just be walking in the park."

Ella could see a gaping gulf between them. There had to be a way to obliterate the past which, ironically, was blocking the way ahead.

She was not intimidated that there was so much of "before" – eight years of cat and mouse; enough time for Olly to have married and become a father; time enough for her to have had significant relationships; to have accumulated yet more debt, and to have lost her mother.

Olly realised suddenly that he was starving. He reached for his watch, saying "Sorry El. So sorry. Stupid of me."

He got out of bed. "Breakfast!" he said, then, picking up his watch, "Too late. Missed it."

Ella said encouragingly: "Look – let's find somewhere in town, pig out, and then have a long walk and let's talk about everything we're going to do together. In the *future*."

Then she kissed him hard on the cheek and said: "Never spoil it Ol. It is bloody wonderful isn't it?"

"It's OK. So-so," he said putting on a hangdog face. Ella giggled and began to drum on his back with her fists.

"Ol, one very, very last word, then no more," she said as she wrapped herself in a big white, fluffy dressing gown, and pushed her feet into the flimsy, hotel-issue flip-flops.

"What we were is what we *were*. What we did or didn't do is history. Let's find a way to give you peace about the past and my past, such as it was. And stop that imagination working overtime. Here. *Now*."

Olly kissed her forehead and said: "Done."

But then, as he reached the shower, he began to picture the first time Ella came to Rhodesia Court looking for Zac; he couldn't help himself.

And as the hot water pummelled him in the privacy of the shower, he thought of the day she was taking books and stuff upstairs to the Crow's Nest and Zac's eyes followed her.

He could hear again the way Zac had said "Mmm...*Peachy*," lustfully, in the way they both talked of desirable women then.

14

"And about bloody time," Tilly said when Ella rang one morning to tell her the news. "You know, I *thought* it was moving that way... We'll have to celebrate soon, after I get this case finished."

She laughed. "Hell would have frozen over before Olly got round to telling me, so thanks. I'm *so* pleased, Ella. Relieved. If things weren't ever going to be right with poor old Jane, I hoped that it would be you eventually sharing the burden of my little brother. That Theo you had was a poppet but I suspect he was a bit of a drip...?"

They chuckled excitedly, like sisters who were close. Ella told her about the flat, about Olly's new job as executive chef at a pretentious new hotel and golf course where fine (but unexciting) dining was part of the rather characterless offering.

"The job's just a fill-in for Ol. Think they were flattered to get him," she said. Olly, she said, had got a long-term plan to run a little restaurant of his own – "A place of *our* own, I should say," said Ella. "The hotel's just taken me on as a waitress. We need to save, and the experience will come in handy...if ever..."

Tilly said: "Look, love. Sorry. The other phone. Got to crack on. Let's catch up properly at my place as soon we've got a result with this court case. Terribly involved business. Pity me – dotty counsel, lots of fibbing and weepy witnesses."

She said again how pleased she was that Olly was in safe

84

hands. "Give him my love and tell him that when you come down for something fizzy, *he'll* be cooking. And I want him to do the ricotta and peas thing. He'll know what I mean."

When Olly came through from the bedroom, looking bedraggled and sleepy, his hair in disarray, she said: "Your big sister sends her love. She's *so* happy about us! She wants us to go down for a meal. She said you'll have to cook, and she says she wants the thing with ricotta and peas."

"Farfalle and peas and pancetta. She goes mad for it. You watch, she'll make me do her some *leche frita* as well. Horrible, floppy stuff. No accounting for taste.... But yes, it would be good to catch up."

Ella was curious about *leche frita* – fried milk? – but it seemed early to be asking for explanations; she'd learned that once you started Olly on recipes there was no stopping him.

Olly remembered using Tilly as a guinea pig when he first made the Spanish sweet of triangles of thick custard. He found them bland, even with the touch of cinnamon but she loved soft smoothness, and the way the crumb coating combined with the dusting of icing sugar.

In Olly's book, Tilly deserved every treat that came her way. He was aware that he could never even begin to repay his sister for all she had done, and continued to do.

It was as if she had held out her arms throughout his life, to steer him away from the edge of pitfalls. She was his sounding board sometimes, his lifeline at others. It was to her, and sometimes her chequebook, that he had often turned in times of trouble.

She laughed off his suggestion that she was a matchmaker, vigilant about who he ended up with. But she *was* watchful.

Preparing a spot of dinner would be a gesture of love, the equivalent of a bouquet, to show that she was not being taken for granted, but of course no "thank you" would have been big enough. He would also take her a couple of jars of his pineapple chutney that he knew she had adored.

Olly sat back and then leaned forward with his elbows, on the small, cheap table with its edges of ragged, lifting veneer. The agent had said the flat was fully furnished. It was – in the style of the late Sixties, and using the original stuff. But Olly and Ella found that they were barely aware of their surroundings. They felt happy, and private. It was home, sweet home; home, cheap home.

During the years after Rhodesia Terrace, Ella's mandolin playing improved beyond measure. She regarded her growing fluency on the instrument as compensation for the bad times. When she had the blues she would take it down and play until the ends of her fingers felt bruised, and her mother was yelling for her to stop. Her skill improved in direct proportion to her misery.

The mandolin hung from a nail beside the only window in the flat. It comforted her to look over and see the sun on it, and she always took it down with a slight sense of excitement.

She had still not quite mastered an especially pretty Sicilian tarantella she had been learning from a book and tuition CD but she never practised this when Olly was around. She planned to play the whole thing faultlessly to him one day as a treat, *her* gift of love, like the food he cooked to please her.

"I gather Tilly's new place is pretty grand," Olly said. "She must be coining it in. Last time she rang I told her that soliciting must pay well." Ella smiled and kissed Olly's tousled head.

Then she said: "You know Ol, if I was in bother with the law, Tilly would be the first person I'd turn to. She's so intuitive and wise. Actually, that's probably why she hasn't got anybody. She could be a bit daunting to most men. You know, being so capable, not appearing to need anybody, a partner... "

"There *was* a bloke, not a lawyer, some sort of social worker I think. It was on and off for a couple of years and then there was silence. She was a bit private about it. Maybe she's too self-sufficient for her own good."

"But she doesn't *have* to have a man," Ella said. "Women can be quite happy on their own, you know Ol. Not me, but some can."

"No, I think that Tilly needs someone. I think the self-sufficiency came out of being alone. I'd be happier if she had someone..."

"But why Ol?"

"Because I want someone to be looking after her as she's looked after me. Just as she looks after everybody else. "

Olly touched the coffee pot and found it lukewarm. He got up but as he began to prepare a fresh pot, he paused and turned to Ella and said: "Tell you what, El. Thinking about it, Tilly's been a mother and dad rolled into one."

He had the opened coffee jar in one hand and a spoon in the other; he was motionless as if struck by this revelation. To his surprise, his voice became tremulous and he felt tearful for a second.

Olly began to describe how, when they were kids, Tilly would step straight in if she suspected that he was being bullied, how she had put her arm round him for the rest of the journey when he had been car sick.

He recalled that when she rang with the news of their mother's death while he was in Italy, in Lerici, working in a seafood restaurant, she had been so gentle on the phone, so full of thought for him, so disregarding about her own pain, just as she'd been when their father had folded up and died on that summer's day at the school sports field.

"It's not that she's always treated me like a softy, El. She once dislocated my finger because I wouldn't let go of a pen that was hers!" They both broke into laughter.

"And three or four times she's taken me on one side and said something like: 'You might not be aware of it Ol, but I have to say you're acting like a prize prick.'

"She was always right, and I always stopped being one. But

not for long! I'd follow her advice any time."

They drank coffee, nibbled at bread and fruit, and talked about the boredom they had endured the night before. It was taking a long time for people to discover the new hotel as a fine dining venue. There had been seven staff on duty and ten customers.

"It was like working in a cathedral, wasn't it El? The silence was deafening. I can tell already, I won't stick it for long. I'm missing the buzz."

◇ ◇ ◇ ◇ ◇

Ella had not spoken to Zac for more than a year by the time she got together with Olly.

He had been due to pass within miles of the flat she had with Theo and had called in for a cup of tea. It had been obvious to her that he had expected her to be living on her own. But with so much of Theo's stuff around it was clear she had a partner.

He was "between women," as he described it, and despite a moan or two about the travails of working with his father, he seemed bright and positive – but most of all prosperous. The clothes – the suit especially – said it all, and the car confirmed it. She didn't know much about cars but his was low, and long, and yellow, and had a top that looked as if it would lift up, suggesting luxury.

Zac seemed to be saying that there would be a day soon when he could strike out on his own, get out from under his father's domination. He hinted that one day a substantial amount of money would be coming his way.

When he'd gone, she pictured Zac as he was when she first met him – on his knees – and remembered with amusement his unrestrained happiness in being a scruff, living in debris with two mad medics, this product of a select school deep in the Dorset countryside.

Olly had not spoken to Zac since they met three months earlier, in an Australian sports bar in the West End. It was the longest spell without contact since they first met. Then one day he rang. It was time they had a catch-up, he said.

Drink had always been involved whenever they were together but Zac was driving that day and had fruit juice. To his relief, Olly found that the conversation flowed, the laughs came, despite the lack of alcohol, and the lack of contact over the past weeks.

He felt the old familiarity returning and he could see that Zac was glad to have him as an audience once more.

The bond of friendship was still strong. They nodded approvingly over attitudes expressed, affirmed decisions taken, and were mutually encouraging over plans for the future. But Olly suspected that the family business was like a manacle, holding the old Zac in check.

After an hour, Zac had looked at his watch, and stirred, as if to go, but had sat down again and said: "To be honest, I want to break free. Dad's great in many ways but we're so different. He's fine on the actual managing but he's not got much vision. He's too worried about risk. Too conservative."

Olly knew that Zac had something else to share, something that had to be said before they left.

"But he's gradually easing out anyway. Then I'll have the chance soon to do things my way. I've got this trust fund, a family thing, in my name, and I get my sweaty little hands on it on my next birthday. It's a very nice stash. It'll stop me committing what do they call it – patricide?"

Outside the pub, they had parted with a firm hug, and pledges not to let the friendship drift, to be back in touch with each other soon. Then they had walked away – and had not been in touch since.

So when Zac rang once more weeks later, Olly was off guard. He had not had a chance to tell Zac that he was with Ella now. It had to be done at the end of this call he said, thinking on his feet.

Zac seemed to want to minimize the small talk. He was now

with a really "good fun woman, runs a couple of wedding hire shops." Everything was looking good business-wise, he said. But he had this mega-mega idea and he needed Olly's viewpoint. He wanted to set aside some time for a proper chat.

Olly knew that he had no reason to be hesitant about telling Zac that he was now with Ella, or to feel guilty, but as Zac talked, Olly found himself struggling to say what had to be said.

"Yeah, Zac, we need a bit more time. Just name a date."

"Cheers matey."

"One other thing. Bit of a surprise for you. Me and Ella have just got together."

There was a long pause and then Zac said: "You mean *together*."

"Yeah. Got a flat."

"Wow, Ol. Shit. Wow."

15

The meeting that marked the start of the most exhilarating months of Olly's professional life was in a coffee shop full of old leather settees and wingback chairs.

The venue had been Zac's choice. "Talk first, beer later," he said when he rang to fix the time and date. "I need you to be thinking straight, Ol. Big stuff. Want to pick your brains, such as they are. Be good to see you, old buddy."

Olly was intrigued. This was a glimpse of Zac the cool entrepreneur. He had always been an occasional opportunist but was now full time. Finding openings was his career.

Maybe he'd just found a big one.

As Olly went to the car on the appointed day, Ella shouted down to him from the upstairs window of the flat: "Give him my love, Ol – and watch your pockets!"

They rarely mentioned Zac but it appeared to Olly that she had been over-eager to know how Zac had reacted when he learned that they were now together.

When he told her, she had drawn her head back in surprise, in a double take.

"Is that all he said? *Wow?*" she asked incredulously when Olly had told her.

"Wow? So he didn't say 'I'm really glad for you both'?"

Olly replied: "No. Because he wouldn't have been. Because he..."

"Leave it Ol. Please."

"Actually he said 'wow' twice. The first time seemed to be shock but the second time he seemed to be talking to himself, just taking the news in. It could have been the sound of his heart breaking of course..."

"Don't be such a silly bugger, Olly."

This hinting at what Zac might feel for Ella was a rare lapse by Olly. Lately, he had been finding it easier to talk about the Rhodesia Terrace days, and his insecurity had receded as his relationship with Ella deepened. Perhaps Ella had learned to avoid saying things that would touch a nerve.

Olly found Zac at the back of the coffee shop, on a sagging settee in front of a low table. He was perfectly dressed for the slightly chilly spring day – casually but immaculately. Olly guessed the terracotta V-neck sweater was cashmere, and that the crisply cut shirt peeping out was from a shirt-maker rather than a clothes shop. There was a file of papers on the table.

Zac showed his big flashing smile, and bent over the table to shake Olly's hand and grip his forearm. "How the hell *are* you?" he demanded to know, looking into his face, meaning it.

"Fine. But God, Zac," Olly exclaimed, "look at *you!*"

"Work uniform, Ol. Like having a decent car – gives the immediate impression that you're a winner without you saying a word."

"Tricks of the trade..."

"Learned it at my father's knee. If you're going to do a deal, you try to get your car somewhere where it'll be seen. People are impressionable, even some canny geezers."

When they had settled and shared bits of gossip about people they knew, Zac said: "Look Ol. I'll be straight. Remember the money, from the... sort of trust, the family thing? Well, they finally coughed up. It's a fair old sum, and I'm looking at splitting from the old man. Not entirely, but getting into something that I can call my own."

He picked up the file, and said: "I've been doing some research. I've had this idea." Olly waited, wondering. He had rarely seen Zac so serious and engaged.

Zac gave a conspiratorial smile as he flipped open the file, enjoying the big moment. He saw expectancy in Olly's face.

"Don't get *too* excited, Ol, because it probably won't happen – or we might not be able to sort things to make it work. But I've been looking at opening some sort of restaurant. A good one, high end. In a nice place."

The news was like an electric shock that activated a bank of ideas and connections, each flashing for attention in Olly's mind. Within seconds his stowed-away ambition was at the front of his consciousness. The prospect of opening a restaurant with Zac almost made him shiver with excitement.

Something told him to react passively, to give no clue to the fervour inside him.

"And you want me to do the fried bread?" he said.

"Silly twot!" Zac said, the business face cracking into a massive grin.

Zac slowly and painstakingly explained that he had studied

the market, followed up successful restaurant launches, and analysed that year's failures. He had looked at locations, studied what the restaurants offered, computed their prices, found out how they advertised themselves.

"I deliberately didn't involve you. Needed to see it all with fresh eyes," he said.

"Do you understand, Ol? If things stack up and I do go ahead, it will be *my* gamble, and so no one else ends up feeling bad if I back a loser. I've learned a lot but obviously you'll know even more, especially about the chef side. Maybe you can help..."

"Of course I can," Olly said, cutting in. He didn't want to sound too keen but he was, wholeheartedly. And it *was* big stuff, as Zac said. Also slightly scary, this prospect of mixing friendship with what looked like a fantastic career opening.

Zac gave a breakdown of his research.

"People get carried away. Faded celebs, ex-footballers, amateur cooks who think they can learn the business side. Some pick silly locations. Within months, the only people coming in are the bailiffs, or the official receiver to shut them down."

He turned to Olly and said: "Look Ol, you can help me not get carried away. Strikes me that the whole business is about the marriage of a concept, creative genius on the nosh side, and business nous. People eating out are there for an *experience*, aren't they?"

Olly was encouraged to hear Zac talking with such evangelistic passion. He was beginning to appreciate Zac's acumen, and revising his thinking of business as some floaty pastime of the rich; it was a job of work, like planning and cooking a banquet.

He felt he needed to endorse what Zac was saying, to match his zeal and show solidarity.

"Actually, Zac, you're bang on about the whole experience being key. You're selling ambience as well as food. You're giving people an *emotional* event, something to boast about later, something to remember..."

"So right. That's the mysterious bit for me, Ol, and it's where you come in."

"Nobody would believe it but poetry comes into it."

Zac gave a snorting laugh and shoved Olly's shoulder: "Christ! Don't say that in front of Dad. It'd fuse his pacemaker. I know you read a few fancy books at uni but..."

"Look Zac. People actually *bask* in the words on menus, especially foodies. Some people read *books* of menus. They love the whole palaver...mulling over what they're going to have. It's foreplay. Anticipating. We'd need to be unapologetically posh. Fancy. People pay for fancy."

"OK. Maybe not as dippy as it sounds. That's just the kind of insight I need," said Zac.

"You'll have heard some people, Zac. They don't say 'Fish stew please', they order, word for word off the menu... 'I'm going for the *caldeirada* of sea-fresh fish with sun-kissed Mediterranean vegetables, combining a hearty main with a briny soup dotted with pasta stars.'"

Zac rocked back laughing.

"Dad would say that's unadultered bollocks. He thinks that all restaurants have to do is to gussie up some cheap chicken legs, or defrosted pork chops with a bit of sauce and give it a fancy name and add a 500 per cent mark-up."

"Well, he's wrong. You need a bit of magic, something that takes them out of their workaday lives. You need to give them *the* ultimate treat."

"Fair play. Dad's a philistine about food. Hates the stuff. Can't stand garlic or any spice except a tiny shake of pepper. Much rather have a biscuit and a cube of cheese rather than a lobster. He thinks that the whole restaurant business is based on the emperor's new clothes."

"Well, you'd be best keeping him out of it."

"I bloody well will, you can count on that! He runs hot and

cold about the restaurant idea anyway. One minute he says that I might as well stick my money in a pan and flambé it, and the next he's weighing up what profit you could get. *He* could get. He says things like: 'How on earth *can* they lose money? Look at these Italian places. All they do is turn a handful of pasta, and a bit of cheese and few trimmings into something people will pay silly prices for'."

They sat back, smiling, both slightly frazzled by the excitement of the prospect of their friendship being consolidated in something so significant in their lives.

"So..." Zac said. Then, "Another?" He got up to bring more coffee.

When he came back they sat silently for a while not knowing quite where to go with the conversation.

Zac said finally: "I've found somewhere that might be right if everything else adds up. *If.* A lovely old red-brick building. It's an old bank that's just shut. It's in a village, a *villagey* village if you know what I mean, with loads of old cottages."

"Sounds promising," said Olly.

"There's money galore round about, and it's just thirty minutes from the city. A million people, a *million* people, are within forty minutes of it. And it's just a five-mile drop-off from the motorway."

Olly's mind began to create pictures; he would probably know the place. But how odd, he said to himself, that Zac had avoided naming the village, as if he feared that Olly might steal a march, leak the secret to a rival. He was prepared to put this down to habit rather than personal mistrust.

They began to talk about Olly's career, laughing together as he recalled people and incidents encountered in a dozen kitchens. Zac described the sure and steady growth of the development company that allowed his father to be less involved.

"He says he wants to ease out but he can't really let go. Well, you know what Dad's like, Ol..."

Ol didn't really know what he was like. He had met Maurice once, when Zac took him to stay with his parents at their London place.

He remembered a bony figure with thinning combed-back hair, a dark man in pristine, light-coloured clothes, with a dachshund under his arm. He had left Olly in no doubt that he was master of all he surveyed. Something about him was lofty and sour, as if a lifetime of acquiring had left him unsatisfied, burned out.

"Don't remember him well really, Zac. Just got a vague picture of him from that weekend," Olly said.

Zac held out the teaspoon and put his finger in the splayed end. "What dad knows about food and restaurants would fit in here," he said. "Bricks and mortar, yes; laws on letting, interest rates, yes. Fine dining, fuck all."

By the time they got up from the table, shook hands and hugged and promised to be back in contact soon, they both felt that they had taken big, exciting strides forward in terms of the project – and pleasurably backwards, to the bond that had been forged on the doorstep of Zac's place in Rhodesia Terrace.

Zac gathered his papers and smiled his massive white smile and picked up the keys to the low, yellow sports car parked within sight of customers drinking their coffee in the window seats.

Olly was half-way home when his racing thoughts about this thrilling new prospect slowed enough for him to come to the calm realisation that at no time today had Zac asked about Ella, or about them as a couple. He put it down to the intensity of the meeting but he did wonder...

That night, Olly spilled out the news to Ella and they had chatted excitedly about the future and the new turn their lives might take. There was so much to speculate about.

He sensed caution in Ella's questions about Zac, how he seemed, whether he had asked about her.

"Funny that, El. He didn't ask. Not about you, or about us. I tried to say that you were doing fine but either he didn't hear me or chose not to, and talked over me."

Olly felt ashamed at enjoying a little pleasure in telling Ella that she hadn't figured in Zac's conversation.

"Head too full of the new project, I suppose," she said. He detected a tinge of spite in her reply.

At last, Olly yawned. He looked at his watch and saw that it was after one. But his head was still buzzing.

"I'll never sleep," he said.

"I'll put you to sleep," she said. "But first, I've got something for you. Just sit back and shut up," she instructed affectionately.

He lay full-length on the settee and doubled up a cushion as a pillow. She took down her mandolin and sat in the chair she always sat in for practice and, after composing herself, she took a deep breath and struck the first chord of a lively tune.

The notes tumbled round the room as Ella, head down, deep in concentration, worked the plectrum with perfect precision, until the final strum.

At the end, Olly applauded and got up to kiss her. She was flushed, thrilled that she had been note perfect.

He knew what she was feeling; it was the kick he got when a guest insisted on seeing him to tell him that they had just enjoyed the best meal of their life.

"Slightly speedy for a lullaby," she said. "But not many blokes get a tarantella at bedtime. You'd never guess, Ol, but it's named after the spider – imagine, lovely music like that. Forgotten why but maybe if you get bitten by a tarantula you do leap about a bit smartish!"

"It was *lovely*!" Olly said, gathering her to him. "That really was something, El. All that practice has really paid off."

He asked her if she wanted a nightcap but she shook her head and yawned a "No thanks." She yawned again, patted her lips with her hand.

"Oh dear – sorry," she said. "I'm absolutely dead beat."

Then she asked, after almost too short a pause: "Did you say Zac was with a woman from some sort of hire shop?"

"Yeah. Bridal hire. He was with her but it's over. Turns out she had planned to wear one of her own dresses in the not-too-distant future and he made a Zac-like escape. He thought she might be a gold digger."

"Oh," Ella said.

Olly yawned yet again. He also felt very tired now, but also content, and optimistic about the future.

As Ella had hung up the mandolin, he put his arm round her shoulder and then, rather unsteadily, they led each other to bed.

16

"A watching brief. That's my role this morning," Maurice said decisively. "Isn't it Tinker?" he added, his voice falling into a soppiness normally used for babies. He enclosed the dachshund's sleek head in his near-skeletal hands and gazed into the small, uncomprehending black eyes.

He placed Tinker down gently, as if he was breakable, onto a cushion beside him, and checked his trousers and sweater for signs of dog hair.

His wife Rachael came in from the kitchen, greeted Olly and Ella with a strained smile, and having taken their preferences for drinks, disappeared again. She was almost as emaciated as Maurice, and as beautifully dressed, and seemed to share his remoteness in manner.

It struck Olly that these people would have felt no emotional discomfort in dropping off a nine-year-old, giving him a perfunctory hug and wishing him well for the next ten weeks of his school career.

"Career" would be a key word. Zac had always said that the family philosophy was that the separations would be worthwhile because they would *lead somewhere*. Zac had arrived at that place.

Olly tried to make small talk with Zac while Ella studied the pictures lining the walls of the apartment. She stood up, turned to Maurice, and said: "Do you mind if...?" gesturing to the main wall which was covered in framed prints and small oils.

"Oh yes – you're the artist. Be my guest," he said. Zac's eyes followed her and Olly noticed. Zac seemed tense. That's how being with the family could make you feel; he remembered that.

The first meeting with Zac as a couple hadn't been as difficult as Olly and Ella had imagined. Zac had maintained his tendency to avoid sticky moments by making comical gestures. As they had hugged at the entrance to the apartments he had wailed, theatrically, to Ella: "But, *darling,* you said you'd wait for me!"

They chatted for a moment, easily and warmly. A dreaded moment had passed.

"Well, one thing, you being what they call an *item* is going to make communication easier," he said, in what to Olly seemed to be Zac's way of accepting the situation, if not giving his whole-hearted blessing.

Ella turned from a clutch of woodcuts she had been peering at and asked whether Maurice had a particular favourite artist. "Yes, one who's dead – and whose work stays popular," he said with no hint of irony. "They're mainly investment. But I quite like that..."

He pointed with a bony finger to a small, gold-framed landscape with the flower-dotted foreground fading from green to blue, and with a church tower appearing vaguely above smudgy housetops. Impressionist, she decided.

The apartment was not as palatial as Olly had remembered it from his visit years before. In fact, the damask settee cover was now noticeably faded except in tucked-away folds, and paintwork had bleached areas where the sun had settled each day. Olly knew this tired look was not the result of reduced circumstances – he guessed that the mantelpiece porcelain alone would pay for a complete refurbishment.

Rachael delivered the coffee and the tea, placing the fine china cups on a coffee table. Her summer dress – deep blue with white abstract splashes – fitted like a second skin over her lean body.

"Would you mind awfully helping yourselves? I'm having lunch today. Do have a lovely meeting. And Maurice – *don't* be a bully, darling. This one's Zac's thing, not one of yours."

Zac sat in a large winged chair, with his father opposite, and Olly and Ella sat side-by-side on the settee. Olly had a new notebook on his knee and a pen clipped to it; Zac held a sheaf of papers.

Zac began by giving background information about the restaurant trade. He then listed the advantages they had if somehow they found a way of pooling resources and launching the eating place he had in mind.

First, he said (graciously, Olly acknowledged) they had an experienced chef who had attracted lots of attention – "The man the magazines called Jolly Olly," said Zac, who was suddenly slightly embarrassed to be briefing people who were his friends. Maurice remained stony-faced, reached for Tinker, and began to play with the dog's ears.

There was the money to invest, Zac said, and potentially an ideal building had been found. That building had plenty of top-floor space that could be converted into living quarters – "If the restaurant went tits up there would be lots of takers for a gaff in such a nice location," he said. Olly noticed with irritation that

Zac had begun to appropriate working class words – gaff and geezer now peppered his language.

As he talked, Zac became visibly excited. He could see that Ella was engrossed and hurriedly tried to think of ways of involving her.

"Then we've also got Ella's artistic talent. Maybe that'll help with the general identity of the place. It'd have to have a total concept that's reflected in everything...surroundings, menus, publicity."

"Count me in," she said eagerly. Olly noticed that she was blushing with excitement as Zac's plans unfolded.

"A key thing, of course – and Olly knows this more than anyone – is where we pitch the place in the market. A good, solid, traditional, place? A potential Michelin star joint with all the gimmicks – is it smoke, and foam and dry ice and stuff, Ol? Or it could be a trendy take on, you know, Pacific Rim, whatever that is..."

Maurice cut in. "Look, it's only my opinion Zac but surely your only question has to be: 'Which sort will make dosh?' And the answer? The sort of place that sold your mother and me that fish concoction the other day. They must be *coining* it in."

Maurice shook his head as if mystified. "A few quid's worth of fish, wholesale. Good fish I grant you. But the name that they put on it... was it ocean something...?"

"...*Trésor de la mer*..." Zac said, grandly. "Treasure of the sea."

"...that fancy name cost £20, times two, plus tax, plus tip! That's the sort of place you want. A place where you sell a few bits of fish to a couple for more than the waiter's getting for a shift."

"Dad! Come off it!" Zac protested. "It did have scallops in, probably hand-picked, and a bit of red mullet. It wasn't your average cod."

Maurice showed no sign of relenting. He ignored Zac and turned his attentions to Tinker.

Zac caught Olly's eye and nodded towards his father with an

expression that said: "Look what I have to put up with."

Zac was tempted to carry on, exploring possible names for the restaurant, and asking Olly for his ideas on what would make it catch the eye of the public, and the food critics. He wanted to rush ahead to talk about the minimum number of tables needed to make it viable, and even get some idea of how the interior might look.

He also wanted a confidential chat with Olly. It would be a delicate business, working out what would be a fair way of rewarding him properly. He knew Olly had debts and Jane and the kids to support, and that Ella had never managed to get her head above water financially.

Perhaps rent free occupancy of the flat and some cash on top? Maybe Ella, who was always brilliantly imaginative and wonderful with colour – and all those mysteriously arty things he wouldn't ever attempt – might even design the interior, and work on a logo idea or two. Her contribution would have to be taken into account.

But all that was for later. He realised that he was hurtling ahead in an unbusiness-like way. He would go into all this away from Maurice.

When they said goodbye to Maurice, Zac led them down to the main door of the apartment block. He stopped on the stairs and assured them that having had this initial meeting, he would be running things.

Hopefully Maurice would not have to contribute financially to the launch and so would have no say in the running of the restaurant.

"So it could be the old Rhodesia Terrace team running the show." He looked at Olly and said brightly: "I can see that Dad and you are poles apart!"

Olly asked whether Zac had any more thoughts about possible names – "We'll need one when we try for some press mentions in the run-up to opening."

"Not yet, Ol. I want to be pretty democratic about that. It's *so* important. We need something that somehow says what we are. Not easy in a word or two but hopefully one of us will come up with something that gets something over about what we are."

"Ella's got a list of possibles," Olly said. "I've been struggling to find a pithy way of describing in a sentence what we're offering. Nearest I've got is 'The finest cosmopolitan cuisine – with a French accent' but it doesn't say enough somehow."

"Nice, Ol. Concise. But the French bit? A bit too froggyish given that it's not going to be actually *French*?"

"Maybe we could say 'continental accent' instead," Olly replied. "But French cooking is still the marker. Still absolutely pivotal despite all the trends that come and go. They lighten the sauces, tart it up here and there, reinvent it. But it's got pedigree. If you give them the best of French cuisine, and the best dishes from around the world that really is some offering."

"Ol, look – I trust you to find the niche in the market. Ingredient X that will make us different, special."

As they reached the front door he said: "All I need to know now is that you, both of you, might be interested in sharing my little adventure – in principle. If you are, we'll get together soon to look at some details. So what do you think Ol?"

"Sounds brilliant. The head's filling with ideas already, and names of contacts who might be useful."

"Good stuff, matey. And what about you Ella? Fancy giving it a go?"

"It's about the most exciting thing I've ever imagined," she said.

For one second the sheer elation of the moment was held in suspense. Olly told himself not to be stupid but there was a timorous voice somewhere inside crying out with some sort of a warning that he didn't immediately understand.

17

Two long, tense weeks passed after the meeting at Maurice's apartment. Olly and Ella had begun to believe that there had been a hitch, or that Zac had got cold feet, or that he'd underestimated the costs of starting the restaurant. After all, they had autumn pencilled in for opening.

Zac could be grandiose. Olly's theory was that perhaps the restaurant idea had been a bit of showing off, maybe for Ella's benefit. Ella believed that the likeliest reason for calling the thing off was that Maurice had argued him out of risking his money.

"Maurice is so shrewd and Zac is so obedient to him," she said, despairingly. She had been bracing herself to hear bad news. It had all seemed too good to be true.

Each day Olly and Ella had become more and more edgy with each other, and had grown sick of speculating.

"It's like waiting for...the result of your exams," Ella said. She had wanted to say "It must be like waiting for the result of a pregnancy test." The idea of having a baby was becoming intrusive, repeatedly coming into her mind at the most unlikely times. Olly had batted back any mention of the subject.

The call they had been waiting for came as they were about to leave for work at the hotel. Olly answered his mobile phone and after a few seconds said: "Yeah, Zac. Great! Will do." Ella froze.

"Cheers mate. Bye," Olly said, simultaneously raising a

clenched fist in silent celebration.

Ella stood open-mouthed. "Well?" she said.

"I think we may have lift-off El!" he said, snapping his phone closed and pulling her to him. "We're going for a meal to talk it over."

"We?" Ella said.

"You and me, and Zac. He especially wants you to be there. He thinks there'll be stuff you could help with. He's always rated you as an ideas person."

"How kind of him," Ella said but the sarcasm masked the pure joy she felt inside.

Olly walked briskly to the car, Ella trailing behind. "Dinner's at a new place in the city. Better book a cheap room somewhere. It'll be a boozy one."

She could see that Olly had been reinvigorated. It was as if his inner electricity had been switched on again after a fortnight's rewiring work. He talked non-stop as they drove to the hotel.

"He said he'd tell me the state of play properly later but it seems Maurice has done some digging and expects to get planning permission, so it looks as if it's on," Olly said.

◇ ◇ ◇ ◇ ◇

The restaurant Zac had chosen was the newest in the city. *La Lavande* was a bright, airy space with a high ceiling pierced by a large globe of tinted, leaded glass panes. The late evening sun flooded the dining area with soft light.

The expanse of the white walls was broken up here and there by heavily-textured abstract pictures which appeared to Ella to have been created by the careless throwing of paint. Lazy. Old hat, she thought to herself.

The décor and furniture tended towards minimalist and the overall starkness was emphasised by the hard, bare, faux timber floor. Occasionally, the scape of chairs being drawn back and forth blotted out fragments of conversation. There was a lesson there.

Zac was sitting, one elegant leg crossed over the other, on a crimson chaise longue in the reception area. He was holding a flute of something fizzy and there was an open bottle in a chrome bucket of ice, and two more glasses on the tiny table at his elbow.

He got up and greeted Olly and Ella warmly, as a waiter – dressed entirely in black except for a lavender waistcoat – stepped forward to fill the two glasses.

"Thought we'd try this place. Oh, and it's all on me, of course. Research. Tax deductible," he said with amusement.

They were led to a table in the furthest corner of the room. The place was almost full.

"I gather this lot got a nice mention in a Sunday paper supplement. I suppose it's like films and plays. Critics can make you or break you," Zac remarked, turning to Olly for his view.

"To some extent," Olly said. "Sometimes, not very often, they tell you where you're going wrong but in general they're opinionated little shits who have to be clever and cutting to entertain."

"Well, what do you think, chef?" Zac said, as they perused the menu in its silky lavender cover. Ella seemed to be more interested in the way the sleeve had been integrated with the menu, and in the typography, than in the food.

Olly said with quiet conviction: "Too many choices. Much too much on offer. They'll have to change,"

"So you can give people *too* much choice?" Zac asked.

"Takes punters too long to order because they're befuddled with all the options on offer. Some will spend twenty minutes chopping and changing, agonising in their minds. Then they regret not having something else they had spotted when they came in. Another thing – they're occupying a table non-productively for so long and staff are having to hover."

Zac flashed a smile. "I'm really impressed Ol. The boy done good, eh Ella?"

"I suppose he has his qualities," she said in an affectionate, world-weary way.

Olly got into his stride. "The other thing is, with a big menu you have to buy in so much stuff. It takes longer to prep for big menus and you use more space storing it and dealing with it all."

There was a nice conviviality at the table now that the champagne had loosened their guardedness.

Throughout the meal, Olly gave a commentary. He pronounced that his sardines stuffed with currants and pine nuts was fine, the squeeze of orange coming through. But Zac's foie gras with grapes on toasted brioche he judged disappointing; the pan, he said, should have been searingly hot to reduce the amount of melting.

"That's a mess," he said.

Ella's duck with blackcurrant sauce was poorly done as a result of another basic failure, he said, almost apologetically because there seemed to be so much to criticise. He said he suspected that the duck breast had been placed in a *hot* pan; this would seal in quite a lot of the fat instead of letting it escape.

"Leaves it a bit flabby. Elementary stuff. The place is full. They're struggling to get stuff out. The pressure's on. They'll be dashing about like blue-arsed flies behind that wall, effing and blinding and sweating like pigs."

He took another sip of what was obviously a very expensive wine, cut through a caramelised fig with the edge of his fork, and felt smug about being at this side of the wall.

Zac ensured that the drink kept flowing and Olly began to recount incidents from his days in kitchens; the practical jokes, the calamities, the nocturnal beach parties in Italy.

It was his turn to show off. Ella had heard it all before but smilingly entered into the jovial spirit; she was relieved to see a glimmer of the old jolly Olly.

It was also good to see Zac so open and friendly, having stepped out of his business persona. She couldn't blame him for coming across as so calculating. It was unreasonable to expect him still to be wacky and outrageous.

The Rhodesia Terrace days were long gone. But as she watched Olly and Zac, hearing the banter, she felt a yearning to be back, and to feel again the pleasing sense that she was at the very centre of the gloriously grubby world they inhabited then.

She sipped her wine and thought about those days and the way she had luxuriated in the attention she had received from Olly and Zac, delighted in the competitive frisson that they thought she was unaware of. She didn't need a counsellor to tell her that she had enjoyed hardly any parental love and so craved affection.

She had missed Zac from time to time before she had been reunited with Olly but had never felt able to mention it. She had missed dear Richard too, and had told Olly only recently.

"Biggus? Yes, that ridiculous name, Biggus bloody Dickus!" she said to herself, aware that the drink was making her feel nostalgic.

Zac scooped the crumbled peanut brittle from his chocolate dessert, licked his spoon and tapped it against his wine glass. There was a slight slowness in his voice –"Well, I suppose we ought to call the meeting to order…"

He explained, between mouthfuls of ganache, that he was on the brink of signing a lease for the old bank.

"I was thinking that if you two are definitely in, I could fit out a flat above so you could live free, above the shop, and we could work out the money side when I do the final costings."

He thought they should go out to the village soon – "Let's give it a really thorough once-over and think where everything might go."

Ella felt she had to check that she was included.

"Want me to come along Zac?"

"Christ Ella! Of *course!*" he exclaimed, gripping her shoulder. "You're key. We really need your input. Bring your camera and then go away and dream up some options, visuals of how the place might look."

The brandies for Olly and Zac had arrived along with the sambuca Ella had been persuaded by Olly to have as a new experience. He had asked the waitress for coffee beans and he dropped some into the glass, one by one.

"Seven beans, seven hills of Rome," he said. "Here. I'll show you how you drink it El. Have you got a light?" he said to the waitress.

Olly lit the coffee beans and then extinguished the dancing blue flame with the palm of his hand. They raised their glasses.

"To..." Zac began. "well, to whatever we end up calling the place! Liked some of your ideas by the way Ella. *La Bouche* was a good one. Tasty, bit erotic. But it's not quite there. Might even end up with *Olly's!*"

Olly couldn't make out whether this was a drunken throwaway line or an idea Zac had really considered. He saw his name above the door, on the menu, on business cards, in advertisements. It would be the making of him.

They chinked their glasses together and sat contented, full, silent. Ella crunched each of the coffee beans in turn. Then Zac paid the bill, and as they reached the restaurant door, he clasped them both, holding one at each shoulder, and walked to the taxi rank at the end of the road.

Olly and Ella joined hands, left him, and strolled through the bright lights of the city to their low-cost franchise hotel.

They found their urge to make love falling away as the cool pleasure of the bedsheets, the warmth of their bodies and the mellowness of their joy overtook them.

Next morning, when Olly checked his phone, there was a text message from Zac. It said in effect that settling on a name had become quite urgent as a catering magazine had been asking about rumours of the venture.

"Finally decided to go for something plain. *Zac's*. At least it'll be me taking any flak! Luv Z X"

Olly couldn't disguise his disappointment; Ella felt let down.

She said, with irritation: "We could at least have talked about it, especially as he said it was going to be democratic. He didn't tell you, Ol – it was a secret – but he *really* wanted it be called *Olly's.*"

"Then obviously his dad has put his oar in and made him call it *Zac's,*" said Ol. "And of course Zac would have caved in." His face clouded with resentment.

"Actually, I'm surprised he didn't decide to call it *Dad's*"

18

When Zac next rang, Olly knew immediately that he had something contentious or disappointing to say. He was far too upbeat, even for these exciting times. Olly could hear the tinny ring of insincerity behind his pleasantries.

"Right, matey, here's where we are. First, good news. We've got our hands on the keys to the place so we can have a good look round. Can you get a day off soon?"

"Easy. No bother," Olly said and then braced himself.

"As we expected, the natives are a bit restless. In the village. But Dad's gone into it all and he's confident he can win even if it means a planning appeal."

"Good stuff," Olly said. And...?

"Another thing – I've been looking at the budget and I think you can seriously look at bringing over your Spanish friend. I realise you'll need a good right hand man. But let's get the lease sorted first and check the cash situation."

And?

"By the way, talking about money, Ella's work on the interior stuff is a godsend – it seems London people won't begin even flouncing around and arm-waving until you show them a grand or two."

Zac sounded as if he was about to sign off but then said: "I know you're tied up next Monday but I want to start looking for some sort of sculpture, some sort of big feature, something for the entrance."

Ol was puzzled. Tied up?

"I've heard there's a reclamation business half an hour from you," Zac continued. "I'm free Monday so I've rung Ella to ask her if she'll come and see what's on offer."

"Zac, did you say I was tied up?"

"Yes. Isn't it your nipper's birthday, the little girl? Ella thought you were due to go back home that day."

"Yeah. I'd forgotten." It was so easy now to forget his children's birthdays.

The line was silent, and Olly began to think the signal had gone.

Then Zac said: "And Ol. I don't want you to overreact or misunderstand but Dad's now going to be involved – just a bit – after all. Just for a year."

"Oh," said Olly.

"I've found I need a bit of a cushion with the money and he offered to put some in with a view to coming out after the first year. I would have struggled otherwise. It'll let you get on with luring El Whiz Kid."

"Oh," said Olly.

"I know Dad can be a pain. But I promise you he'll be kept well away from food matters. You're the chef. I'll keep him in line."

By the time Ella came home, Olly had worked up a head of

steam. He felt a new and deep contempt for Zac and his toadying deference to his father. All that posturing in the college days! And all the time he was the obedient son, with his Dad holding his hand.

Olly couldn't wait to release his pent-up anger. But before he acted he wanted to have his indignation validated by Ella. There had been times in his life when his fury had turned out to be self-destructive.

He sat in the flat, stony-faced. For him the dream was over. It would never work with Maurice, especially as Zac was too weak to be an effective buffer.

Ella went to kiss him as she came in but his face looked forbidding, and so she shed her coat and sat on the settee arm. There was an ugliness about him, he was so different from the Olly she had left in the morning.

"Guess what, El," he said. "After all Zac said, Maurice is going to be around after all, giving us the benefit of his deep knowledge of the catering business."

"Yes, I know love."

"You *know*?"

"Zac told me. He rang to ask me to look at old statues and stuff in some yard somewhere. It's Monday. You're seeing Sophie. Look Olly, we can cope with Maurice. Zac will keep him well out of your territory."

"Zac will? *Zac?* No chance. He's actually *wimpish* in his Dad's presence. I'm losing respect for him, El. He's got no bottle and it sickens me."

"Be patient Ol," she pleaded. "Just think. We're getting a wonderful opportunity. We'll have a nice place in a nice village. We won't have to travel to work. We may have to take a bit of rough with the smooth. When Zac can pay him off, Maurice will be gone. Stick it for a year, Ol."

Olly was standing with his shoulders back against the wall, his head down. He turned to her, and Ella saw in his face a rage that she had not seen before.

He said very deliberately: "So in the first year, Zac is looking to make enough profit to pay back what his dad's put in? But what if we struggle? I see trouble..."

Ella recoiled as he hit the veneered table with his fist.

"What if he can't pay? Will Maurice stay on? It's no good El. I can't pretend. Anyway, how much has his dad put in?"

"No idea."

"Now that surprises me as Zac seems to have made sure that you knew the score before talking to me."

"You're being silly, Ol," she said gently, so as not to stoke his anger.

She walked to their bedroom to give Olly thinking space, time to consider everything.

Today she had seen a side of him that was alarming. He had always been so even-tempered when they were at Rhodesia Terrace. Back then anyone asked to list his qualities would have had "gentle" somewhere in there.

She sat on the bed, trying not to cry, trying to locate precisely the root of Ol's anger. She wondered whether it really was because Maurice was involved after all. Or that Zac always did his father's bidding. Or was it really because Zac had asked her to go with him to the reclamation yard?

◇ ◇ ◇ ◇ ◇

Olly was up early next morning. He had yet to put in his notice at the hotel but had decided to hold fire now that his role in the restaurant venture was in doubt.

He had a busy schedule, calling at the hotel for a meeting with the management team, then driving to see the children, then going back to oversee a banquet for a Japanese company holding their conference at the hotel.

Olly could be grumpy when he was preoccupied but Ella knew this morning's silence was different.

He was hurt, insecure, yet she feared that to speak to him

113

would open the floodgates of pent-up anger.

"I'll be back late, remember," he said. "Seeing the kids, then feeding half of Japan."

He asked the chief executive to be excused for the last phase of the meeting at the hotel, explaining that he needed to be supervising in the kitchen in readiness for the conference banquet.

He stayed only briefly. Three staff members had rung in claiming they were ill. Staff were often ill, he had found, when the long summer evenings came, or when they knew they'd be run off their feet. He would play there game.

When he pulled up at what had been home, the children were playing in the front garden, standing back to back, arms linked, trying to lift each other. Sophie spotted the car first and Olly lip-read her cry of "Dad!" He kissed them in turn, wishing Sophie a happy birthday, pushing away Dylan's attempt at a handshake.

"Dad," said Sophie. "Get ready for some *really* bad news. Jasper's not here."

"Not here?" Olly said. "You mean he's lost?"

"No, dead," Dylan said. "He had a really big lump near his willy."

Olly's head dropped. He tried to keep his face in check, so as not to show the emotion he felt. *Jasper. Poor old Jasper.*

"Look kids, let me have five minutes with mum to tell her some important things and then we'll go for a burger or a walk or something."

Jane was clearing kitchen drawers when he went in. They exchanged perfunctory hellos. She looked haggard today, Olly thought. She turned to her task; he sat on a kitchen stool. He noticed the steel dog's bowl on the draining board. Jasper's lead still hung from the key hook behind the door.

"Jane," he said. "Why the *fuck* didn't you tell me he'd gone?"

She spun round with a look of surprise on her face.

"What the hell was it to do with *you*? As far as I knew, you

114

didn't know he had moved in. You didn't ask *my* permission to live with Ella."

Olly was perplexed for a moment and then it dawned on him that he had been talking about the dog, and she had been talking about a man, the man.

"No, Jane. Not your gentleman caller. *Jasper.* You had Jasper *put down?* Put down without even *asking* me, telling me? I'd have come to be with him."

There was a tremor in his voice and he had to swallow hard. Jane struggled to reply.

"I had to decide quickly. It was last week. He'd been making noises at night and rocking when he walked."

Seeing the level of Olly's hurt, she felt guilty. "As bloody usual I had to take a big decision. The vet said an operation would cost hundreds then next day he said there was no hope anyway."

"Where is he, Jane?"

"He isn't. We left him."

The children opted for a burger lunch but conscious of the time, he had to ask them to bring their milkshakes to finish in the car. He needed to be in the hotel kitchen; he hadn't got full confidence in the staff.

Olly kissed the children on the front doorstep, accepted a wad of drawings from Sophie and distractedly looked at Dylan's collection of football cards. He gave them a £5 note each and told them to get their mum to put the money safe somewhere. He kissed Sophie and said that she must take care of the present he had given her, a simple, inexpensive camera designed for children.

"Take pictures for me Sophie," he said.

When they had gone back in the house, as he walked to the car he saw under the branch of a low-growing bush, Jasper's blue rubber ring. There was not a millimetre that had not been punctured by his locked jaws.

Olly decided at that moment that he would not be able to work that day. He would ring them and tell the truth – that he had just been bereaved. The Japanese would get their food late, if at all, and he knew that he would be leaving the hotel payroll a little earlier than expected.

He picked up the ring, and, in his head, heard again the low, continuous growl Jasper used to emit as Olly swung him round and round, and he heard again the sound of Jane laughing, and Dylan shouting (as he always did): "Presenting... for your pleasure...Jasper, the Flying Dog!"

He gently put the ring into the boot. He felt a little tearful and silly. He knew that taking the ring was irrational but it was a precious memento of how things had once been, of what he and Jasper and the family had once shared.

19

Harry Pygg was content. Very content, all things considered. He felt so very lucky to be a 21st century Pygg. Things had turned out so well, especially lately.

Pyggs had lived out their lives in and around the village for generations, but from what Harry could gather he was the first one to have ended up comfortably off.

The churchyard at St Jude's was crammed with gravestones bearing the names Pygg, and Pigg. But they were all family: to Harry, a Pygg was a Pygg by any other name. He was happy that his dear departed were taking a well-earned rest – and of course that he remained very much alive.

Harry suspected that most of his ancestors had existed rather than lived. He knew for a fact that there were yet more family members lying hidden away in unmarked graves. He felt particularly sorry for these poor Pyggs, who had not had the price of a headstone.

To his knowledge, all the ancestral Pyggs had been part of the labouring classes and, to be frank, his parents were true to type; they never had a sausage. But somehow he had clawed his way, well not exactly clawed, *climbed* up out of muck and into a nicely upholstered retirement.

He had ended up with a decent little nest egg, one hell of a flat-screen telly, and they'd just had a power shower fitted. Unlike the Pyggs of the past, Harry and Esme always had a winter sunshine holiday – it was Gran Canaria again for them this year.

He had a tidy little motor to get them to the airport. Dad had never even driven any sort of car. The old man used the same bike for forty-odd years.

And Granddad, bless him, had been forced to walk everywhere. Walked to work, walked at work, walked all day behind the horses, then walked back. Or rather limped. His foot. First he got it squashed under a dray, and then he broke it cheeserolling.

If asked, Harry would own up to being conservative, with a big C as well as a little c. He had never moved from the village; never needed to. It had worked out. More than worked out.

He and Esme had ended nearly as well off as when they were working, what with the bit of a redundancy pay-off and the pension. And now, out of the blue, there's this new opening, to work as a twosome. *Side By Side.*

Janice had laughed when Harry told her that they'd got the job. "Getting paid for pot washing, Dad? You've been missing out for years, doing that at home for free!"

She said that with it being *Zac's*, such a posh place, if they got a bit of supper it'd likely be snails and frogs' legs.

Esme Pygg was happy and grateful. The struggles had been worth it. Now life was kind.

Like the Pyggs, her family, the Fiddlers, had been around from time immemorial. Esme sometimes thought of them, especially the old ones, the two aunts she remembered clearly.

They all seemed to have had lots of children. They all had gardens. She remembered sweet peas, fusty smells, fat upper arms and the wet kisses. Things had changed so much in her lifetime, not in the actual place because the village itself didn't seem to alter, but in the way people carried on.

Still, she'd inherited some of their ways; Janice teased her about it. One was her habit of passing on observations about life in little packages.

All right, they were old-fashioned mottos but she liked the kernel of truth in things like "A penny saved is a penny earned," and "Don't bite the hand that feeds you." Her favourite was "Count your blessings." She had, and she did.

Esme knew there was a reason the old sayings survived. It was because they helped you get the best out of what little time you had on earth. There were plenty of Fiddlers (and Pyggs for that matter) pushing up daisies under the big yew at St Jude's, reminding everybody that we don't go on forever.

She'd certainly counted her blessings when Harry was made redundant after all those years at the horticultural engineers. But they got through it, thanks to the pay-off. And now they'd landed a nice little night job that meant they could help Janice with the kids in the day, and earn a few bob in the evenings.

True, it was only washing up. But imagine the luck, landing a job right opposite your house! For Esme, every cloud did have a silver lining. Well nearly every one.

Actually, she couldn't help feeling a bit of a hypocrite now because Harry and her had been very vocal about the restaurant plan when the protesting was going on. Very anti. She regretted carrying the placard Harry had made, and shouting so much at the meetings.

She was relieved that the nice lady at *Zac's* hadn't asked her how she had felt when she first heard that the place was opening. Actually, Harry had been worse. A real firebrand. Now he's as quiet as a mouse about it.

To be fair, they *had* over-reacted. She saw that now. Recently Harry conceded that if *Zac's* was only going to have thirty or so places, and people were coming and going at different times, you weren't going to get hordes of people, scores of cars all over the village.

He was right about another thing, Esme concluded. Couples who'd just spent £200 on their dinner wouldn't be the sort to roam round the village afterwards bawling and being sick everywhere like the youngsters.

20

"The thing is, CVs don't give you all you want to know," Olly told the scrawny, nervous young man, sitting bolt upright opposite him at a low table in the half-completed reception area at *Zac's*.

Olly placed the papers on the arm of the chair and anchored them down with an elbow. The interviewee looked crestfallen. The CV had taken ages to collate. He was proud of every line, recording every advancement since his days as a waiter.

"Look, I know you can cook, Ben," Olly said. "I know what you've done at *Gallus Rabbie's* and *Tante Estelle*. But I always need to lift the bonnet for myself and see the state of the engine. It's just my way."

The night before, when the CV was finally complete, Ben had been struck by how many times he had changed jobs in his short working life. What a nomadic business he had chosen to work in. And here he was again, looking for another step up.

Olly felt slightly awkward about the surroundings for the interview, one that was so important for both of them. As they talked, the smell of varnish and sawdust pervaded. Electrical cables dangled. The pile of unopened cardboard boxes beside the low table gave Ben the feeling that they were in the way of the progress.

"I trust what you've written in there," Olly said patting the CV. "But you know that a hundred CVs are bugger-all use when things get chaotic mid-service. You're short-handed, somebody cuts a bit of finger end off, and *every* bloody table wants the risotto ..."

Ben nodded resignedly. He had endured many nights of that sort of controlled panic. Each service was unique; you could never rehearse. "I know the feeling, chef. You've got to have 100 per centers."

Olly said: "So true. Once I got a new sous. Big reputation. I slipped away to take a phone call and I turn round to see a *boeuf en croute* is coming back looking like a very recent amputation in a blood-soaked bandage." Ben nodded again.

"I was the one who had to go out to assure this apoplectic customer that it would be delicious. Once it had been cooked."

Ben smiled, liking this man and his disarming, easy way. He understood why that catering magazine had called him "Jolly Olly."

"It's like this, Ben. It's not *my* fortune that's being ploughed into this place. But it's *my* career riding on it. I need to have the right people."

Olly knew he was at a disadvantage when he was hiring people. He was not as perceptive as some. He had made some terrible mistakes over staff, and they had come back not just to haunt him but to stand next to him at the range each evening.

He didn't enjoy the business side of things; he'd been direct with Maurice and Zac about that. He didn't enjoy interviewing. He didn't like the eye contact, or having to ask awkward questions. He hated seeing people being made to feel uncomfortable, and he'd often ended up prompting the answer he'd been seeking, just to break the tension.

Interviews were unreliable anyway. And taking people on was so hazardous – the industry had more than its fair share of transients, dipsos, head cases, work-dodgers, conmen even, not to mention fantasists with CVs that would win fiction prizes. Ben was different. He was sound.

Olly looked down at his coffee, cupped it in his hands and said: "What I'd really like to know, maybe, is what you had for breakfast..."

On the way to *Zac's,* on his motorbike, Ben had thought he'd rehearsed every answer to every likely question. Now he'd been thrown. He decided that truth was safest.

"Coffee, instant. Marmite and banana sandwich. Wholemeal, sliced. No butter. Dribble of molasses. A combination I dreamed up when I was a kid."

Olly gave no clue as to whether he was favourably impressed. He mused instead.

"Funny what chefs eat away from work. Me? I like good, slow-cooked steak mince on thick, white bread toast, slathered with beef dripping. Poached egg on top. Duck egg for choice."

"Oh, and I love fruit jelly," Olly added, laughing. "Got to be chilled. Nothing fancy – ordinary kids' party jelly. Lime. With tinned Carnation – what my gran called *emasculated* milk."

Ben beamed, his big grey eyes narrowing.

"My grandpa always called a banana a Gertie Gitana," he offered, to stoke up the warmth that was building between the two men.

He had a gnarled look for such a young man, Olly noted. He was as lean as a whippet, kept skinny, Olly surmised, by sheer graft and nervous energy. He noticed that the fingers were scarred, the knuckles prominent, and on the back of one hand there was a patch of skin that resembled crepe. That must have been a very nasty burn.

Ben discerned that Olly was as much an actor in this process as himself. His food preferences had been offered as a leveller. He liked the way he was talking in an open and friendly way, not as if he was The Great I Am, like some chefs he'd worked for. Olly seemed to be asking whichever questions came into his head.

"OK, Ben.... So what would I find in your fridge today?" he said, smiling playfully. Ben shifted in his chair, and reached for his coffee cup to win a moment's thinking time. Again, he decided on a straight answer.

"Not *my* fridge really, chef. The family fridge; I'm saving to get a place. But my stuff would be, well, the beer certainly. And a bit of Gruyere. A head or two of garlic, a jar of anchovies, a bit of unsalted Normandy butter. Oh, and, at the moment, some yeast. Experimenting with some weird breads."

He added hurriedly: "And there's half a Stornaway black pudding. A birthday present. I'd asked for it. The best."

"That all?"

"Well, mum keeps her Prosecco in there. And there's dad's maggots."

Olly raised a quizzical eyebrow. Ben wondered whether he'd strayed too far into informality.

"Maggots?"

"Dad's an angler, chef," Ben explained, tentatively. "Likes to keep his maggots comatose until they meet their doom. For them, our fridge is their Death Row. They're in a proper sealed box..."

Ben was pleased that he had found the nerve to go off script, show a bit of personality. He eased back a little and felt the tension go out of his shoulders. He could see, beyond Olly, the brand new cooking ranges, still wrapped in protective sheeting, and dining furniture swathed in bubble-wrap.

He wanted this job. It could be the big one.

"Tell me - what *wouldn't* you eat, Ben?"

"I'll try anything," he said with conviction. "Not mad keen on sweetbreads or bone marrow. Or cinder toffee. It's the sensation on my fillings," he said grimacing.

"No, chef. Nothing out of bounds really," he lied, remembering the Rouen duck he had eaten out of curiosity in France. It was a step too near barbarity, the bird having been smothered to ensure that it remained engorged with blood. Never, ever again.

"So you're an unfussy omnivore. Good," said Olly. "Because if you work with me you'll taste *everything*. Yes, yes... I know you'll say that you've *always* tasted what you were sending out. But you haven't. But you would if you came to me."

Workmen were coming in the front door now, carrying plasterboard. They were followed by a plumber with lengths of copper piping sloped across his shoulder.

"Right," said Olly, "Challenge! Dream up a dessert for me, one I've never heard of. I'm going over to ask them to give us another few minutes of quiet."

He walked off but was back in what, to Ben, seemed like an instant – all ears, his forefingers making a pyramid beneath his chin. "Right, fire away..."

Ben tried to stay calm. He hoped that what he was going to blurt out really was original but he knew very well that cooking was 95 per cent plagiarism and five per cent inventiveness.

He described how he would take apricots, firm ones, poach them so that they kept their shape; stone them. How he would fill the cavities with finely chopped pecans, and crushed ginger biscuit bound with honey. How he would make a concentrated glaze from other apricots, sharpen it with lemon, and chill the dish before serving it with *crème frâiche.*

"Oh, and I'd do a couple of fingers of shortbread...or triangles, or even little shortbread spoons..." he added hurriedly. "And maybe I'd introduce a cinnamon note..."

Reflecting later on the interview, he liked that "introduce a cinnamon note...." Ben always avoided talking "cheffy" but this was a job interview after all. He guessed the shortbread spoons represented a step too far. Ridiculous; he could see them snapping, scattering crumbs.

Olly tilted his head, then he asked, with a sudden seriousness: "Ben. Have you ever lost control completely during service in a kitchen?" Olly averted his eyes, glimpsing out of the window.

"Yes. Just twice. And perhaps half a dozen times I've been in a situation where everything, *everything* went into meltdown and I was bricking it, so scared I was tempted to run off."

Olly would have experienced that sort of mayhem in the kitchen. He would understand. Of course, he would.

Ben said: "You know how it is, chef. People turn into headless chickens. Grown men shit themselves. I've seen a chef run amok hitting staff with a ladle like that bloke who used to strike that big gong at the start of films. Once, all the waitresses I worked with ran away crying, all of them."

"But you didn't run away whenever it hit the fan? Didn't resign?"

"No. When the lasses ran off I kept cooking and then took it to the tables. Just soldiered on."

"Good. You know you'd be third in command, if you came, and I might have to be away a good bit? The bits of telly stuff, and getting out there spreading the word?"

"Don't worry. I've learned."

"What?"

"To be prepared for every eventuality. To make sure in advance that my food will be fucking *perfection* (he checked Olly's face to see whether the swear word had offended) and to make sure that any lazy arses are kicked *in advance,* so that the food gets where it should be, at the right temperature. That it's delivered with a relaxed smile, and with proper knowledge of what it actually *is*. And that when it hits the table it knocks their bloody socks off. Every time."

Olly found himself startled at the conviction in Ben's voice. With his rangy frame, and his cropped hair and slightly knocked-about features he had the air of a street-fighter.

A pleasant-looking woman in a striped apron approached the table and smiled warmly at Ben as she made space on the table for more coffee. He wondered whether this was Olly's wife, or partner. She was nicely rounded; good living, he supposed. A shade sheepish, or shy, he thought, but with kindly eyes.

"Thanks, Ella," Olly said, then: "Look, Ben. I'll be truthful. I've been wondering whether you're here because you want to get away from *Tante Estelle* and from Philippe. Everyone knows he is an absolute swine to work for. Or whether you actually *want* to be here for the launch of something that's exciting...but chancy."

Ben chose his words carefully. He wasn't prepared to comment on his boss, who was still his employer after all. He said he had come looking for a new challenge not to damn the restaurant he worked in.

Olly was impressed by the dignified way he had responded. He felt he had struck a seam of unstinting loyalty. He took a sip of coffee and asked about portion costing, waste control.

"The star ingredient – the venison, or lobster, or whatever– has to be big enough to *seem* generous," Ben said. "There's no future in ripping people off. Nowadays a mobile photo of a measly portion can be round the world in a minute with a message saying 'Look how this lot robbed me'."

A dinner that cost as much as a weekend break should be so special that the memory of it would endure for years, he said. By way of example, he began to describe a meal that a guest chef had cooked for students at catering college. Olly listened patiently.

"Mr Huang's Peking Duck. I can taste it again now." He

described the crackly skin, the moist flesh, the coolness of the cucumber; the bite of spring onion, and the richness of hoisin against the blandness of the pancakes.

And then a workman shouted – "Can we get stuck in soon, gents?"

Olly shouted an apology and led Ben to the front door which he shut behind him, to muffle the rising cacophony of drills and saws.

"OK, Ben. We'll be in touch. If it's you we appoint, you ought to know that the hours will be shit, and the salary will be fairly shit – at first, at least. But I'll need to go through things with Zac first."

"Oh, so there's a real-life Zac?"

"Yes, he's the owner. A friend."

"So your friend's your boss, chef?"

"Well, yes. But I've not really thought of it that way before. More friend than boss I think. I'll be filling people's bellies, he'll be emptying their wallets."

Olly was a little discomfited by the piercing intensity of Ben's look as they shook hands. It was penetrating. He seemed to be using his gaze to say: You've got a lot on your shoulders; let me help.

As Ben donned his motor-cycle helmet, Olly promised to send "a proper letter" if Ben was selected.

"The situation is this. I hope to hear this week from the bloke I want as No 2. Rafa. He's Spanish and brilliant – and mad. And I'm seeing an Irish lass who's on pastry at *Balchazzar's*. Bridget. Word is she's a bit feisty, so that's encouraging..."

Ben felt a tingle of excitement. He had never been part of a restaurant launch. This was pioneering stuff.

"One thing," Olly said, "we've got two people signed up already. Pot-washers. Husband and wife. A matching pair. Mr and Mrs Pygg."

"Mr and Mrs *Pygg*? *Pygg*? And is Mrs Badger going to be sommelier, chef?"

"No, we've got a nice, mature lady called Laura. The best. Quiet, calm, undemanding. I poached her."

"Rolling boil, chef?"

Olly looked puzzled.

"*Poached* her, chef," Ben said, and immediately wondered once more whether he had gone too far, especially as Olly seemed too preoccupied to get the joke.

Ben started the bike and drowned their laughter as he opened up the throttle. The ear-piercing snort and splutter of the engine was to his ears as sweet as bells pealing in celebration.

He knew he had got the job. He just had to wait for the letter. Then he would take sublime pleasure in handing a month's notice to that ball-aching bastard Philippe at *Tante Estelle*.

21

A pale girl with shining black hair pinned up high above her cobalt blue eyes arrived at *Zac's* just as Janice, the Pyggs' daughter, was starting work as cleaner at the restaurant.

Janice noted the purposeful walk and the new-looking clothes that were just a tiny bit too small. The girl came in and looked around the restaurant with its bare walls, uncoupled radiators, and protruding electrical cables.

Janice made herself useful by wiping light globes that Ella intended to go above the bar. She knew that they would be covered in dust again by the end of this, her first day.

She also knew, within minutes of appearing to get busy, that this would be a cushy little number. Ella was nice and promised she'd ensure that something was worked out if ever child-care became a problem.

This had made Janice feel good but also guilty. Like her mum and dad she'd been very sniffy about the whole idea of *Zac's*. She'd been wrong. They had been absolutely lovely, and she could see already that the place was going to be fantastic, like something from Las Vegas.

It was a bit chaotic in a relaxed sort of way. Olly the chef had even said hello as he walked through. He was a big, happy bloke and Janice liked the way he shouted over "Ella – make sure first that the police aren't looking for her!"

No *side* – and he's so much bigger than she remembered, when he was on television that time.

It had been so comforting, as she sprayed stainless steel cleaner on the already-dusty new stove backs and canopies, to look down from the stepladder and see Mum and Dad in the corner washing the crockery.

Chattering away, side by side. Peas in a pod. Happy as pigs in... well, really content. Ella had let them have the kids alongside for the morning. It would be different when the place was open.

Ella had got Dad to prise open some wooden crates and he was carefully taking glasses, and plates and little terracotta vases, clearing straw from them and handing them to Mum, who was plunging them into the big sink.

Esme and Harry called on Janice and the kids most days. There didn't need to be a pretext or a reason, although there often was; the delivery of new socks for the kids, the swopping of TV soap magazines, the return of a bit of ironing Esme had done to help her daughter out.

When Esme and Harry called that evening, the children were in their pyjamas. They were shouting above the noise of the television.

"They're bloody *hyper!*" Janice said inclining her head towards the girls, one of whom was now crying, having been knocked down. Esme made tea while Janice shouted: "Bed! *Now!* If you go up right this minute, do your teeth *properly*, you can have a go on the Xbox for *ten* minutes".

Harry and Esme had settled on the settee, side by side, each holding a mug of tea at chest level by the time Janice came down. When they sat like that, Janice was sometimes struck by their similarity; they were growing into mirror images of one another, same expression, same double chins, same sort of specs.

Janice turned the TV off and announced: "A *very* interesting day over there..." Harry and Esme tilted forward slightly in eager expectation of Janice's revelations. "*Very* interesting..."

Janice described how as she had been vacuuming the reception area, a young woman arrived and Ella took her to a table next to where all the wine was going to be. Olly was there having a coffee.

"She was small and really smart in a black suit. So *loud*, though. Nerves I expect. Really funny accent..."

Janice said that it was clear that the woman had come for an interview for one of the cheffing jobs.

"Irish," said Harry. "I heard Ella on the phone saying to somebody how her grandfather had been Irish, and giving directions from the railway station."

Janice seemed determined not to have the rich essence of her story diluted.

"Anyway, there was loads of wool coming out of the new carpet so I stopped to clean it out of the vac and you could hear what was going on. Bit of a ding dong!" She mouthed the words "ding dong" silently as if someone involved might be listening.

"No!" said Harry, incredulous. "*Ding dong*?" said Esme.

Janice said that she had vacuumed for a few seconds more and stopped again to clear out the machine again even though there was no need.

"You could hear them from where I was. Olly was saying ever

so nicely that he was going to insult the woman by asking her something and she snapped, saying that she'd probably have to insult him back. It was like they were sparring.

"They were talking about chips. Chips! In a place like that! I think Olly had asked her about the way she cooked chips. I thought she was going to go ape-shit. She said something about coming a long way to meet a so-called top chef, and didn't want to be talking about chips."

Janice had assumed that Olly must have stuck to his guns because after she'd worked on the carpet a minute or two, the woman had gone red and Olly was saying something about seasoning and the woman had said sea salt, *fine* sea salt because the big stuff just rolled off."

Janice said she had left the vacuum where it was and had walked past the table, pretending to look for some dusters but really to catch a little more of the conversation.

"When she said 'fine salt' Olly was really pleased, and said something about attention to detail. Then she looked right into his face and said, *really* sarcily: 'I do a lovely feckin' ....that's how she said it... 'I do a lovely feckin' soft boiled egg, chef. Want me to talk you through it?'"

Janice had heard some laughter. "Then they started to talk in a really friendly way. She was on about cooking in hay and seaweed and Olly was talking really nicely."

Harry Pygg looked thoughtful and said: "So really, he'd been testing her mettle...?"

Janice mulled this over, feeling slightly miffed that she had missed this rather obvious fact.

"But there was another bit of a do..." Janice said.

"*Ooer*," said Esme.

Janice said: "Ella brought some coffees to them and when I started sweeping again, Olly took the woman into the kitchen area, showing her all the bits and bobs."

Janice explained that she was wheeling the cleaner past

the entrance to the cooking area just as Olly was talking about equipment.

"He was carrying over a new water bath thing to show her and he said to this woman 'Bridget, could you just move that spinach off the counter' and she said, 'Sorrel, chef. It's sorrel, not spinach'.

"Anyway, as he put it down she said, cool as you like: 'Cheap trick, chef'."

Janice continued: "I think he was starting to say sorry and explain that it was his way of making sure about people."

She said: "I thought I'd give the new front door fittings a bit of a polish. I'd got the brass cleaner out and I was already out there when they came out. They were talking about her train home. She seemed to be apologising for being a bit fiery. I could hear Olly say that he loved women with bollocks."

"With *what?*" Esme asked.

"Bit of spirit, Mum. Anyway, the taxi arrived and I heard her say that she liked honesty. 'I like to be straight. I do things for real, chef. No pissing about,' she said."

"Bit of a wildcat..." said Harry.

"Yeah, wild. But you had to hand it to her," Janice said.

Esme and Harry and Janice drank up and she gathered the empty cups as her parents rocked and then heaved themselves out of the low settee. Their favourite TV soap would be on at 8 30.

They always followed it, enjoying the ups and downs and ins and outs of each storyline. They spoke of the characters as if they were real.

As they walked the short step home in the dying sunlight, past the old cottages with their cascading front-garden trees, cropped lawns and pots of perfect flowers, they reflected on today's little drama at *Zac's*.

This was better than any soap, Harry said to himself. They looked forward eagerly to future episodes.

"Sounds as if it might turn a bit lively," Esme said with relish.

"You know, Ma," said Harry to Esme, "one thing about being not very important is that you're *invisible*. It's like servants in the old days – their ears must have been flapping something chronic. I mean, look at our Janice today. There she was, seeing and hearing everything but they forgot she was there."

Esme said: "Remember what you used to say when Janice was a nipper, Harry? 'Little Pyggs have big ears...'"

◇ ◇ ◇ ◇ ◇

Late that night, Olly and Ella ate spaghetti up in the flat and reviewed progress. This updating had become something of a habit as the opening night loomed. They felt almost like a king and queen, drinking their Malbec, and discussing courtiers and developments in their little kingdom.

It had been a long day (they all were nowadays) but *Zac's* was taking shape. Olly had begun to feel that he had a grasp of what the restaurant would be, and how it would present itself.

Ella had been busy doing watercolour visuals of colour schemes and any day now, with the basic building work almost complete, they would start the transformation.

Olly had put to the back of his mind Zac's trip with Ella to look for a focal point for the restaurant entrance. He knew his imagination was too active. He no longer associated the sculpture with the trip. He no longer pictured Ella and Zac together in the car, having coffee, debating whether to buy the rusted, sheet steel wild pig, running on tiny legs.

"Loved the Irish girl!" said Ella with relish. "Wonderful! All the feckin' this and feckin' that. And the Pyggs make me laugh. They're like identical twins. Hope we don't grow to be so alike!"

"Inbreeding I expect," said Olly, twirling spaghetti. Putting on a rustic voice he said: "We only 'ave a small gene pool round these parts."

Ella asked whether there had been any message from Rafael. She really hoped that he could come over. Olly really rated him. So experienced, and, by the sound of it, so entertaining. She would feel reassured if there was someone to share the burden with Olly.

"The trouble with Rafa is that he's so bloody *indecisive*," Olly said, suddenly annoyed that he had not received a reply to his last text. "He'll be wrapped up with some girl. Woman-mad! When he phoned he asked whether I'd lay on a posh Englishwoman with blonde hair and a rich father."

"You're not laying on any woman. Unless it's this one," Ella said laughing.

The wine bottle was empty. Ella fetched yoghurts from the fridge and then put them back.

"Let's have a nightcap instead. I think we've still got some grappa."

Grappa. The word conjured up that night in Italy, after his shift, when he was desperately low. A girl with breasts that he always saw in his mind as pannacotta mounds.

And what was it that Rafa had brought out one night, when they nearly became hospital cases? Bacardi something. Bacardi 151. Seventy per cent. Seventy bloody per cent! It had a metal cap on the bottle to stop it catching fire. But that was then...

They took their grappa to bed.

Ella said: "Just thought – I suppose I really am going to have to call you chef, once we're open for business."

"Of course," Olly said with affected pomposity. "It befits my high office."

They had a moment of silliness, talking nonsense, undressing, play fighting in the dark. Minutes later, Ella began crying out as if in pain. Then there was only the sound of a sigh, and the murmur of breathing, as the night closed in on them.

As he fell asleep, Olly felt Ella's lips touch his ear and heard her whisper "Very nice. Very. My compliments to the chef."

22

Zac rang next day. He'd been studying Olly's email about suppliers and thought they ought to do a tour, meeting them, haggling, setting up accounts – "How about it Ol? I'll be the bad cop, you can be the nice one with that smile of yours."

He had noted that Olly's preferred fish merchant was well away from the more local suppliers, making it impossible to cover them all in day.

"Let's have an overnighter, matey. Sort the lot out. Few beers. Boys' night out. If you can tear yourself away from Ella that is...."

And so a few days later, Zac's sports car pulled up and he and Olly set off. Immediately, away from the restaurant – away from Ella, away from Maurice – they felt a sense of release. They laughed, lapsed into familiar obscenities, talked about sport, about women, and – apart from when they were in meetings – they didn't mention *Zac's*.

Towards the end of the day, Zac phoned ahead to book a couple of rooms in a country hotel. They met in the bar for a couple of pre-dinner drinks, ate enormous steaks, and took the remains of the second bottle of wine into the hotel bar. Zac was happy with the day's deals, Olly in thrall to his icy stubbornness in negotiation.

The mood was even more buoyant now, and the conversation was rolling, tumbling. It was like old times. They were the last customers in the bar, surrounded by silence, and overlooked by a bored and yawning barman.

Olly saw this as the perfect time to raise his concerns about Maurice but it seemed so negative, so ungrateful even, after Zac's hospitality, after all the laughter.

Zac said suddenly: "Look matey. I want to know you're all right. Always say if there's a problem. Is the flat OK?"

"It's fine, Zac. Bags of room. They've done it out really well."

"Just one thing...do you think you can stick Dad for a bit? I know he must drive you mad..."

"Can't promise but I'm going to try to resist the urge to cut his balls off and turn them into a terrine."

The explosiveness of their laughter made the barman recoil. And then the silence returned.

Olly, breathless with laughter, said: "One day, Zac, you'll walk in and see me with a knife at Tinker's neck, saying to your dad: One more negative comment, Maurice, and the dog gets it!"

The laughter shattered the peace again. The barman sighed. They were at the giddy stage. He hoped upon hope that they wouldn't order another drink so he could get to bed.

"And how's Ella bearing up?" Zac said, with what seemed to Olly to be studied nonchalance.

"We're OK. Bit of friction here and there. Stress. She'd like a kid but it's not the right time, and maybe for me it'll never be the right time. But you know Ella; she really is something special."

Olly offered this as bait. He waited for Zac to give some clue about his feelings for Ella.

All he said was "Yeah, I know," after draining the last of his brandy, but he seemed distracted, Olly noticed. Was it distracted – or rueful? Or nostalgic? Or regretful?

"Thanks for a brill day, matey," Zac said, at the top of the stairs. He clasped Olly's shoulders and they said goodnight.

23

Something – and I can't remember what, it was so inconsequential – set me off on the well-worn track of recrimination, after Ella and me had spent a long but happy day sorting out kitchen equipment and helping to unpack tablecloths, crockery, utensils and pans.

The painting of the walls was being started next day. The scheme with the Moroccan colours had won the day. The Pyggs were in their corner, chuntering away and washing the stuff we'd unpacked, then storing it where it needed to go.

In the early evening Zac dropped in and asked me whether he could "borrow" Ella to go off and look at a brass rail for the bar area. It had come from a Victorian pub, he said, and he feared it might be snapped up if they didn't swoop in and buy it.

The grudging tone of my agreement – if my approval was ever needed – for Ella to go along, seemed to surprise him. He looked perplexed.

"Never mind, if you're pushed, I could..."

"No, go Ella. No pressure here," I said.

Later, when we were about to go up to the flat, glad to get away from the smell of emulsion, something was said. It was a pinprick of a thing that grew in moments into a throbbing wound. I didn't raise my voice but my tone must have changed because Esme Pygg's scrubbing stopped, as if she was concentrating on listening.

Ella and I ate together but we were so angry with each other that neither of us could finish our pasta. We went to bed silently, unable to bring ourselves to say goodnight, and slept back to back.

I was too befuddled to remember, as I came out of a deep sleep, that I was still bearing a grudge. I was off guard. The thaw was like spring coming. I melted when Ella cupped the point of my shoulder with her hand and kissed me between the shoulder blades, then pressed her naked front to my back. Sulking was a lonely business.

Nothing had changed, of course, but we both knew that, whatever the emotional turmoil, we had to stay together to work together.

Zac's must open soon. This stark imperative nudged our troubled love into a corner, something to be sorted after the launch. We knew we were propping up the whole edifice; if either of us let go, it would fall.

Until more tranquil times came, I had to keep my nerve. To try to find redeeming qualities in Zac. To find a way of tolerating Maurice, and even the unlikeable Tinker, and to get over the loss of Jasper, a proper dog. I had to forgive myself for being an absent father, to deal with Jane's financial demands and convince myself that money was only money, after all.

But – most important – I had to be gentler with Ella, to trust what she said and not insult her with my pathetic jealousy. To understand her yearning to be a mother – "you know, *some* day," she would say, pathetically, and I would feel bad. I always stonewalled when she had raised the subject.

Also, I'd just learned that when *Zac's* finally opened, I'd have to go over the top alone – without Rafa, my one-time Spanish comrade, at my shoulder. He was *apologetico* but he had just fallen in love, *mucho* in love, and could not bear to leave his lady and come to England after all.

Adore Rafa as I did, and admire his cooking as I most certainly did, clearly he was still infuriatingly unreliable, and I had been left *profundo* in the *mierda*.

Thank God for eager beaver Ben, who had rung when he got the letter hiring him and sounded like a child on Christmas morning. And Bridget. Feckin' feisty Bridget! She was fully on board and raring to go. It would be tough but we would manage in the kitchen until we saw how well *Zac's* was doing, and saving Rafa's salary would delight Maurice, have him forgetting his dicky heart and cartwheeling round the apartment.

Then Zac began dropping in on us, fretting about the interior and talking over drapery and fittings. We still seemed a long way from turning Ella's watercolour design into reality.

Zac and Ella had been downstairs looking at the new, golden sign, the individually letters propped against the wall in the reception area, awaiting fitting. I joined them as they pulled away the bubble wrap of the Z. They looked at each other and, wide-eyed, marvelled at the way a handwritten "Zac's" had been transformed into a waist-high 3D version.

"Well, Ol? What d'ya think?" Zac asked. "It really looks like gold but I think it's 22-carat plastic."

"Lovely job," I said. "It shouts quality. It looks as if someone with a giant tube of gold paint has squeezed the letters out freehand. Letter by letter."

We went upstairs and Ella and Zac sat opposite each other, poring over paint cards, discussing the placing of lights. They agonised over the new menu folders, and the terracotta bowls, and the cutlery samples, the gold thread *Zac's* logos on the napkins.

"This is shaping up *so* nicely mate," he called to me as I busied myself around the flat, making coffee, staying uninvolved, so that Ella would feel that this really was her part of the project.

I had been fine. But when Zac began to show Ella photos on his phone of three half-moon tables she had asked for, to run along one side of the restaurant – each table holding a huge dried flower arrangement – suddenly I felt excluded.

Ella went to the bedroom, and, returning, said: "This one's flax, the red one, and this one's hydrangea, both dyed. I'm getting *masses* of them. Won't they look superb, Zac? Look!" she said, holding one of the orange hydrangeas against a paint card.

"Yes, but what about *this*..." Zac said, scrolling forward on his phone. He was showing Ella a photo of an old carved screen he had found in an antiques shop. They could have been a newlywed couple deciding how to decorate a flat.

"Now, I've got the *perfect* place in mind for *that*," Ella said.

It was then that the feeling I used to have, back in Rhodesia Terrace, returned – the times when Zac and Ella played chess. It was like a tide rising inside me. As Zac left, he gave me the usual bear hug, then looked into my face and said: "Now where's our Jolly Olly today?"

I said that I was fine, just anxious to get the place open and to get cooking. Part of this was true – I *was* keen to see Zac's open. But I was far from fine.

"Don't worry Ol – it's all going to be OK. Cheer up, buddy boy. We're moving like a train now."

The day had started with gentle reconciliation and love-making. Then I had taken a walk thinking that I could shed a little stress.

Each day I had looked up the hill that was the landmark for the village. It was so inviting, with its flank of bracken and clumps of trees leading up to a topping of firs. So I took the gently winding path and, near the top, looked down on the village.

Suddenly, my knees were buffeted by a dog's nose, and then another dog pushed its flank against my legs. Behind me an elderly man called them to heel. The dogs were Irish setters; playful, the colour of conkers, their feathery ears never still. Suddenly I missed Jasper.

The man, a country type complete with oiled jacket and knobbly stick, extended a hand for me to shake.

139

"I know who *you* are but you don't know me. You're the restaurant man. I'm Gus. I'm so honoured to meet the devil incarnate," he said with a wheezy laugh.

We stood and talked with ease about food, and the countryside, and we laughed over the rumblings that the arrival of the restaurant had caused.

When I said I had to hurry back to *Zac's*, he shouted after me: "Welcome! Never mind that lot down there!" he said pointing his stick to the cottages below.

Ella was pleased that I'd had a break from the restaurant, had some fresh air, and explored a bit of the countryside. "It's Haig's Hill," she said. "One of the Pyggs told me."

We were fine throughout dinner but then I misinterpreted something she had said when I harked back to the days when we were at Rhodesia Terrace. When I asked her to clarify whatever it was she took it that I was probing again in my paranoid way. So the evening ended with raised voices, accusation, my despair. The monster in me had stirred again.

After the worst was over, Ella – her face puffy, her eyes red – curled up on the settee, looking like a wounded animal that had retreated from the fray to heal.

"I want you to listen to me Olly," she said. "I've been through a great deal in my life and that makes me pretty fearless about the future. I've had to be patient but I have a limit and it's been reached."

"And?" I said. She pulled cushions on to her as if she could feel the cold coming from me.

"And.... Well, wouldn't it be a shame if you lost me, and I lost you, because of some warped notion you can't shake off? This obsession with the past, *my* past, this possessiveness? Don't have any doubt, Olly, I would survive because what I expect from life has never been great. But I know that you would never get over me."

And so we went to bed, silent and heavy, and lay back to back once more, listening to each other breathing.

"Just one more thing," she said. I lifted my head off the pillow to hear properly. "You were jealous of Zac today. Although that stupid little smile was there as usual, you were writhing inside. And all we were doing was trying to find ways of making *Zac's* beautiful."

She was right. Did it really show as plainly as that?

"What you don't know is that the entire interior of that place, the final design, started with you. Your bloody hair," she said, her voice sliding into tearfulness.

"I took the colour of your bloody hair as a starting point and created the whole thing around that shade, then got everything to tone in, all that deserty look, the browns and reds and earth colours."

"I'm flattered," I said coldly.

"I hope that knowing that it was a kind of tribute from me makes you feel like shit." It did.

Then she said with a sniffle: "It's not everybody who gets a restaurant designed round their hair colour!" She seemed to intend this jokily, taking the fire out of the argument, offering me a chance to reciprocate. But I still had harder things to say.

"Look, Ella – I know that you find it easier than me to go along with Zac and Maurice, but I think it's going to drive a wedge between us. I hate to see you kowtowing."

"Kowtowing? But it's *their* place, Olly. We live in *their* building. *They* pay us. It's our big chance. And Zac is your friend, believe it or not. Maurice will be gone one day and then Zac will be his own man."

"No chance," I said, "Zac will always be the monkey and Maurice will always be the organ grinder. Zac has been trained to dance. Conditioned reflex. He's not allowed any fancy footwork of his own ..."

"That's nonsense Olly. He needs his dad's input and a bit of his money to get the thing started.

"He's just having to play along for a while."

I moved even further away from Ella, so that not one part of me was touching her. I wanted to say something that would hurt, and bring her back to my side and I had something saved up. I needn't have raised it – like a fist, to hit her with – but I did.

"Listen to this then. You know what I overheard Maurice saying, when they were looking at your fantastic, *free* design? I was behind him, and I heard him say to Zac: 'It's OK. But watch her. Don't let it end up looking like an Egyptian knocking shop.'"

Ella didn't respond. But I couldn't leave it. I had to know that I had hurt her, got her back on my side.

"I wasn't going to upset you with that. But now I've told you, are you offended? Fucking furious? Or are you quite prepared to take that kind of philistine shit?"

"Yes," she said, coolly. "I am prepared to take it. For the good of us both."

"Well, I'm not. I told Maurice then and there that I'd heard what he'd said, and that I wasn't familiar with the interiors of Middle Eastern brothels but I'd bow to his superior knowledge."

"You bloody idiot," she said, throwing off the duvet and stomping through to sleep on the settee.

"He didn't like it. Zac's face was a picture," I shouted after her. "I did it because I was angry for you," I said.

"Well, don't be. I am *me*. Ella," she called back, furious. "I don't *need* someone to be angry on my behalf. I don't *need* your bloody chivalry. Could be that I don't *need* you."

Suddenly, I was afraid.

"If you're interested, what I do need is what I've never had. A family."

24

The knife was one of the most exquisite things I'd ever had in my hands. A mere utensil but dazzlingly beautiful, like a piece of fine jewellery. So surgically sharp you could probably shave with it.

You could see in an instant that it had been made with love. The dappling in the steel above the razor cutting edge caught the light like the scales of a fish turning in sunlit water. The knife was heavy, yet somehow light when handled; perfectly balanced.

As soon as I opened the package I knew that it was Japanese, that it had been created, layer by layer – perhaps 60 of them – in that place where samurai swords had been made for hundreds of years. I also knew that it had come from Tilly – even before I saw the *"Go Olly! – love, T"* engraved into the deckled spine.

The handle was made from magnolia wood, I read, before taking the descriptive card from the box and slicing off a corner just to enjoy the knife's lethal sharpness.

I'd hankered after knives like this, to add to the personal collection every good chef accumulates. Once, years ago – at a food fair where I was doing demonstrations – I called at a stand where a Japanese chef took a huge mooli radish and pared a slice so thin that when he held it to his face you could see his smile through what resembled damp tracing paper.

I wanted to call through to Ella, who was in the bedroom, to show her the gift but we had slid once again into minimal communication. I feared that any reaction from her, however kind, might taint this special moment.

If Ella and I had been speaking, I wouldn't have dared to let her in on a thought that hurried through my mind as I closed the lid on the knife box. Bizarre. For some reason, I saw Maurice's dog, and associated it in some worrying way with the knife. Tinker, a *sausage* dog.

But making this sort of linkage unsettled me because the reason for the subliminal coupling was as plain as day. There was no avoiding it; something in me wanted to see Maurice harmed.

The question was: How normal is a thought like that? Is that sort of, albeit fleeting, connection an indicator of future intention? I'm a chef, not a psychologist so I had no answer. But it bothered me.

That afternoon I took another walk up Haig Hill. I was truanting, in a way. Zac and Maurice were due to visit to check on progress, and to draw up a list of guests for a pre-opening evening of food and drink. I'd left with Ella a list of people I wanted to see there – food suppliers, a couple of chefs, two or three cookery writers, a wine merchant, a cheese maker, the producer of the regional TV show I'd done bits for.

I had also asked Ella to contact all the *Zac's* staff and invite them to a get-together the following week, whenever Maurice and Zac could come over. We'd give them drinks, and I'd set them the challenge of coming up with some special party food for the preview evening we were calling A *Taste of Zac's.*

Not only did we need to feel like a team, I wanted some allies around me. Silly, but I felt outnumbered in my daily dealings; me versus Zac and Maurice, me versus Jane, with Ella having a foot in each camp. The gift of the knife reminded me that I also had Tilly as an ally.

Once I stepped off the road and began to climb the hill, a balmy wind got up. It was soothing, and the browning bracken was so inviting, I could happily have lowered myself into it and found oblivion in sleep.

I reached the top, walked through the trees on a springy bed of pine needles, breathed in the spicy aroma from the trees, enjoying the gloom of the place, then re-traced my steps. As I went down the winding path, Gus was coming up, struggling a little against the gradient, the dogs encircling him at bewildering speed. Gus waved his stick and waited for me to reach him.

"Hail, chef!" he said, and we fell into easy conversation, like old friends. He was carrying a freezer bag full of blackberries, and we talked of sloes, and cobnuts and mushrooms. He confessed, with a bashfulness that didn't quite eclipse his pride, that botany and field trips had been his life.

His rheumy eyes, pinched features and blotchy complexion seemed out of kilter with his youthful enthusiasm.

Gus said: "If we can get our walks to coincide some day, I'll bore you rigid showing you what's up here – stuff that nobody really cares about nowadays."

Beside the path, was a section of rough wall of stacked buff stone. Gus was edging towards it. He appeared to need a rest. He tilted himself back on to a flat, protruding stone and I found a perch of my own next to him.

We talked of my travels, his regret at having lived so long in the same place, of not having been adventurous. We talked of music and memorable meals, and, he began to rail against the iniquities of *nouvelle cuisine* –"I used to leave places *starving* and had to rush home for bread and cheese! Everything you got was a flaming starter!"

We shook hands, and as I set off down the path he shouted, "Good luck with it all, Olly!" I knew he meant it sincerely. He was a sound, wise, humane man, I could tell. I had gained one more ally. Now it was nearly a fair fight.

◊ ◊ ◊ ◊ ◊

The painters' van was leaving as I approached *Zac's*. Work on the place was due to finish and, before our last little flare-up, Ella had told me that today she planned to take off the plastic covers that swathed practically every surface, and remove the thick cotton sheeting that had been covering the new floor.

I resolved not to spoil her magic moment, finally seeing her watercolour design made real.

She was changing into old jeans and tee shirt as I walked in. She looked guarded as I went to her but responded as I squeezed her, and added one more "Sorry" to the growing tally of apologies.

"It's finished. Downstairs," she said, holding in her excitement.

We went down into the empty restaurant that still smelled of wet paint and newness, and stood in the centre of the dining area.

We took polythene sheets from wall lights, then foam sheeting from the top of tables, then we eased off sleeves of bubble wrap from chair backs. We lifted hardboard sheets to reveal the new bar, and cut the tapes holding foam around the brass bar-rail.

Ella made a little noise of self-congratulation as she gently lifted the tent of plastic from the first of her big arrangements. I could see that she couldn't wait now to see the new zigzag floor exposed. We hurried to roll up the overlapping squares of cotton sheet.

"Olly – do *not* look until we've got all the rubbish out!" Ella said, panting as she gathered various bits of the protective cocoon the restaurant had been wrapped in for weeks.

Suddenly she said urgently: "Olly – the *boar!*"

They walked to the restaurant entrance and drew a bedsheet from the richly-rusted sculpture of a hefty boar, trotting daintily on tiny, inadequate legs. It had been cemented onto a small pedestal by the builders.

Once the last of the coverings had been taken out to the back, Ella took hold of my hand and we walked, eyes to the front, to the back door to view the restaurant in all its splendour.

I felt like a patron watching a huge painting unveiled at

last, after a long and frustrating wait. And what was before me certainly looked like a work of art – the red and orange of the walls, the sand-coloured ceiling, the matching desert tones of the dried flowers, the brown warmth of the woodwork.

Ella's face lit up with the most ecstatic smile. She looked the place over with wonder, as if it was a cathedral.

"There! Now how's that for a knocking shop?" she said pulling me to her, reaching up and kissing my chin.

25

"The trouble with feckin' finger food is you never know where the feckin' fingers have been! Isn't that the God's honest truth Ben?"

Bridget's wild yelp of a laugh cut through the hum of conversation, the whirr of a mixer, the shuffling of dishes and rattling of pans as *Zac's* finally came to life.

Ben – scrubbed, and shaven-headed and in crisp whites – was touring each work station, to oversee the prepping of an array of delicacies for the *A Taste Of Zac's* evening.

Bridget – with Poppy, a trainee, at her shoulder, silently looking and learning – was well ahead with her contribution.

Last night's get-together had been everything Olly had hoped for. He could see staff melding into a team. There had been plenty of wine. Zac had made a short, halting speech saying that a big adventure would start next day with the taster event, and that they were privileged to have Olly at the helm. He held up his drink and said "Good luck!"

Olly had asked each member of the cooking team to bring him a list of imaginative, colourful, easily-eaten morsels they might make, to show the variety and quality that customers could expect when the restaurant opened.

"Only Esme and Harry are excused!" he had announced and everyone turned to look at the Pyggs who stood side-by-side at the bar rail dressed in various shades of beige.

Olly had weeded out some of the more extreme ideas submitted, and some titbits that would be tricky for guests to eat...

"No *millefeuille*, Poppy love. Think of those pastry flakes falling everywhere!" he said with a laugh to put her at her ease. "And I see dribbles of egg yolk down cleavages with that one," he said kindly, handing back her list. "But ask Bridget to get you doing your fish cubes with the masala coating and then let me have a taste. Use firm fish so people can spear them."

Ben had come up with scores of ideas. As he read out his list, Olly had given him instant verdicts on each suggestion – "Crab tart" – *"Yeah, but a bit predictable?"*; "Lady's Thigh Kofte" – *"Yeah, just on the sound of the name but let me taste"*; "Oyster cromskies"– *"Yes, please."*

Ben was relieved by the time he had come to the end; he knew Olly had been impressed.

"Oh, an idea for the sweets, chef – little hot doughnuts with rhubarb and ginger and custard piped in, or passion fruit inside" – *"They sound good..."*

When, later, the wine had washed away any trace of shyness, the staff gathered in the bar area where Olly sat on a tall stool so he could see, and be seen.

He raised his glass, held it aloft and said: "This event tomorrow is going to be *yours*. I'm going to be the bloke in the tall white hat, behind that glass, at the range, doing flamboyant stuff with flames, even if there's only a bit of brandy in the pan. We're putting on a show, remember."

There was a ripple of laughter. Two village girls, who Ella planned to train, stood with her. They were rosy-cheeked and wreathed in sleepy smiles from the wine, and when they laughed it was too loudly.

"The flambé thing will be for a bit of drama. The rest of the time I'll be shaking hands and kissing women." He paused and looked thoughtful – "I must get *that* the right way round tomorrow!"

Ella was dazzled by this confident, authoritative, Olly; she could tell by the way the staff laughed that they were thinking: "It's going to be fun here." He was showing trust in them and he knew they would not let him down.

Charismatic was the word that came to mind, listening to him. And he looked so striking up there on the stool, exuding confidence, his burnished hair shining under the bar lights.

His touching words of welcome to the staff, his slightly scary warning that there would be no excuse for anyone not giving their best, or not supporting another team member, made her feel proud.

He looked severe when he warned that if ever the mobile phone of a member of staff went off within earshot of a customer, that phone would go in the stockpot.

Somehow, out of seeming chaos, and despite all the conflict, Zac's had become reality and she couldn't wait until the guests for the taster evening arrived next day.

She would be watching their reaction to the interior as they walked in. The colour scheme had turned out just as she had dreamed. She had never had any feeling to match the pride she had allowed herself that morning down in the deserted restaurant.

She was placing a single arch of red crocosmia in each little terracotta tube on each table when she stopped, looked round and was about to let out a cry of sheer joy.

It was only when she spotted Janice arriving at the door that she managed to stop herself. She went upstairs to make coffee. Perhaps it was all going to be all right after all.

Next afternoon, with all the ingredients safely delivered, Ben toured each station carrying the master list of approved dishes to be served during the taster evening.

Bridget was getting Cassie, the rawest member of the kitchen staff, to taste her plum sauce which was to be a dip to go with her pork crackling straws. She would do her sage toast fresh, to order.

Bridget began easing bite-size globules of glassy, chilled brawn from pig-shaped moulds. When Cassie tried to help, the brawn slid out and fell at her feet. The girl looked appalled, put her hands to her mouth and began to cry.

"And this little piggy went – *splat!*" Bridget said brightly, laughing manically. "No bother, Cassie. It's been a bad day all round for the piggy that this brawn came from. Started this morning with me taking his ears off and boiling his feckin' face."

◇ ◇ ◇ ◇ ◇

Everyone agreed that the taster night had been a huge success.

When Olly had waved the entire Zac's team out from their various stations, and thanked them, the guests had risen as one, clapping and cheering.

He did the same on the opening night, when every seat had been taken and when service had gone like a dream. He had opened a home-made congratulations card from Sophie and Dylan just before the first diners arrived and had taken it down to the kitchen and propped it high on a shelf, to see it and for it to be seen.

Their drawing showed Olly holding up a trophy, and hordes of little people round him, as if at a football stadium, with cartoon balloons above their heads and, inside them, the words "Dad! Dad!"

That would be Dylan's idea, he knew; everything was football related in his life at the moment. In capitals at the top of the picture was: THE WINER. Maybe he meant THE WHINER, Olly said to himself ruefully. Out of the mouths of babes...

Inside the card was an envelope and in that a note from Jane with news that came as an unintended present. She wished Olly well with the project and said that if it helped with future planning he should know that she was going to sell up and move back to the North East, to be near her parents and to free up some of the cash in the house.

She would be a seeing a lawyer and asked whether Tilly would be the one to contact when her solicitor needed to arrange for his share to be transferred to him.

"You won't believe what houses round here are fetching now," she wrote.

Ben had taken over cooking the last mains for Olly, so that he could visit every table. Having had the news of the impending house sale, and the promise of freedom that money brought, he did so with a lightness of heart.

Any concerns he'd had about how the new *Zac's* would be received were allayed immediately. Here was vindication at every turn – hand-wringing, praise for the décor, rapture over one dish or another, promises of return visits.

Tilly had brought a partner, a suave and attentive man, and she glowed with pride in being the chef's brother as she introduced Olly. A couple of times later, she made exaggerated expressions of pleasure as Olly watched her sampling food.

"Delish," she mouthed to him at one point, across the room. He remembered the little Chad Valley cooker and those tiny discs of fried cheese.

Zac and Maurice and the family had a table of eight and he could see them luxuriating in what he had created, taking the credit, but he was so elated this didn't irritate him as much as it might. People knew that *Zac's* was really *Olly's*.

Meanwhile, Ella was walking on air. The interior had been

praised as highly as the food.

Olly and Ella were still down in the dining room well after midnight, alone except for the Pyggs, who muttered away in their corner as they scrubbed and wiped.

Ella looked at Olly over her champagne glass and said: "Well, Ginge...?"

"Incredible. Wonderful. Almost worth it all. Almost," he said.

She poured him another brandy and they sat, hollow with exhaustion, intoxicated as much by their triumph as by the drink.

Ella kept her lips close to her glass and said in a little girl voice: "Let's stick with it, Olly. Please."

This sounded to Olly like provocation. Imagine, bringing this up tonight. Imagine – getting me to think about the future with Maurice and Zac at this sweet moment. He glared threateningly at Ella, who flounced off upstairs.

The Pyggs shuffled out a few minutes later and he poured himself another drink.

◇ ◇ ◇ ◇ ◇

He trudged upstairs, and fell asleep on the sofa. He woke constantly, finding he'd been dreaming, repeatedly, of Monika's list of flavours. It was like watching some surreal film, the words rolling, rolling...

...honeyed, astringent, cloying, briny, mealy, peppery. Flowery – *Aunty Tina's bosom.*

Gamey, floury, pungent, chalky. Aromatic – *The smell in the pines at the top of Haig Hill.*

And salty. *The top lip of that holidaying girl in France. The taste of Jane.*

Oaty, brackish, buttery, fusty, malty. Cleansing – *Italian beer from the fridge after service at the seafood place.*

Crispy, smoky. Numbing. *Dipping my tongue into Dad's whisky when he went for a pee.* Velvety – *Inside Jane's thigh.*

Bittersweet. Herby – *The smell on the sea breeze from the*

lunchtime barbecue in France. Bland, fishy. Dissolving – *Guido's citronella sorbet.*

Bittersweet. Effervescent – *Illicit Andrews Liver Salts that sent bubbles up the nose.*

Unctuous, arid, brackish, mellow. Heady – *The smell of night scented stock after my shift, and my cigarette smoke outside the pub in Kent.*

Sour – *Maurice.*

Yielding – *Claudia's pannacotta breasts dotted with vanilla seeds. And spinach – that time when she saw in the shiny splashback that she had been talking to me with spinach on a front tooth, and her running off, humiliated.*

Musty – *The smell of Jasper coming in from the rain.*

Ferrous – *The taste of blood that seems to be leaking from...is that roadkill? No, it's Tinker.*

Peachy – *Ella.*

26

Never in my life have I needed a walk as much as I did today. Ironically, I'd reached a crossroads of sorts before I even set off.

Ella reminded me that in a few weeks' time the restaurant would have been opened for a year. A year! We should have been in celebration mood.

We'd established *Zac's* as a destination for the best food, served by the most efficient and happiest staff, in the loveliest surroundings. But peel back the glossy skin of the apple, and you'd find mush, rot, and even a couple of grubs gnawing away at the remaining sound bits. Zac and Maurice.

Over the months since *Zac's* opened, I'd drawn on my love of Ella to control my paranoia over Zac and her.

Here I am linking their names, but the coupling comes not from evidence, not even from reasonable suspicion. It comes from inside my sick head.

Over the months I've also strived to find a way of working happily with Zac, but he has remained the wretched go-between for Maurice, his mouthpiece, his friendly spy.

Zac's was doing fine. We had a heavy flow of bookings, a couple of more – than – approving crits in the papers, an interview in a county magazine, and a mention of *Zac's* on regional TV when they challenged me to show how to make three family meals from a single big chicken.

And Maurice? We have locked horns at every meeting. I see him as ungrateful, grasping, vulgar, cheeseparing. He sees me, I'm sure, as careless over costs and fanciful, arty-farty, too fussy by half. He holds my creative side in contempt, while Zac admires it as a baffling gift.

But I know (and Zac knows) that the place is only still operating after nearly a year because people want to come to eat the food we cook, I cook, in an ambience that makes them feel they have been transported.

I say this without conceit: They also come to see Jolly Olly waving his ladle in greeting from behind the glass divider.

Maurice doesn't give credit where it's due because, for him, life's not about giving anything but about taking.

And this morning, The Young Master (as Ben hilariously refers to Zac, without chastisement from me) informs me that Maurice will be sharing our adventure for another year, and not leaving us to it as he had promised. A year.

The message came by email. Zac had the wisdom to be well away when he lit the fuse.

Although as we reach our first anniversary we will be profitable, theoretically, it seems there won't be quite enough in the pot to pay back Maurice's full investment. Besides that, I believe, Maurice wants to continue simply because he enjoys being a meddlesome old bastard.

So today I really am facing a dilemma. To revert to my literary mode, let me invoke a metaphor...

One finger on the signpost at the crossroads I'm facing points to Resignation (from Zac's). Beyond that lies Separation (from Ella). And beyond that Privation (I'd be homeless – and I'm still skint).

No, that's the one I want – Confrontation.

But first a walk. Fresh air, squelchy turf, heavy breathing, and then the reward of a view. That and a chat with Gus.

We were sitting on the old wall at the foot of Haig's Hill, basking in late-summer sunshine, with clouds gathering and moving slowly towards the village. I was thinking of Jasper, wishing he was here, running wild with Gus's hounds.

We'd walked for an hour, stopping for Gus to poke his stick around, to rabbit on, and me to listen and learn.

Now, on our rocky perches, we were talking about fugu fish, and Jack O'Lanterns, and how a mushroom could be bioluminescent. Gus talked of the names people had assigned to fungi, the warnings in the names.

He remarked that it seemed wrong that members of one family of mushrooms that could kill you should have such a pretty, feminine name. Amanita.

"Could be the name of a sexy flamenco dancer!" Gus said, and was immediately overcome by a wheezing laugh. "And actually, Muscaria is damned pretty, the red one with the spots. It's Phalloides you shouldn't tangle with. Death Cap."

We concluded that eating fugu fish and eating mushrooms was similar, not unlike Russian roulette, although we agreed that, with mushrooms, there were far fewer bullets in the chamber, so to speak, and many more harmless squeezes of the trigger.

"But just imagine, those fugu chefs train for three years to make sure your dinner doesn't kill you!" I said. "Bloody bizarre."

"And Sunday walkers all over Europe go out, bring back a bag of mushrooms for tea and pop their clogs within days. Now that *is* barmy."

Gus thought for the moment and said: "Olly. You're a chef. What does this fugu *taste* like anyway? Is it ambrosia, paradise on a plate?"

"Tasteless. Virtually. That's what I was once told. The piquancy is in the risk of it killing you."

Gus shook his head, nonplussed, and then peered around, checking that the dogs had not strayed too far. They were bouncing around in the bracken which with the change of season had begun to match the brown of their coats.

"Actually, Olly, thinking about it, all mushrooms are edible. But some only once!"

We sat with the sun on our backs. Eventually he put the question I had hoped he'd ask.

"And how are things generally at *Zac's*?"

Gus knew that I was in crisis. I'd once hinted that Ella was a defender of Zac and Maurice, and that this was a major problem for me. I knew he was saying: "Tell me. Trust me. Let it out."

And so I let it out. I described how Maurice and to an extent Zac had no appreciation of what was at the heart of a restaurant, and how I had created *Zac's* with minimum outlay. Almost despite them. And how they wanted more.

"Here's a little example Gus. You'll know we serve kobi beef? Wagyu. It costs a bomb but it's superb."

Gus said: "They say it's the best. Comes from cattle they feed with bottles of beer, doesn't it?"

"And they get a daily massage," Olly said. "Anyway, Maurice sees the price on an invoice and says 'That beef you get, Olly. It's nearly as dear as bloody gold. Not a lot of margin there"."

Gus grabbed the chance to sound supportive. "But people *come* to Zac's for things like kobi beef. You're exclusive. You can get rump in any steak house."

Exactly, I said, relating how Maurice couldn't see that it was not about filling people up in the cheapest way possible. It was about celebration eating, romantic eating, creating memories, being pampered, about getting – for one night in a blue moon – a taste of the best the world has to offer.

"'But I maintain it's still only beef,' Maurice said. And you know what, Gus, I really did feel like taking a knife to him..."

"He's beyond education Olly. Vulgar. Don't waste your energy by being angry. But sounds to me that eventually one of you will go. I hope upon hope it's not you..."

Gus called the dogs to him but seemed in no hurry to go. They lay panting at his feet. There was something comforting about being near dogs. When I was with Jane, and I fell into one of my dark moods, having Jasper lying on my stockinged feet had been more heartening than any word from a human being.

As we prepared to say goodbye, I felt outrage welling up inside me and wondered whether I could really open up to Gus, without breaking down. He made it comfortable enough for me to spew out some of the acid I was carrying around with me.

"You know what, Gus. After I'd run that place on a shoestring, put it on the map, got some branded preserves and chutneys going for extra revenue and worked my proverbial arse to the bone, my friend sent me an email."

Gus looked at his feet so that I knew I wasn't being observed; he did that.

"Zac sent me this 'hi matey' email saying he was coming over. Nice and informal. Attached to that email, by mistake, was one that wasn't meant for my eyes one that had been sent to him by Maurice."

"Oops. Another of the inadvertent truths that social media

can leak out..."

"Maurice's message said that the end-of-year figures weren't bad but maybe things could be tweaked further, and maybe he, Zac, could arrange a little chat with Olly and get him to rein things even more."

"Oh dear. So Dad's clearly in charge. He sounds like the worst sort of accountant, and I must say, Zac sounds to be rather spineless."

"He is Gus, he is. It's been a revelation. He was once so bloody outrageous, so funny and carefree. But who am I to talk? I used to enjoy a bit of a laugh..."

"Seems to me Zac is neither a friend, nor a boss. It's a funny old mix. Finally, he has the power. Friendship has to stretch a long way to bridge the gap between you."

"Exactly Gus. But I know I have power too, different power. Zac envies my freedom from money-chasing. He'd like to be expressive, imaginative. He envies my cooking and he envies Ella her talents. And he envies me having Ella."

"Does he?" Gus said, intrigued.

I stood up. Work was waiting. We had about 30 bookings. I said I had to hurry off and shook Gus's hand.

"Thanks for listening, Gus. You might have just saved me from going completely doolally.'"

"Good. But just be careful, Olly. Think hard and long before you act. Don't be rash. If you do feel the need for revenge, remember that advice about it being a meal that's best served cold."

As I stepped it out, down the path and onto the main road to the restaurant, I remember feeling prepared to face whatever was coming but I knew not to expect backing from Ella.

She would say, as she had said several times: "Bite your tongue Olly. Look – you're skint. I'm skint. We're skint. They hired us to ensure that *they* never become skint. It's the way of the world."

27

"Richard? *Biggus?* You mean they're coming *here?* Shit!"

Olly was striding upstairs, huffing and puffing, from the restaurant to the flat, Ella in his wake.

"And not just him but Bridezilla – and *baby* bloody Biggus?" He stopped, extended his arms, head tilted up to the heavens, palms up, almost speechless.

"Christ, Ella... what the hell were you *thinking?* Biggus. That's *all* I bloody need!"

At the top of the stairs, he turned and said curtly: "Look. Ring them back. Make an excuse." Then, self-pityingly: "Christ! Haven't I *enough* on?"

Ella followed Olly into the flat. She looked downcast but was not especially bruised by Olly's vehemence, as she would once have been. He was like that most of the time now. Frantic, driven, unreachable.

She was about to ring but stopped. "No, Olly. Too late. They'll be here in two or three minutes. It'll look odd. They're back from the States, on holiday. She said something about Mexico..."

"For *God's* sake Ella..."

"They were driving and suddenly saw a sign. Impulse. Come on Ol – I could hardly say no. They won't be able to stay long. I just didn't think fast enough. Sorry."

In fact Ella didn't want to turn down the chance to see

Richard and the baby. She would tolerate Vi, as she came with an otherwise pleasurable package. She put the kettle on and got out mugs and coffee, and a glass; perhaps the baby would like some milk.

Olly made a short and bad-tempered call to a fish supplier, and immediately afterwards, Laura, the sommelier, rang from a wine merchants' for a decision on cases of wine that slightly exceeded her budget.

"Just do it, love," he said almost too calmly, and then closed his phone.

"Ella, just keep them here till I'm back," he said, hurrying to the door. "Need to check on prepping, and get some invoices to Zac. We're not getting the hake or the cockles this afternoon. Bungling buggers."

"Steady Olly."

"No. They're fucking well sacked, and now we're a main down...."

Olly reminded Ella to check that as diners looked at the menus, staff should say sorry that the hake main was unavailable and add: "Chef wasn't happy with the quality of the fish delivery today."

She heard the brisk clickety-click of his shoes as he descended the stairs, a heavy man breaking his natural speed limit. It couldn't go on like this – *he* couldn't go on like this.

Ella went down to wait outside for Richard and his wife to arrive, and to lead them up the back stairs to the flat.

Vi was driving. Richard, now much balder than she remembered him, was looking towards a baby seat in the back. Vi got out, they embraced briefly and then Richard eased his now-prodigious bulk from the seat, and hunched up awkwardly against Ella's welcoming cuddle.

"Richard! How great to see you. To see both of you!" Ella said.

Richard responded by pointing with what looked to Ella like a smirk of self-congratulation to the baby seat where a toddler sat contentedly chewing a toy bus.

"Oh, and *baby!*" Ella exclaimed, reaching in to the car to discover a miniature Biggus Dickus; round-faced, bald, self-absorbed, mouth over-moist.

"Vega," he said. "You're little Vega aren't you? *Aren't* you? Yes you *are!*"

He undid the belt on the car seat and cradled the toddler, clutching her protectively, shielded her head as he moved out of the arch of the rear door.

"This is Aunty Ella," he said, flipping her dripping bottom lip with his forefinger. "Aren't you going to say hello? Come on – show her your bus?"

Was this really Richard, the Biggus we knew and loved? Surely not – the once-solitary, disengaged misfit living in his own head, now nose-to-nose with a baby, chortling and gurgling and looking every inch the loving father; *and* properly dressed. Thought had gone in to what he was wearing. A vivid butterfly had sprung resplendent from a dull, grey chrysalis.

When Ella had made coffee and given Vega milk, and had apologised that Olly was tied up for the moment, Vi sat up very straight in her chair and began to pronounce.

Ella saw a resemblance to an oracle in her stillness and flat delivery. It was as if she were reading a list of number-plates of her beloved old buses.

"They think the world of him over there. They love his Englishness. I think they've got him down as a bit eccentric," said Vi.

Richard was on the floor now, blowing to make blubbery noises on Vega's bare belly as he changed her nappy. With each fleshy raspberry noise, she squealed hysterically with delight.

Innocents together, Ella observed to herself as she drank in the picture of joy, and felt tears prickling, seeing how the baby had woken something inside Richard. She felt sorry to know that for so many years the feelings he was showing now had been locked inside him. When Richard stood up, Vega clung to his legs.

"Ricky's not Biggus over there, you know," said Vi. "In Mexico. They came up with a new name. They couldn't understand the jokey nickname you lot gave him. They said it sounded as if Ricky was some sort of dinosaur!"

She droned on. "One of the other professors chose the new one. He said 'Ricky, every guy here has a special name, even the girl guys! You're cute and cuddlesome, you're like that little English bear, in the scarf, the one who rides the train…We're gonna call you Paddington'."

Ella was struck by Richard's sartorial transformation. The greyish assortment of woolly jackets and badly-fitting trousers of old had been replaced by expensive tan chinos, cleverly cut to disguise the chunky thighs and full bottom. His silky shirt, showing an almost luminescent desert landscape and flowering cactus, was dazzling.

Most unlikely of all was the Texan neck-tie with an aquamarine stone set in silver. As Richard stooped, Vega took hold of it, and when he saw that Ella was looking at it he said: "Do you like the bolo? Most of us wear them in the faculty. They gave it to me. A Tex-Mex thing."

The door to the flat opened and Olly hurried in, wiping his hands on his apron. He grasped Richard by the shoulders, then pumped his hand.

"Sorry I wasn't here. Welcome home!" Olly said, looking Richard up and down. It took him a second or two to absorb the change in Richard's appearance.

Having given Vi a peck, he got down on one knee and said: "So *you're* baby Biggus!" and then looked up at Richard and asked: "What do you call him?"

"Her," Richard said. "Vega."

"Sorry miss," Olly said, smiling at the baby.

"Vega. Brightest star in the constellation. And we should

know. We've got one of the biggest telescopes in the world down there. Sees through dust."

"We? Down where?"

"Didn't you know I'd switched interests? I'm helping to measure cosmic microwave rays and galactic nucleii. University of Mexico. Gran Telescopio."

"God! We've come a long way from Rhodesia Terrace haven't we...good on you Richard."

The small-talk seemed to be limping along. Ella wondered whether, now that Richard was a bit more "normal", they had all been left high and dry, conversationally.

At the mention of Zac's name, Vi stiffened slightly and remained silent. Could it be, she wondered, that Richard had talked about Zac, and the stunts and the taunts. Could it be that Vi regarded this as having been ritual humiliation?

Olly briefly gave news of Zac ("every inch the businessman now") but Richard showed no interest either, gathering Vega in his arms and sitting with her on his lap, alongside Ella.

"Can I?" she asked, and Richard very carefully placed the child on Ella's knee.

While Vi, Olly and Richard laboured at being interesting for each other, she whispered and teased and invented simple games for Vega. The child settled between them, Vega holding Ella's watch, and Ella and Biggus each holding a plump, firm leg.

"Isn't her skin *wonderful*!" Ella exclaimed. She marvelled at the tiny fingernails and opened the deep crease where the baby's arm met her hand, at the wrist. The clarity of the baby's big, pure eyes held her in rapture.

"Oh Richard! I want one! *Want* one!"

Without warning, Vega slid gently from Ella's knee to the carpet. Richard looked down, and Ella looked down, and both – at the same precise moment – realised that they were now holding each other's forearms.

Richard contorted in embarrassment as if he had been buzzed

by a belt of electricity. Ella laughed wildly, pulling her cardigan to her, and rocking to and fro. Olly spotted Ella's camera on the mantelpiece and said, by way of diversion, as Richard seemed so discomfited: "Come on – let's have a picture!"

Ella and Richard sat together with Vega between them, and Vi sat, erect as a poker, on the end of the settee. She seemed to have no familial connection with Richard or the baby, or perhaps she felt excluded by the bond that Richard and the little one shared.

"Look, Ricky is absolutely besotted!" she said, with no hint of affection or approval. "I can see I'll have to arrange a time slot to see my own daughter as she grows up!"

It occurred to Richard to show a little curiosity in Olly and Ella. Etiquette rather than real interest or concern.

"Are you enjoying the cooking?" he asked Olly, looking up in turn to Ella. "I suppose it's nice just to work in the evenings." If *only*, Olly said to himself. "The diners seem to be happy, so that bit of it is fine," Ella said.

"I used to really like your fried bread," he said without enthusiasm.

Olly looked at his watch and began thinking of stuff they'd need for the duplicate main course. He wondered whether he'd been a bit too ambitious with that night's menu. There was some very labour intensive prep involved. But then he always felt a certain nervousness in the run-up to the first diners arriving.

He had been waking up, sweating and alert for a few nights. He felt like someone besieged, someone not daring to sleep.

There was a knock at the door of the flat. It opened and a voice said: "Sorry chef. We need you for a bit if you can spare a minute..."

Olly returned to Richard, and said: "Sorry old friend, I'll have to love you and leave you. Great to hear that you're enjoying life and that you now have this little one to keep you out of mischief." Richard nodded mechanically.

Olly didn't, couldn't, kiss Vi, but he waved. He then waved to

Vega and said, without a trace of sincerity, that she was lovely
–"No wonder your mum and dad named you after the brightest
star going, young lady," he said.

Richard looked puzzled. "No, Olly, she's not *actually* named
after the star. We picked the name way back, when we went on
one our Bus Cavalcades," Richard said.

Vi cut in. "Yes, we were both totally blown away by this
brilliant streamlined dream in two-tone blue."

Richard blurted: "Bedford SB *Duple Vega*. We're talking
a Fifties *classic*. Curved waistline, streamlining. Removable
windows. Toast Racks, some of them were called, because of the
way the seats were."

"Oops, my mistake, Vega," Olly said, adding, with irony, and
a touch of mockery, that was lost on all, including Ella, who was
dreamily absorbed tickling the back of the baby's neck: "You're *so*
very pretty it's no wonder mummy and daddy named you after
an old blue bus."

28

"What you need is a nice, clean headshot," Mick said as he drew
the gun from the canvas case. "Not as easy as it sounds, even
with this little number."

He slapped the beech stock of the rifle and ran his hand down
the barrel with satisfaction. "She's got a silencer, so neighbours
won't be a problem. You'll get more kills when it's dark and
they're roosting."

Mick loved his guns, just as his dad loved his guns and his grandfather had before him. Guns and wild animals and trespass were what they'd always been about. That, and being on the wrong side of any countryside law drawn up by townies.

But Mick knew that, like some animals and plants, his type was becoming extinct. He was the only one for miles now keeping ferrets, and some of the new people coming in, people like this Olly, wouldn't even know one end of a gun from another.

But each to his own, he said to himself. He liked Olly even though most people he knew were "anti". He put that down to suspicion.

Actually, Mick hadn't cared whether the restaurant was there or not. But he was sure that now he'd got a foot in the door, in the winter it would be an outlet for as much game as he could shoot. That was one of the reasons he was seeing Olly all right today.

The bit of gardening he'd done at *Zac's* paid for his tobacco, his Saturday bets, and his ammo but he'd have done it willingly for a couple of pints and the pleasure of being out in the fresh air getting dirt under his fingernails. Life wasn't all about filling your wallet.

He held out the rifle and said: "If we weren't here, right on the street, with the old folks place just over there, I'd have let you do the job with my up-and-under. Fair old bang but a lovely pattern. It'd be instant, so you wouldn't need to worry yourself about just wounding them. It'd just be – *crump!*"

Olly took the gun, tentatively, looking to Mick for advice on how to handle it.

His hands were shaking and his voice was weak with uncontrolled emotion.

"It won't hurt you!" Mick said, believing that Olly was fearful of the gun. In fact the trembling came from fury over Zac's latest email, and anger at himself for having just stormed out of the flat when Ella had been trying to explain herself.

It seemed to him that he was in a minefield. Wherever he

trod there was peril. The draining, dog end of the marriage, the future of the kids. The threat of losing Ella. The bloody bank, the staff he felt so responsible for.

Olly had often come out to the garden for a few minutes to sit and calm down. Today the peace had been elusive. His eye had fallen on a veg patch where yesterday there had been two rows of pak choi. This morning, there was nothing left except a few shredded leaf veins.

The destruction in the garden was the flame that lit the gunpowder – a silly thing that didn't really matter in the scheme of things, yet it had sent him raging for a few wall-kicking moments.

It wasn't the first time that the pigeon nuisance had made him react over-dramatically. A couple of weeks before he had draped a net over some kale, and had come down one morning to find a pigeon trapped inside the net, having decimated the young plants.

He had swung the net round and round with the bird in it, and hit it violently against the wall. Then he had shaken the twitching bird out into the dustbin.

Today, when he saw the row of pecked-over plants he had pulled out his phone immediately and found the phone number Gus had given him, Mick's number. Gus had said that he was the man for pheasants – and for sorting pigeon problems.

An hour later, Mick had biked over, delighted at the chance of introducing someone else to the pleasure of shooting.

"That's it – lift her to your shoulder," he said. "No – front hand further forward. She'll give you a little kick. You get that even with a pea-shooter like this."

Mick, a lithe, sunburned figure, quick on his feet for a middle-aged man, had placed a plant pot on a post at the far edge of the restaurant garden.

Olly asked: "One thing Mick. Is there a better way. More humane. Poison maybe?"

167

"Forget poison. There is this stuff, if you can get your hands on it, that you put down that makes them wobbly. It's supposed to stupefy them, as if the little sods are not stupid enough."

He held the gun up so that Olly didn't back out.

"The idea is that you give them the old one-two while they're feeling squiffy but usually they've flown off. Anyway, putting poison down is no fun. Usually you're putting it down in carcasses to kill foxes. This way, with a gun, at least you get a bit of sport."

He was anxious for Olly to fire his first shot, to be blooded.

"Go on," he chided. "Go on!" He thought: This Olly chap might be a bloody good cook but he's a big silly tart with a gun in his hands.

"You can't *hurt* anybody Olly; you've got big tall walls so you could shut your eyes and not worry. Let her go!"

Olly squeezed the trigger, and just when he thought that the gun was not going to fire, his shoulder was jolted very slightly and he heard a crack. Mick was beaming. The clay plant pot had been split in two – "Bugger me! Dead-eye Dick!"

Olly managed a smile, and let out a sigh of satisfaction. This was good, this feeling of holding something powerful and using it, especially as it probably wasn't quite legal. He had decided earlier that it was best not to clarify the legal side with Mick; ignorance equals innocence.

Mick slipped the gun back into the canvas bag, and drew out a cardboard box of ammunition from a pocket at the back.

"This should do you," he said. "Keep it as long as you like. Me, I like to get out with the old twelve bore."

Olly took the gun and propped it against the door leading to the dining room. He thanked Mick and promised to add a few bob to his next payment for gardening.

"Don't get upset if killing them is a bit messy. Even I'd struggle to get clean killer shots with that. Surprising how much they bob about, and how quickly. You might sometimes go through the neck, or shoot the beak off, or send them flapping about with a hole somewhere but you can always...you know..." he made shapes with his knuckles, to suggest stretching and twisting,

"Or the old..." He stamped with his boot on the flagstone path. "Don't worry about them. They're rats with wings, flying shit spreaders."

For some reason, in his mind Olly saw Maurice and Tinker and found himself saying: "Out of interest, what would something like this do to a dog, Mick?"

"Well, for sure it'd make it want to bite you!" he said, with a staccato laugh. "Well, let's say it would make the bugger jump a mile."

Mick was a pragmatist about life, and Olly could see that he regarded him as an urban wimp.

"Stop worrying about what the bloody *pellet* does. Worry about what the bloody pigeons do to your whatever it is."

"Pak choi. It *was* pak choi. Kale and cabbage..."

"Feed them. Tempt them close, then try for that clean headshot. If you miss, and you mostly will, and they're hit somewhere else, finish 'em off any way you like. You can pick them off better at night but it's not the same, sport-wise."

When Mick had biked off, Olly went into the kitchen and came back with a handful of puy lentils. He cast some about and sat still on the garden bench, trying to take stock.

He felt that his problems were closing in, vying with each other, but it was the email, the email from Maurice that wasn't meant for him to see, that was still rankling.

He had given enough ground, and enough dedication. Ella had given enough in time and stress and support for him. There was a limit to the obligations of friendship, and anyway, obviously Zac now saw people as resources more than old pals. Olly decided that from now on he would respond in kind.

It wasn't as if the restaurant wasn't ticking over nicely. The food was a success. Customers were coming back. The costs were under control – in fact you couldn't provide fine dining anywhere as cheaply.

There was the new bit of profit from the weekly *Lunch With Olly* promotion. There was Bridget's *Zac's Kitchen* bottled chutneys. Ella had done the interior design for no reward except personal pride in seeing people's faces when they walked in.

Even this bit of a veg plot was going to cut the cost of garnishes, and more unusual vegetables (he looked forward to being able to say *"...gathered this morning from Olly's restaurant garden...")*

So Zac's was a success. If there was any shortfall, it revealed a fault in Zac's masterplan. Any failure to produce the return they had calculated was in *their* spreadsheets, *their* marketing, or in *their* meanness.

He would tell them: There's no more blood to be squeezed from the stone.

The pigeons were showing interest now, bobbing at the edge of the scattered lentils.

He studied them and started to think of Mick's description of damage – shattered beaks, the flapping dances of death performed by the wounded. He was alarmed to find that he was not in the least appalled by the prospect of seeing this, here in his peaceful haven, the garden.

He had taken three shots, all of them misses, and was waiting for the pigeons to circle and settle again when he looked up at the window. There was the shadowy, slightly bent figure watching from the window of the retirement home.

He put the gun in the case and went in to the kitchen to oversee prepping but he knew he would be back soon. He could quite understand why Mick loved what a gun could do. It was like pointing a magic wand.

He pictured that plant pot, the way it had cracked in half. One gentle squeeze and – what was it Mick said? *Crump!* Putting down poison wouldn't have been half the fun.

29

When Ella came out into the morning sunshine, wearing her dressing gown, she found Olly on the garden bench, the gun between his knees, the ammo box empty.

When she rushed to him, he was motionless. He hadn't responded to her cry of relief as she found him.

"*Jesus* Olly! I was *so* worried!"

She took hold of the gun and drew it away from him.

"How long have you been out *here*? And what are you doing with *this*...? Olly..."

She eased the rifle to the floor and, as she lowered her head, noticed that the paving beneath the bench was carpeted with grey feathers.

Olly's face was expressionless but he was lucid, although a little vague, as if he had been momentarily concussed. She sat holding his hands while he stared ahead. She asked him to go in, to get some coffee, but he sat as still as a statue.

She searched his face anxiously. Was this a stroke? A moment of insanity? Something serious going on with his brain? She asked him to tell her what day it was, and he answered correctly, and with a little snort of a laugh.

"Testing me out for a bed in there?" he said, pointing to the residential home. He squeezed her hand to reassure her as he said this. She was white and trembling.

"Just a funny turn. I'm fine," he said wearily. He looked as if he was coming out of a deep sleep, willing himself into action. "Suddenly it all seemed, well, weird, as if I was spinning away.... Can't explain. But it's fine now."

Ella led him back to restaurant door and they walked upstairs to the flat. Olly fell into the settee. As Ella prepared coffee she began to question him.

"Did you take anything last night, Ol? Any tablets? A lot of drink?"

"No. Just a brandy, maybe a treble."

"Did you fall at any time? Do you remember getting up this morning, and going out there in the dark?"

Olly was drowsy now and he knew that his irritation would increase with every question.

"Look, Ella. Forget it. It was just a funny sort of fit. I remember everything from last night, down in the restaurant. Everything. But I can't seem to get past the point where I'd turned everything off and shut everything down and started to come upstairs. Maybe I shut *myself* down."

Ella joined him and sat on the edge of the settee, both her hands holding one of his. He would reassure her. He began to describe the previous evening.

He said that he knew that they had rowed, and that she had hardly looked at him throughout the dinner service, keeping exchanges purely professional. By the time he'd gone up, after he'd had a solitary brandy in the dining room, she'd been asleep.

He remembered that the fish man had let them down and so the seabass ceviche had been taken off the menu but they'd dropped off a few langoustines as a sweetener and Ben had served them butterflied, as a grill special.

It was all perfectly clear in his memory. There had been few takers for Bridget's stuffed squid and she had been disappointed. She could be caustic. Celtic angst, he put it down to.

"Yes, and I remember Bridget's little spat over the Pyggs. Clear as day."

Olly said that Bridget asked the Pyggs to wash a potato ricer. The Pyggs had either not heard her, or had chosen to ignore her, and when she went to their corner and asked for it, it had still not been washed.

Bridget didn't care for the Pyggs. She had told Olly that she thought they had a conspiratorial air, that they were capable of mischief.

As she had left the kitchen, she had looked contemptuously towards them at the sink in the corner and said: "Will you look at them, Olly.... Tweedle feckin' Dum and Tweedle feckin' Dee..."

Olly took another sip of coffee. "I had to laugh, seeing them on their fat bums on those high stools." Ella was pleased to see that there was now some colour in his face, the sandy complexion replacing what had been a waxy whiteness. He was back from wherever he had been.

Ella gathered his hand once more.

"See, I remember every detail..." Olly was warming up now. He wrapped both hands round the coffee mug. "Happier now? See – I'm OK."

"Yes, but the gun business...? Getting up in the night, sitting out there killing bloody pigeons...what were you *thinking* Ol?"

"You've got me there. Seems a bit batty, even to me, except that I really hate the little grey bastards."

"Could have been sleep-walking, I suppose," Ella said. There was some relief in her voice. Sleep-walking. That was plausible. Olly said Sophie did that all the time. Maybe it was hereditary. That was the explanation she would cling to.

Olly, meanwhile, was finding it especially inexplicable as to why he had taken so many shots, so many that his arms had ached. Dozens of pellets had gone from the box which was now empty. More puzzling was that it had seemed at the time that he had been watching someone else doing the firing out there in the twilight.

Things were coming back. He remembered having woken,

and feeling restless. He remembered checking the time on his phone. It was around four.

He had re-read an email received the previous night. It was from Jane. She was pestering about money, and listing dates when he might see the kids, and passing on a holiday date – "We're all going away for a week," she wrote.

All? Was that her, and Dylan, and Sophie? Or the family, plus The Man, the man who would be swimming and laughing with the kids? The man who would be on the beach, carrying the inflatables, then buying a pub meal for them all and sleeping with Jane.

It must have been after reading the email, he reasoned, that his mind closed down. He remembered the first light of dawn and an incident that seemed to release the tension in him. It was when he nailed a roosting pigeon, not with a headshot but a disabling one to the body and saw the breast feathers ruffle.

It was good when it fell and flapped and began to spin. It had been so pleasurable to pin its wings to its throbbing body, to lay it on the flagstones and feel the bones crumple under his foot.

From that moment there was nothing – until he heard Ella's voice... "*Jesus*, Olly. I was *so* worried!"

She was still worried. The theory that Olly had merely been sleep walking seemed suddenly inadequate. It was something much more worrying but she couldn't avoid mentioning the day's workload.

"You ought to get a nap, Ol. You've got another heavy one, forty covers tonight and Ben's off and the new girl will need to find her feet. I've got to do the specials menus, and it's nearly time for the deliveries."

"I'd forgotten. There's no time for a sleep. I ought to get organised."

"I'm *really* concerned about you Ol," Ella said softly. "*Zac's* is not worth killing yourself over." She decided that she wouldn't mention getting a doctor's view, not yet. But she would be watching Olly's every move from now on.

"You mustn't let the sodding pigeons become an obsession, Ol. Let them have what they want or get somebody in to clear them," Ella said, putting her arm round his shoulder.

"Of course. I've been stupid," he said, knowing that the flattening of the pigeon was not the end of it but was a taste of things to come. The memory lapse was inexplicable, probably something medical but hopefully he could now keep everything in check.

Then terrifying thoughts crowded in on him.

"What if I'm going a bit bonkers?" then "What if it had been *people*, and not pigeons, that I'd got bead on with that gun this morning?"

That thought was in the mind of the police sergeant who was now tapping gently on the front door as Olly and Ella went back into the restaurant.

"Need a chat sir," the sergeant said, looking round the empty dining room.

They sat across from each other at a restaurant table and the sergeant, having refused coffee, to emphasise that this wasn't a social chat, explained slowly and carefully that a resident on his way to work at dawn had looked down the path towards the garden and seen a man with a gun.

"So muggins here had to rush over with an empty stomach and sit up there in a bedroom at the residential home, watching, to make sure that we didn't need to trouble armed response."

The sergeant had the thick accent heard in the local villages. He also had what Olly thought of as a rural look; many people round here seemed to have a reddish glow to their faces. Olly fancied that here might be a gamekeeper bred from generations of poachers.

He waited to hear what he might be charged with but felt such lethargy that he didn't really care.

The sergeant outlined the law on gun possession and declared that even using low-powered guns could represent a breach – "In fact, just inducing fear in someone by merely *showing* a gun is serious... even this low-powered thing that Mick let you borrow," he said pointedly, with a glance at Olly.

"Yes. It'd be Mick," the sergeant said smugly. "It's a small place and I know who's who, and what's what," he said.

There was a final lecture summarising matters and leaving Olly in no doubt that he had been close to being charged.

"Right. Lesson learned. Matter closed," he said, rising, and offering his hand for Olly to shake, as Ella came out from behind the glass partition where she had busied herself with unnecessary jobs, while listening anxiously to what the sergeant had to say.

"Nice. Very posh!" the sergeant said, surveying the dining area. "Must come here some time with the wife. Some of the locals have given you mixed reviews. Funny, because most of them haven't been in the place! But we'll come some time. My wife loves all that foreign stuff."

Ella led the sergeant to the front door having brought him the gun as he requested. Olly went out to talk with the driver of a delivery van that had just pulled up.

As the sergeant began to get into his car he turned back and, nodding towards Olly, said quietly to Ella: "Seems in a state. Must have been a nervy time, getting the place going. Is he OK...you know...?" He waggled a finger near his temple.

In a world in which everyone said exactly what they meant, Ella would have replied: "Of course he's not OK, sergeant. Olly's cracking up. He's morbidly jealous. He's overstretched. He's being badgered by his wife. He feels let down by his best friend. We rarely have sex because he knows I want a baby and he doesn't. In short, sergeant, his golden dream (our dream) has turned into a crock of shit."

But instead she replied: "Fine! He's OK," laughing and hugging herself.

Then she said: "You won't believe it, sergeant, but normally he's really cheery. I think he's just over-reacted a bit to the pigeons nicking his precious bloody veg."

30

Olly was in no doubt. If Tilly had known about this week's squalid little interlude she would have told him: You, Olly, have acted like a prize prick. If Ella had found out, she would have stepped out of his life like a shot. But then she seemed set to do just that.

As it was, he was already being punished for his monumental stupidity. Guilt. The guilt arrived to make him squirm at the moment of waking, and it jabbed at him at random points in the day. It was worse when it came to him as he was watching Ella; loyal, industrious, tolerant Ella.

The episode would join the handful of old embarrassments that would pay him uninvited visits from time to time, flooding his mind, like dye turning water pink. He was safe, in the sense that no one need ever know about what happened with Cat, but somehow that was little consolation. *He* knew what he had done.

Only the Pyggs had been around when, insanely, he had got involved with what in retrospect was more like freestyle wrestling than hot, swift, urgent sex, something that had moved into the past tense for him since the start of the running conflict with Ella.

Looking at it now, he realised that he hadn't even wanted sex, not really. It was idiotic. He had wanted revenge, to get at Ella, yet she could never know of this vengeance. What was even crazier was that if it was revenge, and not just hormones, she had done nothing to deserve it.

He was practically sure that the Pyggs had seen nothing even if, in their prurient way, they had got a sniff of it, so to speak. He agreed with Bridget about the Pyggs. There was something slightly sinister about them. They gave little away but, he suspected, gathered much of what went off around them.

The day before the incident, Ella had been loving and acquiescent, going as far as her self-respect allowed in conceding points to Olly. But once more he had been unreasonable, returning to the old, tired topic of Zac – and whether "anything had ever happened."

It was becoming an illness. She had exploded. Her diatribe ended with her putting her contorted face into Olly's and screaming: "And what *if*, Olly? What *if*?"

Next morning, as Olly was preparing his demo for the lunch group, Zac had rung and, after the usual faltering preliminaries, had asked what Olly thought about having Ella alongside him as a "sort of" manager.

"A sort of *what*?" Olly had asked indignantly.

Zac explained that he had thought that it could ease the burden on Olly if Ella got even more involved than she had been. Looking at invoices, helping with ordering, that kind of thing.

"And have you broached this idea, which is probably one of your dad's, with Ella?"

"Yes, she's up for it, if it's OK with you. Actually it wasn't Dad's idea, not entirely."

"Well, it isn't OK and you must have known that. You actually want *Ella* to keep an eye on me? Look, if you make her any kind of manager, you've lost me, and I guess Ella would go too. Or maybe not. But from me the answer is no way Zac. No fucking way."

He went to confront Ella. Olly fumed over the fact that she

had not told him of Zac's divisive little plan.

Olly found her painting, something she had not done for months. The little figure with the open mouth – singing, crying, pleading – was back, set against darkness.

31

Over the years, at times when I've been under the cosh, I've felt my self-control uncoupling. It's as if, to escape the unbearable, I try to self-destruct.

Sometimes, I've gone for the bottle; sometimes I've erupted like a volcano, showering everyone with my rage. Nearly always, though, I'd seek oblivion with a woman. But it really is as if isn't me at all but a second Olly taking over.

It has happened several times on my cheffing odyssey, before I got *Zac's*.

There was a bad episode in Portofino, and a nightmarish time up in Applethwaite when, while the snow fell and the guests sang carols, a sweet young trainee I had turned to, and then abandoned, took a paring knife, went to her room, and gave herself a set of cuts for Christmas.

Once, in Brittany, sleeplessness and homesickness and the tormenting of a violent chef made life too much to bear. It was as if I was watching someone resembling me, tipping the glass back, hurting some lovely unstable girl who wanted the kudos of having slept with the English sous chef.

Something similar happened with Claudia, in Italy.

I'd just heard that my mum had died. I was skint. Guilia, who I was in love with, had become disillusioned with the restaurant job and gone back to Turin to study.

Claudia, silent and intense, worked at my elbow. I remember she would lift the wire basket of *fritto misto di mare* from the oil and shake it fiercely as she might a disobedient child. There was protest in that action, the fierceness of the shaking.

I surprised her late one night in her room in the staff quarters, by bursting in seeking drink. Shy as she was, strangely, she did not seem to regard this as an intrusion.

Claudia had black eyes, and a suggestion of dark hair above her top lip and in front of her ears; the faintest smears of charcoal dust. She was intriguing, so introverted, so fastidious about attending mass. Above, pinned to an arch in her room, was a crucifix and on the wall a picture of her family beside a photo of some religious statuary.

Claudia's face and arms were scattered with inky imperfections, tiny black moles. It was as if someone had flicked black ink at her. For me, they enhanced her solemn beauty, and I had always wondered whether they spread over her entire body.

When she came to the door that night, unsmiling and unsurprised, she was wearing light pyjamas. She turned down the sound from the TV and pointed to the arch leading to the kitchenette saying: "Grappa, somewhere. Have it Olly."

When I turned round she was on the settee and she was opening the flimsy pyjama top. She tilted her head back on to a cushion and closed her eyes quickly, as if overtaken by some drug.

My curiosity about the moles was satisfied. Her breasts hardly flattened as she lay back. If I was back at uni, doing the creative writing unit of my English course, I'd describe them as pannacotta hills spilled from concave moulds, dotted with chocolate hundreds and thousands, with summits of sun-dried berries.

We hardly spoke during, or after, what could never be

described as love making, more half-hearted aerobics, performed silently except for a few small animal noises.

We resumed our duties next day in silence. As we flipped squid and swordfish steaks at the hot plate it struck me that the whimpering soul beneath me the night before had not been Claudia at all but some sort of spiritual night visitor who had moved in to inhabit her.

I guessed that the second Claudia (just as there was a second Olly) allowed brief, merciful release for this dour Catholic enigma working beside me.

Sometimes my mad bouts didn't involve alcohol at all, but led soberly and directly to a woman, often someone unsuitable, or unattainable. Someone like Cat.

I didn't really know Cat, except as a competent slicer of shallots and rabidly keen amateur cook, but from the start of the *Lunch With Olly* thing she had looked at me in a certain way. She was teasing and had something of the little girl about her but I could see that there was a core of steel under the inviting softness.

This week, Olly No 1 – rational, reliable, amusing, jolly even – moved over to allow Olly No 2, the deviant doppelganger, to seek sanctuary in a warm, safe place, hopefully between the breasts and the legs of someone equally needy – Cat.

Truly, I really didn't feel that it was *me* involved. The notion of being unfaithful to Ella had not even occurred to me since we had begun to live together. It was not desire; it was more like reprisal.

Given a few moments of eye contact, growing longer and more meaningful over the session, I find myself turning purposefully towards buttery, sun-browned shoulders nudging out of the white, starchy, sleeveless cotton dress.

Then I find myself showing this young and slender mother-of-two, a sparky woman with blonde corkscrew curls, how to use a balloon whisk, my hand on hers, making her blush and laugh, in front of a dozen other women, who smile indulgently. Some are plainly miffed by the extra attention she is getting for her money.

Within a minute of the rest of them leaving, and with the Pyggs clattering away in their corner, washing the pots and pans, I have led her towards the garden to show her...what? The artichokes I think I'd said, pathetically.

Just outside the door leading to the garden, I unzip the back of the white cotton dress, and I'm unhooking her bra without expertise or great enthusiasm. Thirty seconds later, I'm involved in a slapstick attempt at sex on the bench beside the herb patch and overlooked by the retirement home.

One of my clogs falls and bangs on the flagstones. We are both tugging at my apron, the last barrier, when Esme Pygg suddenly calls from the kitchen: "Chef! The veg man's on the phone!" I've since wondered whether Esme had first peeped round the door to find me, and – taking in the appalling spectacle – retreated and *then* shouted to me.

So – the *interruptus* without the *coitus*; the shame of intention without the pleasure of the sin. And piled on top, the penance of imagining Ella's pained and puzzled face. And on top of *that*, the feeling of having been recaptured by cruel reality; that nothing has changed, and there really was no escape.

There were still invoices to sign, tomorrow's mains to list and describe, so that Ella can present the menu in her flowing italic hand. When I look at my phone there will be an apologetic email from Zac to answer, rotas to look at, an excuse to invent to fend off Jane's appeal for money.

Then there's the question of my resignation – and my future with Ella, if a future exists.

As always, the release had been in the anticipation. The tan, the flattery, the shiny teeth biting on that parmesan crisp. Then my nose buried in her tickling, perfumed hair. And her whispering, over the clang of pots and pans: "I don't do this kind of thing, but I think we're both allowed *one* tiny sin don't you...?"

The restaurant tonight will be only half full because people are on holiday, or unwilling to face a drive, and be inside on a hot evening. I'll leave things to Ben and Bridget once we've prepped and I've checked everything. I have to tell Ella that I plan to throw in my hand.

I get the book to check on future numbers. The *book?* I insisted on the old-fashioned book, against Maurice's moaning, because I think customers feel that it's less impersonal than a computer. Computers are for accountants not cooks.

We're almost full for a couple of days (did you hear that Maurice?). As I flip ahead I see that there was another booking today, for a few days ahead. A table for two. It's in the name of a Mrs Hirst, full name Mrs Cat Hirst.

32

Tilly was about to leave her office when Ella phoned, apologising through tears that she had been forced to ring when Tilly was at work.

"Olly's going to chuck it all in, Tilly. He's in a state," she said, hoarsely. "I'm very worried about him."

Tilly could hear soft sobbing and said, a second later: "I'm coming to see you."

"No Tilly! Not all that way! You can't. I just need someone else to know how he's acting..."

"I'll come. Sounds to me as if you're on suicide watch..."

"No Tilly – it's not like that. But he's a time bomb at the

moment. He's cracking, I know it..."

She explained that things had been bad for months. "He sees me as being in league with Zac and his dad against him. I'm not. I just want it all to work. He makes me feel disloyal. I feel bad now, ringing you behind his back but..."

"You were right to ring, love. Can you do tomorrow morning? Make an excuse to him and then text me with a meeting place."

They met in a busy coffee shop in the market place of a town roughly equidistant from Tilly's London home and *Zac's*. Tilly looked serious as she touched Ella's hand, and settled at the table in the crowded corner.

Ella said: "Sorry Tilly. You must have had to cancel work things..."

"It's only work. What's a half-million-pound fraud case compared to a bit of Olly bother?" she said. Ella's laugh in response seemed forced. Tilly knew that Ella was strong and capable. There must be something very serious going on.

Tilly was used to listening to clients but this was different. She felt anxious about what she was about to hear; this concerned Olly, not a client. Although she feared what she was about to learn, she wanted to know everything. Everything had to be brought out and dealt with. She'd found that through her job.

Ella decided to abandon any sense of duty concerning confidentiality; she would come clean, for Olly's sake, and so she spoke – softly and unemotionally – about Olly's obsession about Zac and his belief that they had once been intimately involved, about the pigeon killing, about their differences over starting a family, about the towering rages.

"It really is like living with a crazed person, really Tilly," Ella said, gravely. "And yet, in the restaurant he's marvellous – calm, like an orchestral conductor, getting the best out of all the staff, charming the customers."

Tilly didn't respond. Her silence invited more details but she had heard enough to pick up distant echoes of the young Olly; the sweet boy who could turn feral if slighted or mistreated.

Ella seemed to be building to the climax that had led her to ring. Had Olly attacked someone? Tilly could wait no longer.

"So what's Olly done Ella?"

"Nothing terrible. Yet. But it will happen. He feels let down, especially by Zac. He regards him now as a spineless creep and he's told him so. He never expected anything from Maurice. Anyway, now they've asked me to do some paperwork, bits on pricing and invoice checking but Olly sees me being *their* person, a potential snitch."

"Are you concerned about, you know, what he might do to himself. Is it as bad as that?"

"I'm more concerned about what he will do to others. He's turned into a snarling animal. He's probably ringing them now to say he's quitting. All that effort gone to waste...and what about Ben, and Bridget and the girls. What about *us*?"

"Yes, but you can understand Olly's reaction. He's the chef after all. Might Zac be trying to drive a wedge between you with the manager business?"

"It's possible. He can be devious. Or it could be that the idea of me as a sort of manager is Maurice trying to trim the buying bill, to get yet one more drop of blood out of the stone."

Tilly didn't reply, sensing there was more. And there was. Tilly leaned forward. The café was noisy and she was hanging on Ella's words.

"Thing is Tilly, I'm carrying round a secret that would push him off the edge. To tell him would destroy him, wipe *us* out, probably – yet to not tell him makes me hate myself for my disloyalty."

Tilly braced herself for the news she was sure she was about to hear – that Olly had been right, and that Ella and Zac were lovers, or heading that way. If they had been close once, it shouldn't be a serious matter now. But if there was something going on now, much as she loved Ella, she would have found it unforgiveable.

Ella said: "Zac took me out in the car a couple of times looking at stuff for the restaurant. Olly hated that but it was innocent, I made sure it was strictly business. But at the end of one trip, he stopped the car and confessed something."

She explained that Olly and her had always believed that Zac owned the restaurant and that Maurice had put in some money to give the business a start. That was why Olly felt resentful at Maurice's interference; he believed that Zac was the boss but acted as if he was his dad's puppet.

"And the true situation?" Tilly asked.

"Zac was never the main investor. It was bullshit. His dad was – is. Zac admitted to me that despite everything his dad had said about restaurants being bad investments, Maurice knew someone who was raking off nearly 30 per cent a year, and he wanted some of the action. He saw an opening."

She told Tilly that Zac knew that Olly and his dad would not get on, and so he set himself up as a buffer, hoping to keep the peace and buy his dad out once the business was doing well. He daren't confess to Olly, even though things were falling apart.

Ella could see that Tilly was putting everything in place. She was nodding, while her forensic mind examined every element of the accumulating information.

Tilly made a pained face showing her distaste for the full picture as it formed in her head.

"So...in short, this Maurice used his son to draw in Olly, at a time when he was flavour of the month in chef circles. Then he used *your* skills to create the ambience of the place, and exploited Zac's friendship with Olly to run the place on a shoestring."

Ella thought for a second and then said simply: "Yes."

"But, worst of all, Zac lied to Olly at the start. He baited the hook and then reeled him in. And then relied on Olly's good nature to half kill himself making the business a success."

"Yes."

"So, in effect we have here a pair of charlatans, one manipulative the other a posturing wimp." She tutted in abhorrence and Ella saw a muscle in her jaw pulse. She looked down at her empty coffee cup and said, absently: "Poor Olly."

Ella had begun to feel bad that they had been at the coffee shop table for so long. There were customers around the door, waiting to come off the windswept street. They left and stood outside, surprised by the change in temperature, the plunge into the first really chilly day of autumn.

Ella said: "So what can I do, Tilly? If I tell Olly what Zac said, he'll want to kill him, not only for the lie but for telling me, not him, his best friend. Olly's going to leave anyway, I know it, and I wouldn't be surprised if he went down and wrecked the bloody place, and then hunted Zac down. I think he's capable..."

"Not sure that even Olly at his worst would go down that road..." Tilly said, a little uncertainly.

"But he has to know, love," Tilly said softly. "You owe it to him. If you two are strong as a unit, if you really do care for each other, you'll get through it. What if at some time in the future Olly found you'd been hiding what you knew about the business set-up, about Maurice's grubby little plot?"

Tilly said that one lie always led to another. She was now implicated just by listening. If Olly rang her at this moment and asked where she was, and who she was with, she couldn't have admitted that she was with Ella, who is saying you've been hoodwinked by your dear old mate.

"You have to tell him, to keep things open, or the lies will finish you," Tilly said. "I don't mind being the messenger but that wouldn't really help. It's you and him and the truth. Hint to him that maybe I could help sort things. And ring me any time, day or night."

Ella knew that no one knew Olly like Tilly but the fits of temper weren't the boyish tantrums she'd heard about. Tilly hadn't seen the incandescent outbursts over the last weeks.

Ella knew that there was one thing that Olly couldn't stand, and that was being deceived, having his sincerity abused. He hated treachery in any form and had sacked people on sight if they had been disloyal. It seemed to turn him into a different, and very dangerous, person.

◇ ◇ ◇ ◇ ◇

As Ella was driving back to *Zac's*, Olly was walking down Haig's Hill with Gus. They had pottered around in the woods, Olly unloading his troubles, Gus listening and making affirming noises occasionally to show that he understood.

Gus had felt that he was a spectator, seeing the last twists and turns of a serialised tragedy being played out. Today's episode had centred on Olly's confrontation with Zac.

Zac had finally shown a little spirit and repelled Olly's attack by reminding him of the financial risk he and his father had taken and had almost shouted down the phone: "Look Olly, we're all pissing in the same fucking pot here. "

Olly told Gus that it had been so good to hear Zac had some fight in him. Olly said he had come back with: "True, Zac. But the trouble is your dad's missing the pot and pissing on me."

The recent warm, wet spell was over. A cold was moving in. But the few days of late-season humidity had yielded a flush of mushrooms when it had looked as if the fungi season had finished. Olly had no interest in gathering any – what was the point?

When they reached their perches on the wall, they sat for a moment in the silence, and the dogs settled at Gus's feet, without being called, as if falling in with an old habit.

"So it's the big one coming up Gus. The fireworks go off tomorrow. I'm going to talk with Ella, then ring Zac tonight and tell him that I'm resigning but promising to work on until he can get somebody to take over. I would never leave him in the shit although I know that feeling isn't reciprocated."

Gus knew that Olly had thought things through and there

was nothing for him to contribute but his good wishes and a supportive clasp of his arm.

"Maurice and Zac are due to come tomorrow afternoon anyway so I can tie things up. But Ella's my big worry. Before they come I have my adoring ladies for their lunch session. While the world falls apart I'll be guiding them through the perils involved in making a hot smoked salmon and puy lentil tart."

As Gus nodded, it struck Olly that on recent walks, he had done all the talking – poor Gus taking it all, soaking up all the grumbles and the anger.

"Look Gus, I'm so sorry that I always go on so. Selfish. You're my head doctor. But don't worry, I'll soon be moving on."

"You're welcome Olly."

"But how are things with you? I never ask."

"Pretty good. The chest has been playing up but they're getting to the bottom of that. Can't say that you and Ella going isn't a big blow."

"Not sure Ella will be going Gus. She has a mind of her own as you know."

"Oh dear. Is it as bad as that?"

"Yes, it really is as bad as that."

33

Olly was awake before dawn and half way up Haig Hill when the rising sun flooded the bracken with golden light. There was no wind, and he walked in a silence broken only by the fall of his boots on the wet turf, and the rhythm of his breathing.

He realised he was marching, but felt no compulsion to hurry. Strange – he felt like a man with a purpose and yet, overnight, ambition and aspiration had evaporated. He so wished that Jasper had been at his side, on this last walk.

Today he wanted to avoid Gus. Today the lovely old boy would be spared his non-stop monologue. Anyway, the time for talking was over – nearly. Zac and Maurice texted to say that they'd call at the restaurant late in the afternoon on their way to a London meeting.

Olly breathed in. The walk was therapy, helping to clear his head after last night's emotional turmoil, and strengthening his focus on getting through the day. He had to be prepared for the last showdown with Zac and Maurice.

After dinner with Ella the previous night he had told her, matter-of-factly it seemed to her, that he'd rung Zac to say it was over. Zac had asked for time to speak with him, to explain things, to make an offer. Olly had merely offered to listen, when they visited.

Ella had cried when he said that he had made the call, and then she had broken her own news, that Zac had confessed about the investment.

She did it gently, and diplomatically, and in an even, objective way; not excusing Zac for his lie, saying she understood how Olly felt about being betrayed, and then she begged, almost literally begged, for him to reconsider his resignation.

"This place, this is the first place I've felt was a destination. I've had a job. I've had you. My talents have been used. Save us Olly, for my sake."

Olly had sat like a statue in his chair, staring ahead. He was blank-eyed, playing with a fork. He seemed to be somewhere else. He appeared to Ella to be in shock. She knew that their whole future rested on her words, and it made her tremble.

"Olly. Zac wants to make it up to you," she said, doggedly, as if a careless phrase, like a missed foothold, would send them both careering to ruination.

"He lied to you, yes. But he says he thought that the restaurant would give you the break you needed. He really did want to call it Olly's but as we know now, his dad held the trump card."

Olly had appeared not to be hearing. This was not what Ella had expected and she didn't know whether to regard it as Olly's dumb acquiescence, now he had resigned, or that his head was constructing some terrible response for some later date.

She stood and went behind his chair and encircled his chest with her arms.

"He's ashamed, Ol. and he'll do anything to repair things. Frankly Ol, I think it's more important to him to keep you as a friend than it is to keep Zac's, or even to keep in with his father. He really is breaking away from his dad. He so values you."

Olly turned to Ella and responded with a smile that she interpreted as cynical, and sinister.

"He told me you represent something he's never had before. I think he sees in you bits of what he would like to be. Look: he owes you, Olly. He wants to make amends. Take what he offers. Use him, as he used you. Stay."

Olly was in the pine plantation now. Although there was sterility underfoot, the carpet of fallen pine needles having accumulated and stifled any growth beneath the trees, there were clearings where pools of light fell and greenery flourished.

The sun was higher now and stronger when each time he emerged from the gloom beneath the pines. He stopped at the next clearing, one he had visited several times with Gus, and sat on the stump of a felled pine.

He drank in the smell, breathed the cool air, enjoyed the feeling of being cut off from the world. He wanted to live there, just where he was.

In a damp corner he saw a flush of young mushrooms, glowing like a cluster of small orangey lights in the shade of the overarching trees. They made him think of Gus, who would at this moment have been looking over his glasses, poking them with his stick, the Latin name and the common name rolling from him, the habitat described.

He re-lived, with amusement, Gus's fury over the new breed of fungus-hunters pulling up specimens to examine them, then discarding them, and damaging the growing system irreparably. Gus abhorred this trend; middle-class, untutored foodies rampaging through woods with their identification books, having been inspired by some TV chef.

"You've got a lot to answer for, young Olly!" he said. It had been a chance for Gus to have a rant for a change.

Half-heartedly, Olly gathered a handful of the mushrooms, the smallest and most tender looking, and slid them gently into the front pocket of his all-weather jacket. They'd be the last of the season, the last he'd ever have from Haig Hill.

By the time he reached *Zac's*, Ella, looking pale and strained, was going from table to table in the empty restaurant placing three small, perfect, tangerine-coloured dahlias in each terracotta tube. She had grown them in a corner of the vegetable garden having bought the corms in spring.

The varietal name, *New Baby*, had been irresistible, as had the colour of the flowers in the photograph on the carton of tubers.

Ben had set out the equipment and ingredients, and the *Lunch With Olly* aprons, and was now busy preparing lamb noisettes for the dinner menu. He was whistling while he worked, so happy to be a key person at *Zac's*.

Olly knew that the worst moment facing him was telling Ben.

◇ ◇ ◇ ◇ ◇

Nine of the *Lunch With Olly* regulars were at their posts when Olly started a quick demonstration of filleting a whole fish and removing pin bones. He left a couple of bones in a fillet of the big cod deliberately, and asked four of the party to stroke the fish fillets and confirm that all the bones were out.

Even in his black mood he could see the comical eroticism in the exercise and soon the women were laughing suggestively.

"You can go home and tell your husbands that the best bit today was stroking chef's cod."

When the laughter died down and the fish had been pronounced bone-free he said: "Serious point ladies. There are still bones...here," he said, pulling them out with tweezers. "Big enough to choke granny."

He loved this role as part-entertainer, part-educator. He loved the laughter that came from bright women with their shiny-white teeth, their tans and their stunning clothes.

When he had finished and moved on to his salmon tart recipe, and nine rolling pins were moving in synchrony, Cat came in looking like a potential film starlet. The peppermint green bodice of her dress clung to her and her tan ran down evenly from her forehead to the rounded tops of her breasts.

She looked as if she had turned up for an audition but Olly decided that he wouldn't be thrown by her stagy entrance. What had happened on the garden bench had no more significance in his mind now than a fleeting fantasy. It was something he wanted to bury as deeply as possible.

He could see that it was not the same for her. He could see that steely interior; something in her frown. Fear not, Olly, he said to himself; remember you are about to move away, and out of her dreams.

He could feel an invisible blanket falling on the group, muffling the conversation. He noted the sidelong glances, and the absence of warmth in the greetings. Group dynamics were endlessly fascinating. In a textbook, this would be called The Cat Effect.

"So sorry, Olly," Cat said with an exaggerated breathlessness. Not *chef*, Olly. She was telling the class something.

Other members of the party were sharing ovens for the blind baking of their pastry. Cat was well behind them and she held up a hand to Olly for help. He waved to the Pyggs who were just arriving. He felt their eyes following him as he went to her side.

"Bugger! How *do* you stop it tearing, Olly?" she said as he bent to repair her pastry. She whispered imploringly: "Coffee after?"

"Sorry Cat,"Olly whispered. "Big meeting straight after this. Owner and son dropping in."

She had looked at him as if he'd insulted her; stepped over some boundary.

When he'd finished the session and the members of the group had gone to their nice shiny cars carrying their hot salmon and puy lentil tarts in their nice ovenproof dishes, he went to greet Ben.

They had a bond that had dissolved difference in rank; Ben had become a friend who happened to call him chef. Bridget was also a friend and fierce defender of Olly and the restaurant. Laura was silent and loyal and brilliant; the young ones were a delight.

Ben had put the lamb away and was helping Bridget to assemble steel bowls of salad stuffs and garnishes for the evening service; chilling puddings and assembling sauce ingredients.

Ben called to Olly as he left to go up to the flat.

"Are these your mush chef?"

"Yes. Pop them out of the way somewhere Ben. We've got a visitor later. The Young Master. He likes his mush."

Bridget cupped her ear. There was so much noise, some of it coming from the pot-washing Pyggs, dropping glass rolling pins on to the draining board.

"Can't hear for the mixer, chef!" Bridget called. "Were you saying that the young masturbater is dropping in?"

"Steady," said Ben softly. "A step too far, Bridget. Olly's talking about the boss."

"It's himself, the boss, that I'm talkin' about," she said. The scorn on her face spoke volumes.

She'd told Ben she'd had Zac down as a feckin' shyster from the moment she saw him.

34

"So – no Maurice?" Olly asked as he led Zac into the garden. He said this in a disinterested way. He had resolved to keep the conversation unemotional, flat, factual. After all, everything had been said, except goodbye.

The air was chilly and the garden had begun winding down. The sun was waning even though it was only mid-afternoon. It seemed to Olly to be the right location, somehow, for a farewell.

"No. Had to cry off. Tinker's ill. Really ill, I mean. They're at the vet's with him," Zac said solemnly. "Actually Dad's not too chipper himself."

Olly resisted an urge to say that he was sorry to hear that, mainly because he wasn't sorry.

Olly and Zac had passed the Pyggs in their washing up corner on the way to the garden; a pair of inquisitive faces, two pairs of glasses tracked their walk, then two wet hands waved ingratiatingly.

They sat on the garden bench, Zac in his fine wool, navy overcoat, Olly swathed in an old, oversize chunky sweater.

Ella brought out a big pot of coffee and a scarf for Olly. She barely spoke and moved swiftly back into the restaurant. It was uncomfortable to be there, between them; the edginess was palpable.

She noticed that Zac had laid a document on the end of the bench. She hoped that inside it somewhere was cause for hope but she knew that the enormity of Zac's deception had ruled out any chance of reconciliation.

But then, an hour later, when she had expected the two men to come in, to shake hands, and silently start on an agreed process of uncoupling, personally and professionally, they emerged relaxed and chatting.

Ella watched through the glass partition wall of the kitchen where Ben and Bridget and two of the trainees were paring and chopping and mixing. Olly's face had brightened and Zac seemed to be spinning some yarn, underlining points with gestures.

She went to the garden and texted Tilly. "Peace in our time," she wrote, quoting somebody or other, she couldn't remember who. "Z and O meeting and talking like friends! No anger. Unbelievable! Will keep you posted XXX."

She went back in and, taking napkins out to the tables, she heard Zac say that he'd let Olly have everything in writing but that he'd better be off.

Olly insisted that he have a sandwich, something. He'd got ninety more minutes driving. Zac resisted and then, taking out his phone, relented: "OK. Ten minutes then, Ol. Suppose I'd better check on Tinker."

Olly mouthed to him: "Got a few fresh mushrooms. Four minutes?"

Zac covered the mouthpiece and said: "Not the rubbery meaty ones you gave me last time...? If it's the little yellowy ones you do. And only if I get fried bread with them..."

While Zac spoke on the phone, Olly joined Ben and Bridget in the kitchen and within a minute had mushrooms sizzling with garlic in a pan. He called to Ben, asking him to fry two slices of baguette in another pan, and to get Ella's tortilla from the fridge.

Lately Ella had made it a rule to have something to eat mid-afternoon, and her busy daily schedule dictated that it be quick, and cold and portable. She loved the plainness of the egg and the cubed potato. Simple food, such a change from the rich dishes around her all the time.

As Zac ended his call, Olly's phone buzzed. It was a text: *"Can I see u? – C."* He texted: *"Sorry Cat but no."*

Olly called Ella over to a corner table and she and Zac sat down together. He felt his phone tremble and looked down. Cat's message said: *"Not used 2 people saying no."* Olly felt a chill. There were shards of broken glass beneath those expanses of downy, tanned skin.

Zac asked: "Ol – OK if I tell Ella about what we've decided? Or do you want me to leave it so you two can talk later?"

"No problem. Tell her," he said, looking reassuringly at Ella.

Ben delivered the mushrooms and the tortilla to the table and Bridget, unsmiling, brought a carafe of water and glasses.

Olly excused himself and went into the garden to send a message telling Cat that "it" had been a silly mistake and that "it" wouldn't be fair to people they were with.

He rang the meat supplier, and replied to a young rep who had been toting for the business doing the restaurant laundry. Another text arrived before he could go inside. It was from Cat.

"Don't start things UR not willing to finish," it said. It was

unsettling and he wished once again that he hadn't been beguiled by a cosmetic smile and those bronzed breasts. Spooky threats were not sexy.

When he returned to the restaurant, Zac and Ella were in animated conversation. He joined them and they went to the front door

Ella gave Zac a hug and then the two men clutched each other.

"Manly hug?" Zac said.

"Manly hug," said Olly.

"Thanks for the talk. Really appreciated it. Be in touch."

Olly had forgotten to ask for the latest news about Tinker. Not only that, Zac had mentioned that Maurice's health had worsened but Olly had not cared and this must have shown.

Ella took hold of Olly's hand and, leading him back into the restaurant, said: "So you're going to give this profit-sharing thing a bit of thought? That's bloody brilliant, Ol. Brilliant! And Maurice really *is* pulling out. Great."

She squeezed Olly's hand and said: "I'm so proud of you." But for the rest of the day, beneath the frothy elation and relief of knowing that they might stay at *Zac's,* lay a troubling question that came back to Ella time and time again.

It was: What happened to Olly's anger. Where did it go?

35

Ella woke up nauseous two days later – and was delighted. She was thrilled by the urgent churnings that sent her scurrying to the toilet, where she knelt and thought of babies.

The truce she had come to recently with Olly about her yearning for a child – their tacit agreement simply to avoid talking about the matter while things were so fraught – was for her a victory.

It meant that she was vulnerable to the chance of conceiving, and that if, just if, she was lucky, it had not been entirely her responsibility. It took two to tango, and Olly knew exactly what the situation was.

And so the morning sickness came to her as a gift from heaven. She retched and rejoiced at the same time.

She would have to have a proper think when she felt better but a pregnancy really was a possibility. There had been a time, a few weeks ago, when for a few days Olly had managed to put aside his grudges and had been soft and sweet and approachable.

Olly came up from the restaurant for breakfast and found Ella at the table with her head in her hands. Her face was the colour of milk.

"What the hell's happened to you, El?" he said, pulling up a seat next to her and putting his hand on her shoulder, pulling her hair from her face.

"Just some sort of bug," she said weakly. He brought her a glass of water but before she could drink she had to hurry away. Even as she gagged and coughed she celebrated inside her head. She would go through this every morning for nine months if necessary if only...

Olly forced Ella to go back to bed and to keep her phone next to her. He had deliveries to see to, and three days' menus to work on. He had to order everything and there was always so much to think about.

He envied owners of cafes offering half a dozen alternatives – simple bacon breakfasts, toasted snacks, cakes – especially on days like this when he was under pressure.

Today he would have to source yams and okra, calves' liver, red snapper and spinach, pork belly and Agen plums. Short beef ribs. He needed to speak to the cheese lady. He would need a couple of pomegranates and more vanilla pods. And figs; he planned a compote to go with the new season pheasants Mick had left on the doorstep, the price scrawled on a cigarette paper and tucked under a bloodied head.

"Just ring if you need me, El, and I'll be up," Olly said. "Don't worry about tonight. If you're still bad, Laura can do front of house and I'll get one of the girls to help on wine. Sleep."

She lay still, thinking about babies and about Olly and what he might say if her hope was indeed fulfilled. The feeling of nausea had subsided but her head ached now, and she had the ache in her bones and the shivering that she remembered from episodes of flu.

She woke from feverish dreaming and vomited before she could get out of bed. She was too weak to sit up but managed to reach for the phone. Olly was up instantly and rang the GP. He was to take her to the surgery.

She answered the doctor's questions as best she could but it was a struggle. She leaned against Olly, who stood beside the chair in the surgery. He found himself answering for her as the doctor, a soft-spoken young man with a gentle, sympathetic manner, tried to eliminate possible causes for what he was sure was food poisoning.

"So, none of the usual suspects...no soft cheese? No raw egg but cold omelette yesterday. The omelette is not guilty. But this soup you mention...this bui...(he abandoned his struggle to pronounce the name)..."

"Bouillabaisse, doctor," Olly said.

"This leftover soup you had late last night had mussels in it – and any oysters? They can be bad, mussels and oysters. Norovirus. And you have the symptoms that might point to norovirus."

"Mixed fish and, yes, some mussels," Olly said. He felt Ella press herself more firmly against him, her head lolling from time to time. "You've been ill after mussels once before haven't you, El? France." He felt Ella nod.

The doctor asked whether any restaurant staff had been ill, and then said: "Ella, could it be possible that you are pregnant?"

Ella began, "Possible but..."

"Unlikely," Olly said.

"We'll eliminate that," the doctor said, turning to his computer. "But I think I will find the bui..."

"Bouillabaisse"

"...is to blame rather than a baby."

Olly left with a prescription, and an instruction to bring Ella back if she was not better next day. Ella left with the feeling that she was dying but – what felt worse – confirmation that she was not expecting a baby.

Two hours later, Ella rang down to Olly who was prepping in the kitchen. The weakness in her voice alarmed him. He handed over dinner service to Ben and half carried, half led Ella downstairs and to the car.

At the hospital, in a side room in the emergency department,

Olly answered more questions from the registrar about foods, while Ella huddled in her coat, her chin down, face a ghastly white.

She asked for water and Olly could see the doctor's concern as she drained the glass.

"When did you last pee Ella?"

She shrugged, and whispered "Not sure."

"I suspect your kidneys are having a hard time. We'll do tests. Could be that something's poisoned you. I'll be back soon. We'll get some liquid into you, start to sort this. Might help if you two could write down everything you've had in the last 24 hours. Everything."

When he returned, the registrar said to Olly: "I understand you run a restaurant. Have you had any other reports of illness? Staff, customers?

An hour later, Ella had been admitted and toxicology tests were underway. Olly stood at the gap in the plastic curtain around Ella's bed and watched nurses attaching tubes to her, and taking blood.

He stole a minute to go to the entrance to the department and ring Zac, who had left a message.

"Olly, mon frère!" Zac sounded delighted to hear Olly's voice. "Seen the review in the Your County magazine? Eight stars. Nice one."

"Zac. Can't talk. Ella's ill. Really ill. I'm at the hospital."

"Shit! She's *ill*?"

"We're open tonight but if this is as bad as it looks I might have to talk tomorrow about what we can do until the emergency's over. Could be food poisoning. Could be in the restaurant. Environmental health might have to get involved."

"Sure man. No worries."

"Have to go..."

"You get off Ol. Keep me in the loop. Seems a really bad time all round. Tinker snuffed it at the vet's and Dad's gone downhill fast. Stomach pains, sickness. I think it's an ulcer. He eats like a church mouse. He's been like this before when he's lost a dog. Mum says that it's grief. Pets are his people."

"But Zac. I'm not sure you realise. Ella's *very* ill. I'm sorry but Tinker's a dog. It's serious – I can see by the way the doctors are looking at her."

"Shit mate. I didn't want to compete or anything. Give her my love and listen: Anything I can do, you ring, OK?"

36

Ella seemed to be sleeping. Olly was pleased to see this, and reassured to see the pipes, the equipment. Something was being done.

As he sat feeling helpless and full of regret about the way they had been, how the restaurant had in one sense made them, and begun to destroy them, a grey-haired, pink-faced doctor stepped through the curtains and asked Olly to go with him.

The doctor, who had an air of seniority, steered Olly towards seats in a corner of the open-plan department where nurses hurried to and fro, and preoccupied staff peered at computer screens. He brought a plastic cup of water from a cooler and pulled a plastic chair round to face Olly.

"You must be tired of questions but we have to go over things again to make sure what we're doing is the very best in the circumstances."

"Of course. Fire away," Olly said.

The doctor said: "When did Ella last eat mushrooms?"

"Mushrooms? Long ago. I've given a list of what's she'd had in the last two days. No mushrooms. She doesn't even like them particularly, except as part of some dish or other."

"The thing is, our toxicological tests seem to be showing orellanin. That's a particularly nasty poison found in certain fungi."

He peered hard into Olly's eyes. It was not suspicion but the look was interpreted by Olly as suggesting that the doctor believed that something had been left unsaid.

To Olly, none of it made sense. How could someone who hasn't eaten mushrooms be poisoned by them?

Mushrooms...

He saw himself in the glade, in the pool of sunshine on top of Haig Hill gathering mushrooms for Zac. Chanterelles. Silently, he counted with his fingers the number of days since Zac's visit. Four days. None of this can be anything to do with the chanterelles.

The doctor sounded almost irritable: "We must get to the bottom of this, and quickly. The tests are being repeated."

Olly asked whether orellanin occurred in any other foods and learned that it didn't – "I think it might be chemically related to some ingredient in a nasty weedkiller. But then I'm not a chemist."

So Ella couldn't have been poisoned, actually *poisoned* by someone interfering with her food. Anyway, the very idea was ridiculous. Everyone, *everyone* loved Ella; as he said this to himself, he was overwhelmed with his own love for her, and fear that he would lose her.

He chastised himself for moving into the realms of silly speculation but his mind raced from one incredible scenario to another. It simply didn't make sense.

A nurse at a photocopier held up a printout and waved it as a signal to the doctor who moved to the copier and began reading.

Olly felt the buzz of his mobile phone but ignored it; he was absorbed watching the doctor's reaction to what he was reading.

The doctor came back and sat opposite Olly and said, solemnly, as a lawyer might: "Sorry to persist but when was the last time that anyone, anyone has eaten mushrooms in your company, or in your restaurant. Disregard time intervals."

He looked closely at Olly this time more searchingly than before, as if to suggest that he knew that Olly had not been totally open.

"I suppose that the last time I served mushroom was when I did some chanterelles for a friend, my boss, the restaurant owner. I did him a few, on fried bread. He's as right as rain. I've just spoken to him."

"Now...when was that, when he had the mushrooms?"

"Four days ago. But he's as fit as a fiddle."

The doctor maintained his steady stare, as if Olly's demeanour suggested that he was struggling to take things in. Shock did that to people.

"As a matter of urgency, I'd like you to get in touch with that person and urge him to come here immediately. He might be in grave danger. Please let me know that he's on his way and I'll make sure he's admitted."

This gets crazier and crazier, Olly said to himself. It would take Zac at least an hour to get to hospital. All for nothing. It was Ella who was ill and not Zac. He was ashamed when he felt tempted to add, in his mind, the word "unfortunately."

Doctors knew so much it seemed presumptuous to doubt them but – Olly reasoned – it was a bit of a tall order to link the chanterelles to this bizarre drama.

He rang Zac who laughed off the suggestion that he come into hospital. Olly persisted and said: "The specialist wanted you to know that if you didn't get checked there was a possibility you might die." It had the desired effect.

Then Olly saw that Ben's father had sent a text, and that there was a missed call. He would read it and reply later: he urgently needed to be with Ella, to look for a sign of improvement.

But he was overcome with curiosity. When he looked, the message stopped him in his tracks.

It said: "Sorry but Ben spewing all last night. Wanted to come in but real bad actually crawling about. Didnt want to let you down thinks it was mussels. Keep you posted."

37

The doctor was firm. "This young man must come in now, of course. We'll arrange an ambulance. Please stress it's precautionary, it's in view of what's happened to Ella. We really have to work out what's been happening."

Olly rang Ben's father briefly, told him that Ella was ill and passed the phone to the doctor who said that he would simply like to check on Ben's symptoms.

When Olly went to Ella's bedside her eyes were open but she looked distant. A nurse was reassuring her and saying: "We'll soon know exactly what's wrong." Ella said thank-you in a tiny voice. When she saw Olly she managed a half-smile but seemed too weak to speak.

Beside her was a big machine and he could see that blood was passing through plastic tubes coming from it.

"Doctor has put Ella on dialysis," the nurse said gently to Olly, who froze. So it's as bad as *that*?

"Don't jump to conclusions," the nurse said, noting his

shocked expression. "Doctor wants to give the kidneys a bit of a holiday and flush a bit of her badness out!"

Olly tried to speak but no sound came. As Ella slipped into oblivion again he took out his phone and started to key in words, fearing what he might discover.

"Chanterelles" took him to other mushrooms and clutches of terrifying words..."*dangerously similar"* and *"shared habitat"*: and *"easily mistaken"* and on to *"Fool's Webcap."* Gus had mentioned Fool's Webcaps, pointed them out with his stick.

The internet journey ended with the exhortation for worried mushroomers to seek help fast, and the heart-stopping fact that in the case of poisoning by the mycological genus *Cortinarius*, the first unspeakable symptoms lie undiscovered for up to three weeks. By that time all the internal arrangements had been made for death.

Putting aside the unfathomable poisoning of Ella and possibly Ben, did that mean that Zac was a candidate for serious damage or death?

This was madness. Olly decided that the analyses of samples had been wrong. They'd got the wrong poison – surely. Things like that sometimes happened in hospitals.

Nevertheless, Olly frantically searched for more information on mushroom poisoning. He grasped eagerly at *"charcoal treatment to absorb toxins..."* and *"encouraging experiments with extract of milk thistle"* and *"treatment with corticosteroids."* Then came the heart-stopping *"No known antidote."*

He could not read on. His eyes were filling with tears. Closing his phone, he strode back to Ella's bed, pulled the plastic chair close and held her hand, carefully avoiding the shunt, holding her finger ends. He wanted to be in bed with her, holding her.

The doctor came in and said: "Your friend's arrived. You're right – he looks in fine shape. Come on, let's have a talk."

He led Olly to a small room where Zac sat, holding a cup of water. He stood and with his spare arm pulled Olly to him and said: "Bear up mate. We'll sort this together. It'll be fine."

It was the warmth in what Zac said, and the way he said it, that released a torrent of tears, Olly covering his face with his hands, embarrassed.

The doctor sat on the desk but then, as Olly cried quietly into his hands, pulled up a chair so he was as close as possible.

"Your young friend Ben has just arrived and although he has to have tests, and probably some treatment, he's quite bright. It's possible that he just had a simple stomach upset, quite coincidentally. But we'll have to check him for poison."

He said that what they all should be pleased about, in all the doom and gloom, was that Ella had presented early, and this meant that what treatment was possible had started, and that Ben appeared so perky and reported that his nausea and shivers had eased.

"We're looking at research but we know that generally there's a relationship between the amount of poison consumed and the degree of damage you get." Seeing Olly's anxious, attentive gaze, he said, "*Can* get."

"And the other good news is that you, Zac, steered clear of the mushrooms – and that finally we can make sense of it all!"

Olly looked up astonished. *"Steered clear of the mushrooms"?*

"Sorry, mate, you missed me saying what happened that day," Zac said chirpily.

The doctor sat back. Unresolved problems irritated him. He was relieved to have Zac's description of what happened, and he was sure that Olly would be stronger when he knew that there was a rational explanation. The poor man had a great deal to face.

"Remember I was going on to a meeting, Ol? Well, when Ben brought me the mushrooms, they really did pong of garlic. I thought: I can't go down there reeking. Anyway, Ella offered me her omelette with the bits of spud in – nice and plain, did me fine. I had a bit of the fried bread and Ella tasted the mushrooms."

"Did she have all of them?"

"No, she just nibbled, sort of, out of curiosity. There was some left when I went."

Then Olly had a flashback. He remembered frying the mushrooms and having to go, and asking Ben to take the plate out to Zac, and Ben cutting off a bit of the cooked mushroom with the edge of a fork, drawing in air as he ate it because it was scalding hot, and saying: "Needs salt chef. And if it was my dish I'd mix in a splash of cream."

Dutiful Ben – following orders, tasting everything. And he could have been dying at this moment as result.

No, not as a result of tasting, as a result of me being careless and stupid, Olly said to himself. Me going up there thinking I was an expert on mushrooms, not checking to see if the gills were wide, not checking to see whether there was a trace of a cobwebby veil, the veil that Gus had shown me when he pointed to the webcaps with his stick.

He berated himself. The punishment – Ella being so ill – fitted the crime because he will suffer the guilt for the rest of his life. He resolved that if Ella were to die he would follow her.

The doctor was anxious to get back to other patients. He stood up and said: "So, gentlemen – bingo! Chanterelles in disguise, I think. The mycology man says that telling the nasty guys, webcaps, from chanterelles, can be problematical."

"I made a terrible mistake, I know," Olly said gravely.

"Well, what I say is: Stand up the liar who never made a mistake," the doctor declared, patting Olly's back. "Now let's get on with the damage limitation..."

Olly and Zac were left in the corridor as the doctor hurried off.

"Look, don't worry about the restaurant, Ol. I'll go and see them all. You just think about Ella. Good to hear that Ben's out of the woods."

"I don't know what to say."

"Don't say anything Ol. But you know, I really didn't think you hated me so much that you'd to try to see me off with that dodgy lunch!"

Zac laughed. Olly remained silently desolate, his head down.

Perhaps Zac had stumbled across some unspeakable truth, one that it was too terrifying to confront and as a result had been turned into a joke.

Olly said to himself: "No matter how much I despised Zac and resented him, I could never have done that. I could never put down the poison, like Mick does with foxes." But he knew that it was just the sort of thing Olly No 2 might get up to...

38

When he went back to the ward, a sudden surge of weakness came over Olly, making his knees slacken under him. It was the feeling of abandonment. Ella was no longer in the curtained room. She had gone, within minutes.

This special sort of terror was familiar...

It was Tilly forgetfully leaving him to walk home alone after school and him taking the wrong turning. It was being barged and losing Dad in the crowd that summer in Southend, and roaming around for hours, finding his way back to the bed-and-breakfast while they searched and searched down at the beach.

It was when Sophie choked, almost died, on a piece of apple, while Jane was out shopping, with Dylan laughing as he turned her upside down, begging for help. It was Dad falling dead next to the car that day, at the school sports.

If, when he had planned to be a writer, Olly had been challenged to find a word to describe this feeling, he would have failed; there wasn't one that captured the frightfulness of it. But if he'd been asked to invent a word he would have said *aloneness*.

It was the experience of losing touch with whatever anchored you in life, stopped you being in terror of being set adrift, like being pushed back and letting go of your dad's hand.

In panic, Olly checked that he was in the right curtained bay. He was. But Ella had gone and the dialysis unit had gone. There were two nurses making up a bed which might or might not have been the one that ten minutes earlier had been there, with Ella, propped up, piped up, wan and weak, her head sunk helplessly into a supporting pillow.

He stepped away from the curtains to look round the open plan department. There was no sign of her. He asked the nurses what had happened to the patient who had been in the bed, and one said: "Sorry. Not sure. We've just come on. I'll check. Was she due to be discharged?"

The nurse went to a corner where there were desks and a clutch of computers, and a notice board showing initials and times and other information. He could hear the nurse asking a colleague for Ella's whereabouts, and for a dreadful moment thought he heard the word "resus." Resuscitation? So they were fighting for her life somewhere...

When the nurse came back she said: "Mix-up. Sorry. She's in *Renal*, two floors up. She might still be in the lift."

Renal. As the relief washed over him, like a warm bath, he wondered: Was this a place where very sick people went to be kept alive, or where sick people went to get better? He feared that Renal would be a coping, and not a curing, kind of place, a place where people sat with their life-saving machines wondering what the point was in staying alive.

He walked upstairs and as he reached the doors to the ward

the lift doors opened behind him and there, on the trolley, was Ben. Olly leapt forward as the porter tried to push the trolley out of the lift, and at the same time tried to stop the doors closing.

"Gents! Let me get this thing out!" he shouted but Ben and Olly were oblivious as their hands clasped and their faces radiated joy, like soldiers who had gone into battle and found themselves still alive at the end.

"I am so sorry," Olly said.

"What for? I'm as fit as a butcher's dog, chef. It's cleared up. But Ella. Tell me."

"Ella's bad Ben. She's in there somewhere."

It was Ben staring hard and reaching out and grabbing Olly's arm that proved unbearable. Olly began to cry again, his face a still, sad mask. "What have I *done* Ben?"

Ben squeezed Olly's arm, hard, almost aggressively.

"Look chef – you made a little mistake that's had a big outcome. But that doesn't stop it being just one *little* mistake like we all make. She'll come through chef, you watch. She's a strong woman."

The porter looked impatient. Every day there were emotional events like this: death bed goodbyes, pre-op prayers, cries of the doomed, joyous smiles when eyes opened and there was light and life and a nurse promising a cup of tea.

A nurse took Olly to Ella's bedside. There had been a change. There was some colour in her cheeks and she looked to have a sleepy awareness of where she was.

He held her gently by the shoulders and kissed her forehead and pulled a chair to her bed. He was tearful again, and started to try to say that he would give anything to swap places.

She shook her head. "Don't say anything Olly," she said breathlessly. "Not now."

She turned her face to the hospital window as if looking for some revelation.

"But I just don't understand. You could have killed Zac..."

she muttered as if more puzzled than condemning. "I just don't understand..."

"And I don't, El. It was as if it wasn't me involved. Must have been stress. I know I'll have to live with it so don't worry, I'll get my punishment. But I just want you to be well."

Ella fell asleep almost immediately. He fetched a sandwich from the hospital café. He brought a second chair and placed it facing, so that he could put his feet on it. He tried to settle his big frame on the flimsy chairs but it was excruciatingly uncomfortable.

An old adage passed through his head – the one about making your bed and then having to lie on it.

◇ ◇ ◇ ◇ ◇

Zac did what he had always done, for some years anyway, when life was too much, when Dad had been too much, when he was sick of striving to get the edge on business deals, tired of having to come out on top to live with himself.

He went to the Bliss Spa. As usual, he would shower first, then swim until he was breathing so furiously he was shipping water, and lie on a poolside couch –and then go from hot room to the pool, glide gently for a length or two, sit in the steam room and put on his eye mask and lie in the meditation suite.

The routine, relaxing as it was, never quite flushed away the dross of a really bad day. Often the knowledge that by being more hard-faced, there might have been just a bit more to be squeezed out of a deal, would linger like a bad taste, sometimes for days.

Zac knew that he had been bred to win in business, not just to succeed. He also knew that it was expecting too much to think that today the regime would do anything but relax the neck a bit and refresh the body.

He chose the hottest spot in the steam room and lay his towel on the warm tiles and shut his eyes listening to tiny dripping noises and feeling sweat and steam mingle in minute rivulets down his body.

The glass door swung open and through the steam he was disappointed to see that it was someone he knew. His much-needed peace and quiet – to come to terms with Ella's illness, and his dad's illness, and Tinker – had been denied.

"Zac boy!" said the young man, his premature baldness casting doubts about the youthfulness of the chubby face beneath it. "How goes it?"

"Trev," said Zac. They shook hands and sat side-by-side like two Roman senators in a bathhouse, comparing health and wealth and ways in which they would vouchsafe both of these.

Trevor had yet another estate agents' office opening, and had plans to start a really cool web site service for landlords and tenants. Normally, Zac could have matched him boast for boast but today he would have to give Trev the satisfaction of knowing that he'd not only had a shit day, he was having a shit life.

"So Maurice is ailing, poor fella?" Trev said, wiping sweat from his eyes with the corner of his towel.

"We thought it was his stomach. It's his chest. He's had an X-ray that showed something but Dad being Dad paid for another at a more expensive clinic hoping that the extra money would mean he'd get a picture without the nasty dark bit. He didn't. It's bad."

"Poor bugger. Sorry to hear it Zac. But, anyway, how's the restaurant doing? You know Melanie and me went for our anniversary? Brilliant! Cracking chef."

Zac described how everything at *Zac's* was up in the air, how he'd just left the hospital, how Olly's reputation was now up the swanny.

Trev punctuated Zac's commentary with "*No way!*" and "No *fucking* way Zac!" until he was struck mute by Zac's description of his visit, and what had happened to the mushrooms Olly had cooked, and how Ella and then Ben had fallen ill.

"Zac. I want you to tell me again. Are you saying that this chef cooked mushrooms for you and that it was only by chance that the other two dipped in when you changed your mind?"

"Yes. They were too garlicky. I had a meeting straight after."

"So how well have you been getting on with this Olly?"

"Not so well. We've been bosom buddies for years, but Dad kept rattling Olly's cage, didn't really appreciate the great work he'd done. I was piggy in the middle."

"But Zac – those bloody mushrooms were meant for *you*. Surely you can see that! It could have been – no, it *should* have been – you up there in the City Hospital with pipes coming out of you."

Zac found this idea ridiculous. He was feeling slightly overcome by the heat and put his head in his towel over his head and protested through the curtain of material: "No, Trev. Not in a million years. Olly's been terribly stressed. I saw that. So *angry*. Our fault; he had too much on."

"But he didn't need to try to see you off. Bit of an overreaction perhaps, attempted murder?"

"Bollocks Trev! Olly's been brilliant. He just made a mistake. Actually he was trying to give me a treat because we'd made peace. Even did me some fried bread!"

"We'll give him remission for the fried bread then."

Trev was not convinced and said so: "If you want the man-in-the-street view of this, not knowing this Olly, I'd say that he wanted to give you a bad bellyache or worse. Come on Zac – a chef like him shouldn't be getting his mushrooms mixed up."

Zac felt dangerously hot now and so he shook Trev's wet hand and said he was going to find somewhere to chill.

"Go easy Zac. And watch what you eat! Maybe like those old kings you should hire a food taster but I won't be applying for the job."

Zac smiled, raised a hand and closed the door on Trev's laughter. He walked to the meditation room, put on his eye mask and lay down.

He decided to visit Ella tomorrow. It was only now, in the

quiet, that he could really think of her, and examine the anxiety he'd carried about her since he heard the news. She was so wonderful, a mixture of kindness and integrity and ambition and talent. He hadn't come across many women like Ella.

They could never have become a couple, he knew that now, but it was what he had wanted. Ironically, in getting close to her for one weekend he had revealed himself to her, and in doing so she put him at arm's length.

So all he had was a memory of that weekend, and although she had never mentioned it since, she would also carry that memory but (he suspected) with some regret that it had ever happened.

It was in a college break and it was his birthday. Olly was away, Richard had not yet joined them.

Ella had no money even for the fare back to Milton Keynes to visit her mother and planned to spend a couple of days painting. Zac was at a loose end; all the college people were away.

He took Ella for a drink at the pub in Tanganyika Road, and by closing time he had persuaded her to go with him next day to a matinee at a theatre in the West End, and then go on to a hotel where there was some sort of murder mystery entertainment that involved guests in identifying the killer.

"All on me, El. The folks were extra generous this year for the birthday. I really need someone to help me spend it."

"Sounds brill," Ella had said and then, quickly: "And the sleeping arrangements?"

"As you prefer madam," he remembered saying. "Rhodesia Terrace rules can apply if you want. Pyjamas under another layer of clothing, big socks and four paces apart."

"Yes then. I'll come."

Being so much younger, Ella was less trained in hard drinking and after a couple of half pints there had been a noticeable softening in her demeanour. He'd hoped upon hope that next morning she wouldn't cancel.

But, no – that night Ella had dug out her best dress, pressed it, found a pair of passable shoes and next morning they had set off on the Tube.

The show was mediocre, dinner excellent, or seemed so through the alcoholic haze that surrounded them. They laughed through the meal; Zac remembered having shone, as he sometimes had at parties.

Ella luxuriated in what for her was a new and heady experience – good food, waiters fussing, fine wine and the fun of playing out a silly drama at the hotel with convivial, half-pissed strangers.

She had chosen to sleep on top of the bedclothes but at some time after they'd fallen asleep she found herself being pressed to Zac and not being able to resist pressing back. The next moments had been fierce and urgent and all over before either had surrendered to enjoyment of their bodies.

Ella had left the bed and was shuffling about trying to find her clothes. He'd called to her: "Come back El. Let's just lie together. That would be the best bit for me."

"No, Zac, I'll just nap on top of the bed. That shouldn't have happened."

"But it did. The horse has bolted," he'd said, laughing. "Come back El."

She didn't and from then had always avoided being in intimate situations with him, and quick to point out that there would never be a chance for anything physical happening ever again. And it never had.

Re-living that weekend, beneath his towel and behind his eye shield, and having the time to think deeply, he was struck by a truth about their relationship that had never occurred to him. He had *bought* Ella that weekend. Bought her with wine, and a nice meal and a show, this young and needy girl.

He had bought Olly too, enticing him with a fib, getting him to build the restaurant with Dad's stingy budget, getting him, a friend, to create an asset for them. And in doing this he had bought Ella once more, exploiting her good nature and playing on her vision for *Zac's* and their need for a home.

There had been a rake-off from their friendship. He and Dad had creamed off a percentage.

"Now I owe them," he said to himself. "I owe them big time."

He began applying his mind to salvaging the most he could from *Zac's*. He was sure it would sell as a going concern on the strength of the first year's trading. But he wondered, just wondered, whether there was more to be made by splitting the building into two with, maybe, a really top-notch country wear outlet in one, and a small but high quality Chinese or Indian restaurant in the other.

The area was full of horse-riding people, and folks in tweed hats and oiled jackets: it was a touristy area for country walkers. There was no chip shop, no fast food outlet, for six or seven miles, so a tasteful little restaurant doing takeaways would do a bomb. It should be OK with the planning people; it would just replace an existing restaurant.

Zac took off his eye mask and sat up. Suddenly he was filled with self-loathing. He asked himself: What sort of a bloke *am* I?

Poor Ella might be dying up there at the hospital. Olly's at his wit's end; people have killed themselves in these situations, when they've accidently ruined the life of a loved one.

I haven't even told the *Zac's* staff that the show's over (and it surely is; who wants to eat at a place where the chef poisons you, never mind whether it's accidental?).

And here I am, he said to himself, sitting here like God, planning to wipe out *Zac's* at a stroke, and already moving on to the next earner, wondering whether the garden at *Zac's* is big enough to make a car park for the new Chinese.

It was not an easy fact to face but as he headed past the pool edge to the changing rooms he opened himself up for it, dropping his guard and taking a big punch.

I'm worse than Dad, he said, I really am.

But maybe, he thought, there's a saving grace. Unlike Dad, I'm going to see Ol and Ella all right. I owe them.

39

Olly stirred, stiff and aching, at about three in the morning to find a nurse tending to Ella, checking the paraphernalia surrounding her, easing her head forward and plumping her pillow. She seemed quite alert. She smiled feebly towards Olly.

He edged his chair forward and held her fingertips. Her hair was lank and her speech lazy.

"Does it hurt?" he asked.

"Not now it doesn't. I think what I had before was kidney pain. And my muscles were tender from being sick so many times."

Olly was so relieved to hear Ella speak a full sentence. He took it as a shining omen in a black sky.

"They've tried to explain it all, what they're trying to do, and how they hope it might end up but I can't seem to take it in."

Olly wondered when, exactly, she would ask him how he came to poison her, and why he had tried to kill Zac, because it looked like that. That's what any reasonable person might think. But she mentioned nothing about the incident.

"What have the doctors said to you about me? Is it going to be all right?" she asked objectively, not at all as if it was her life was on the line, or that she might be tethered to a machine for hours several times a week.

He gently squeezed her fingers. "Not a lot, just that it was good that you were sick so early and came to hospital straight away and that you didn't eat a lot of the..." He couldn't quite bring himself to say mushrooms. They were death caps, deadly poison, and *he* had put them on a plate.

"They're constantly monitoring you, seeing if the... (he couldn't say the word poison)... stuff has cleared a bit. Checking how well your kidneys are coping, and seeing if they're healing."

"Is Tilly coming?"

"She's coming today, this morning some time. She's mortified. Tearful for you. And the *Zac's* lot bunch their love. You should see the lovely messages on my phone."

Ella let her head fall back, and her eyes close for a moment and then she said: "How's Zac taken it all?"

"Appalled. But you know Zac, and the way he is about emotions. He's seeing everyone at the restaurant today. He's going to look after everyone, including us – or so he says. We've no worries, Ella. There's no worry but you. I can't even begin to say how sorry I am and how much I love you."

He gazed at Ella hoping that she might return the sentiment. But she just turned to one side and said: "I have to sleep."

◇ ◇ ◇ ◇ ◇

Zac wasn't good at speaking in public, despite all the debating he had been forced to do at school, all that pressure to be assertive. He felt quite exposed as he stood at the bar of the restaurant with the staff round him. The quiet, as they gathered – as requested in his emails – was disconcerting. Everyone looked glum.

He began by saying that the "accident" would mean that the restaurant would have to remain closed, certainly until things "resolved themselves." Then he delivered the phrase that he knew would leave no doubt that *Zac's* was in fact shutting. Was shut.

"Obviously, with Ella's situation uncertain and Olly unable to be sure of his future for what might be a long time, we have to stay closed. Of course being closed for an unspecified spell will be damaging, coming on top of the incident. I'll be frank – there has to be a very big question mark over us."

The message struck home. He heard it in the low hum that went round the room and then died out in the emptiness of the restaurant.

Bridget stepped from behind two of the trainee girls to get nearer to Zac. She was pink with emotion and her chin was thrust forward truculently.

"When you say the question mark's over *us*, Zac, I take it you mean *us* (she swept her hand around) but not you. Because God forbid that *you* shouldn't be able to pay your way." Her blue eyes were icy and she kept them steadily on Zac who didn't answer.

The Pyggs made assorted grumbling noises and Janice tried to reassure two of the young waitresses.

Zac said: "Look, all I can say now is that if we can't survive this, as soon as that is known I undertake to do everything required to the letter."

Harry Pygg held his hand up, as he used to at school, and began to frame a question but Esme pulled his hand down and told him to hush ("Leave it Harry - he's not worth it," she said, just loudly enough for Zac to hear).

Bridget picked up her coat and fixed Zac with another stare.

"You've shut this place already in your mind, so you have," she shouted. "But you haven't the balls to tell us, have you Zac? Come on, admit you've shut the feckin' place before poor Olly knows whether he's on his arse or his elbow and with little Ella at death's door. Come on man, say it!"

Zac blustered but had no ready response to reach for. He decided to retreat and just said: "Thank you all. I'll let you know of any developments."

He remained at the door to lock up as everyone trooped out. As they passed him, the Pyggs gave him the nastiest look they could muster.

When everyone had gone, he looked round the restaurant, speculating as to where a dividing wall might go, and wondering whether it would be best to have the entrance to the Chinese restaurant round the corner, off the street so that there was no clash with the frontage of what would be a really upmarket shop.

He paced the garden one way and then the next and quickly estimated how many cars would fit in the space. It was roomy enough.

Then, in the car, he thought of Ella and for a moment at least was contrite. It really wasn't a time to be thinking of business.

◇ ◇ ◇ ◇ ◇

Olly would always remember – to his dying day, he would say – how Tilly had been when she came to the hospital.

She was calm, constructive, and positive but not before she had leaned forward and held Ella's face and then put her cheek against Ella's and stayed there for a long time. She then placed a huge bunch of orange gerberas at the foot of the bed.

"You dear thing," she said, looking in her handbag for a paper tissue. "We're going to make it right, Ella, just you see."

Then she turned to Olly and kissed him. There were no questions about how, exactly, it had all happened, just promises of support, loyalty to both of them.

She would see that everything was OK financially – "You were right, Ol, soliciting in the evil city pays pretty well," she said trying to normalise things with a little joke. Ella just raised her eyebrows; smiling would have been too much of an effort. She was sleepy again.

Olly walked out of the ward with Tilly and they talked quietly and hurriedly for a moment.

Olly wanted to say how the accident happened but she stopped him. "That's for later Ol. Right now, it's getting Ella back to some sort of health. Surely by tomorrow they'll have some idea about her future...?"

"I'm sure they will."

"I know this is crazy at this point Ol, and I know enough to understand that these things are complex, and that there's waiting lists, and matching and all that scientific stuff. But I would want Ella to know, if it turns out to be bad – and I'd want you to know too – that I'm a big healthy lump and I'd happily give her a kidney."

"Tilly. What a thing to offer. "

"Yes, it's a bit of a far-fetched scenario but I've thought about it and read up on it in the night. No kidding – if it's necessary and I happen to be made of the right stuff, she could have one of my kidneys. I've always carried a spare for times like this. Learned it in the Guides."

◇ ◇ ◇ ◇ ◇

Zac came to the ward next morning with lilies and a card. Another, giant, card arrived simultaneously from the *Zac's* staff and Olly received a text message from Richard in Mexico having sent him a message the night before.

He held up his phone and read out the message: "Please get well soon dear Ella. Celestial love to you at this time, as reward for all the love you give on earth. PS Yes, the bomb bay doors are firmly closed – Biggus XX (ie Professor Biggus)"

Ella showed little response, just the raising of the eyebrows that sufficed to show that she was touched.

"Old Biggus and his bloody bomb bay!" Olly said.

Zac laughed loudly and said: "Imagine him remembering *that* from so long ago...It's actually jokey! I don't remember Biggus ever making a joke. "

They sat inanely smiling, both remembering Biggus, rummaging through the mental memorabilia they had stored, recalling the endearing oddness that added piquancy to their later days at Rhodesia Terrace.

Ella's eyes showed that she was remembering too but she was still weary-looking. She would press the doctors to tell her whether the treatment was helping, whether she might recover.

After she had been examined, given more blood, and had her urine quality assessed, she thought she had heard a doctor at the other side of the plastic curtain talking about a new step forward.

She couldn't be sure but she thought he said that in the next day or two they might see how things went without dialysis. For the first time in days, she felt there might be a way back into life.

40

Olly woke refreshed, stronger. The sun was shining and there was a relaxed Sunday morning feeling in the hospital reception hall as Olly took the lift to Renal. Many visitors carried flowers, and led children into the busy entrance area.

Coming to hospital, sitting around, and then leaving, had become the main activity in Olly's life. He looked forward to it, although he had begun to dread the walk from the flat down to the empty restaurant.

He hated arriving back in darkness to see the tables still set, the napkins folded, fading dahlias in the little terracotta vases.

He thought about his disbanded team, about what had been left unsaid and how one day he would try to explain and make it up to them in some way. Ben. Bridget, Laura. The village girls, the trainees. He simply could not have wished for better.

Olly had noticed that over the past days, on Ella's ward, a community consensus had begun to bind patients and staff. All formality had broken down.

Nurses had begun to ask Ella about Olly, and greet him warmly, and as they performed tasks around her they would ask Ella about her life, about how they'd met, ask which moisturiser she preferred, which TV soaps she watched, what she would do if she won the lottery.

As Ella gained strength she would ask about them, and – rather enviously – what they had been up to in the outside world she was excluded from.

Olly imagined that it was probably quite like this in prison. It was impossible to remain detached; people were curious about people; people wanted to connect.

When Olly arrived he waited at the bedside until Kath, a vivacious twenty-something with a wicked laugh and her head in the clouds, finished sorting Ella's catheter and began describing a wild hen party that she'd attended the weekend before.

Olly was delighted to see Ella was listening attentively, and responding. It had to be a change for the better. Last night, as he left to get a full night's sleep, she had asked him to bring in a novel, her little radio, and stationery.

"Thanks Ol," she said as he placed the bag of her stuff on her bedside cabinet. Was that warmth returning to her voice? That had been the first "Ol" while she had been in hospital.

He was not to know, as he began to dare that Ella would be all right, that *they* would be all right, a second catastrophe was five minutes away.

When Kath and a colleague began to attach Ella to the dialysis machine, he left promising to buy her a magazine from the hospital shop.

He was queuing to pay when he decided to buy a Sunday newspaper, knowing that it would be a long day. It was then that he saw a photo of himself looking out of the front page of a tabloid.

Beside the picture of him – it was the one taken on the opening night at *Zac's* – was the headline: LOVE ROMP CHEF IN POISON RIDDLE – see Page 6.

This is a dream, of course it is, he said almost audibly – or is this insanity?

He bought a copy of the newspaper, folding it to conceal the front page, knowing that throughout the country countless thousands, perhaps half a million people, at some time today would be turning to page 6, something he couldn't wait to do, and yet feared to do.

He found toilets, and locking himself in, stood with the paper open, appalled, reading about rows in the *Zac's* kitchen, verbal abuse between him and Ella, "the sexy frolic in broad daylight" with a cookery course beauty, and finally the poisoning. The mysterious poisoning of his unhappy live-in partner when rare mushrooms found their way on to his stove.

He was trembling. He put down the toilet lid and thought of damage limitation, of fighting back.

This was a new treachery, someone paying him back, or paying *Zac's* back. He thought of Cat and her menacing email. He thought of Bridget and her anger – and was immediately ashamed; Bridget was a wonderful ally.

Ben? Laura? Never in a million years.

Then he smelled Pyggs.

He took the lift to the ward and asked to see the sister in charge. She was very busy but broke off and asked how she might help. He asked to go somewhere private and she frowned in concern; he looked so grey and frightened.

The sister took him to a small bay, away from the hubbub of the ward, and he told her that in a national newspaper today were some ridiculous accusations about him and he needed an assurance that no-one would let Ella see the newspaper or discuss the contents with her.

"It would destroy her," he said.

The sister thought a moment and then said that she would

brief her staff but that she had no means of policing what visitors might say. "If it's some sort of scandal, the place will be rife with it."

By the afternoon, the community feel on the ward had gone. The formality was back. There were no light-hearted exchanges. Even Kath seemed strictly practical now. They knew.

When he left that night, and looked at his phone, the list of messages appeared endless. He feared what some of these might say and decided to ignore them until he was in the flat. He needed peace to assess the gravity of it all.

But he couldn't delay making one call. A cry for help – to Tilly.

41

Tilly sat at the dining room table in the flat above *Zac's* with the Sunday newspaper opened at page six. She had a notebook beside her and she was wearing reading glasses, a recent necessity.

They had spent a couple of hours with Ella, and Tilly had noticed a big change for the better, an alertness. Olly had hoped that with this improvement would come a return to intimacy but Ella still seemed guarded.

She had deflected his attempts to talk about "it" in detail. The shame and guilt lay heavy, yet she seemed unwilling to say anything that would lighten the load. He could not read her emotions or intention.

Back at the flat, Olly watched Tilly from a seat in the corner, one leg draped over the other, slumped low in the chair, biting the edge of his fingernails.

"They suit you," he said. "Thanks," Tilly replied pushing the glasses a little further up the bridge of her nose.

"So what do you see through those new specs, eh Tilly? Tell you what I see. I see me never working again, not at chef level. Who'd want a mushroom fricassee I'd cooked?"

Tilly didn't reply. She was peering down at the newspaper, carefully putting a line under phrases.

Finally she said: "I'll tell you what I see. A libel action. Defamation, clear as day. "

She hesitated, looked over her glasses inquiringly and said: "Unless there are things I don't know...?"

Olly shook his head impatiently. "Wouldn't it be better if we just let it all die down, leave the lies, let people believe what they want. Anyway, don't libel cases cost an arm and a leg?"

"Only if you lose."

"Olly – they've ruined you. Portrayed you as a poisoner and a predatory womaniser. A foul-mouthed bully. That's what Joe Bloggs and his mate would say, down at the pub. They'd say 'He's a dodgy geezer; wonder what else he's hiding.'"

Tilly read through the article again, tapping the point of the pen on each phase she had underlined.

"Look Ol, I know you'll be straight with me. I want to ask you a couple of questions. But do *not* lumber me with things that I might not be able to help you with, things you'd have to tell another lawyer. No big confessions. Just tell me what I want to know, OK?"

Tilly wanted to know about the sex romp woman. Was there a woman, was there a romp. Yes, there was a flirtatious woman but the romp was a farce. It was an ungainly grapple. She asked whether what happened had been seen by anybody; he said that it hadn't.

She wanted to know how violent the rows had been, with Ella, and with Zac.

"Not especially bad."

"Come on Olly. I know you. I've seen your temper."

"Well, loud and nasty but no violence. It was the stress. I'd made things up with Zac before the mushroom business, and Ella and I kept having little phases where we were really, really happy. It was the stress"

She cleared up the business of the "rampage" with the gun; then she wondered who might have had reason to go to the papers.

The Pyggs, he said, without hesitation. "They're a couple who wash up. I could trust any of the others with my life."

Tilly took off her glasses and said: "Would any other people, apart from the Pyggs, believe that you would knowingly serve poison mushrooms to Ella to harm her, as the innuendo in this article suggests?"

Olly said: "God no. The mushrooms weren't for her anyway. They were for Zac. I did them as a treat on fried bread – he loves fried bread. Ella hates fried bread. Had too much of it when we were at Rhodesia Terrace. She had an omelette. But they swopped and she sampled the mushrooms."

She wrote down a few notes and said: "So you can't have intended to harm Ella. Sweet point to us. But Zac....? Olly, again, would anyone have believed that you would knowingly have given Zac something that would endanger his life..."

Olly thought for a moment but before he could answer Tilly held up a hand and shouted: "No! Don't say anything Ol. You might give me a cause to worry. It's criminal to give someone a nasty substance, and a step away from attempted murder."

Olly felt afraid at the mention of crime. There were some vindictive people about, people like the Pyggs, people like Cat.

Tilly said: "Look, I have to opt out but I know someone who'll go through everything with you, a solicitor and she knows a really clued-up barrister, a lovely man. I'll cover this bit financially, you know, the fees, and then we can see what the advice is. I really think we could make the pips squeak."

42

Olly pushed his breakfast plate aside, opened the bulky envelope and found, inside, three cards. One was for Ella, and there were two addressed to him. It was Jane's writing on the envelope.

Her card to him, tasteful white and almost funereal with its embossed message saying "Thinking of You", touched him. *"Devastated to hear about Ella and truly sorry for you. Keep fighting Olly – love Jane X."* A brief fizz and sparkle from the re-connecting of wires snipped long ago.

The card from the children was just a general "Hello Dad" greeting; they had written it under orders and with no explanation as to why it was necessary. Sophie's writing was now cursive and fancy; Dylan's drawing was of an alien in a chef's toque.

As he walked to the hospital he decided that today he would bite the bullet. He would confront Ella, now she was strong enough, about their future and her feelings for him, and he would ask the doctors about Ella's prognosis.

Ella had been cool with him, using her illness as an excuse to defer discussion of the mushroom incident and her plight. He knew that. He wanted to take his punishment from her, and then to see what could be salvaged.

Along the way, there was a big hurdle. He had emailed everyone to beg that they keep the newspaper article from Ella but she was bound to see it some day and learn about his "love romp."

But right now they both needed the doctors, who had been evasive, non-committal, to reveal how Ella would be in the future. Would she need dialysis, a transplant even?

In the event, when he reached the ward, and kissed her, she looked brighter than ever.

She told Olly, with excitement in her voice, that the consultant had just done his rounds and had mentioned, almost carelessly that "the improvement in the chemical side of things continues." The aim, he said, was for Ella to function fairly healthily with her own kidneys.

He had said: "I see you presented quite quickly after ingestion, as hopefully pregnant. You're a lucky lady to have come in so promptly – and eaten so little of the mushroom."

The news had brought colour to Ella's cheeks and it filled Olly with optimism about the future. He kissed her forehead and squeezed her but Ella seemed unresponsive, as if the news was for her alone to celebrate.

Once the nurse had brought Ella her drugs, and left, Olly said: "Look Ella. We're not talking, not properly. You're so cool with me. Maybe the wonder is that you're letting me sit here with you at all, after what happened. But I want you to say how you feel. I want to know how we stand."

The joy fell from Ella's face. She looked at Olly in a dispassionate way and it pained him to feel so excluded, unwanted.

"Look Ella. I wouldn't have harmed you for the world. You know that."

"But what about Zac?" she said coolly. "We would have been going to his funeral if he'd eaten those mushrooms."

Olly lowered his head. The bile was starting to flow.

"I'm not saying you tried to harm him. That would have been attempted murder I guess. And I'm not saying that it wasn't just a bad mistake over the mushrooms, caused by stress because lately I've been expecting you to crack up completely. But I can't get the bits to fit. You *know* about mushrooms. What I'm saying is that I simply do not understand. Nothing can move on with us until I do."

43

By the time the woods had been collected and handshakes exchanged, the tea urn was bubbling away merrily in the Memorial Hall kitchen. The opposition team didn't really care that they had lost: they knew that they were in for a treat. The village was famous for its post-match tucker.

The weekly carpet bowls evenings gave some of the less mobile villagers a chance to get out, to socialise and chat. Someone having double-glazed windows fitted, a child getting measles, a new pregnancy, a dog roaming the streets – these were all topics to sustain lively interest while scones were being scoffed, teacups topped up.

Tonight it was different. The level of conversation was feverish, anxious, speculative. Members of the visiting team stood agog, nursing their tea and feeling privileged to be with people at the very centre of a proper scandal. Heads shook in astonishment and hidden pleasure that "this" had happened here – "*Here!*"

The chatter was of guilt and innocence, near-death and infidelity, intrigue, tirades, kidney transplants, three-in-a-bed scenarios and of al fresco sex in full view of the old folks' home. The talk was also of the Pyggs, two of their own, village stalwarts who – it was generally agreed – had gone too far this time.

An eavesdropper, perhaps an amateur anthropologist, would have left the village not only with a good idea of what the Pyggs were like but also an understanding of this small and ancient community. They only had to listen...

"So the Pyggs must have actually gone to the newspapers! Esme can be a nasty piece of work. I bet she made the move..."

"I speak as I find and I hear that this Olly was a lovely man. Emma who worked there said he didn't eff and blind – not at her at least – like the paper said...."

"The thing is, that Olly chap knew what he was doing. Must have. He was always up Haig Hill with Gus bringing mushrooms back. Notice he picked the nastiest buggers he could find..."

"I hear that Janice wouldn't have anything to do with her mam and dad spreading the dirt. She's a decent girl. Remember the rumour they peddled about the new vicar...?

"That place was never going to fit in here. They're just city types who came to make a few quid..."

"I think it was one of those there love tangles that just careered out of control..."

"It's shut you know. Zac's. The owner came and sacked the lot. But the chef's still up there. Passed him yesterday. Looks like death."

"They say when the old folk looked out of their windows, they were at it hammer and tongs, him in his big hat...

"Mark my words, when they sell up we'll get a bloody nail bar, or a bloody massage parlour, or a bloody mobile phone shop."

The one thing that all would have agreed – the fair-minded and the rabidly judgmental, the censorious and the forgiving, the small-minded and the liberal – as they devoured their jam tarts and salmon sandwiches – was that there was nothing quite as succulent as a really good scandal.

The anthropologist would have called it *Schadenfreude*, in the absence of a English name to describe the delight that people – especially people in a small and cosy community – take in the misfortune of others. Especially people from "outside."

44

Jolyon's chambers resembled a deep brown cavern. The old panelling served as a backdrop for his luminous presence, his glinting intelligence, lolloping blond forelock and his pastel pink shirt.

His jacket was on his chair back and his sleeves were rolled up. He regarded the papers before him as he might have done an overgrown ditch that he was about to clear with furious energy.

"Just stop me if I err, Olly. Put your oar in."

He had the newspaper on his big polished desk, open at page six. He had a sheaf of pens, a big notebook of blank pages, and some papers from a solicitor friend of Tilly's. Somewhere in the papers, Olly guessed, were comments from Ben and Gus, Laura and Bridget, now back in Kinsale. Olly was sure they would have responded to the solicitor's inquiries.

You only had to look at Jolyon to know that you were hiring a very sharp brain. He spoke in long, convoluted sentences, facts gathered in and restrained like lively puppies. Olly suspected that this suave and slender product of good breeding was older than his looks suggested.

"So, Olly, this lot tell their readers that you're a bit of a shit. More than that – that you're a malcontent who roamed the countryside looking for poisonous mushrooms with which to kill your much-loved partner."

He pointed with his pen to the article. "Oh, and look! Evidently you are also the deranged slaughterer of wildlife, a rabid chef mouthing off at all and sundry. And what else? A bit of a goat, at the stove, drooling, primed to mount all the nice ladies coming to you to learn how to make choux pastry..."

Olly didn't know how to respond. He watched Jolyon chuck back the blond forelock and say thoughtfully: "That's what I'd have believed of you, if I'd not known you, and read about you on what they used to call the Clapham Omnibus. Mr Ordinary forming an opinion of someone from what's he's just read, in this case in a *national* newspaper, or the website thereof."

He added, with emphasis: "I stress *national* because this has great relevance. We must remember, as they must, that their squalid characterisation of you was for world consumption. Big audience, big libel, big damage – hence big damages."

Jolyon instructed Olly to stop him at once if any of the facts were wrong but he was about to offer a portrait of a different Olly, and an alternative version of events...

He said the Olly he had in mind was a committed chef of proven talent (National Young Chef of The Year – "long ago, but well done anyway!").

At a friend's invitation this Olly had built a healthy clientele within a year of opening the restaurant for a friend and had done so at ludicrously low cost. Sometimes, quite reasonably, this Olly railed against the meanness of the funders.

This Olly was loved by the staff, who regarded him as strong and fair and loyal, not to say inspirational.

Olly swallowed hard. Jolyon flicked the papers about until he found what he wanted.

He said that the impression, given by heavy innuendo in the article, that he had wanted to *harm* his partner Ella, was wrong: the reverse was true – he wanted very much to keep her alive because he loved her immensely, and he showed it by constantly trying to resolve their differences.

He was also often at odds with his friend and part-funder Zac but he persevered stoically, rebuilding bridges, mending fences. They were seen to hug on the very day that the mishap took place.

This Olly was attractive to women and, one day, a flirtatious – and perhaps neurotic – woman of substance ambushed Olly when he took her out, at her request, to see the restaurant garden. Olly rebuffed her and declined to have intercourse.

Jolyon stopped and his eyes brightened. He was almost salivating over the sweet dainties that would top off this truer portrait of his client.

"Far from being a wicked seeker out of poisonous fungi, a laughable idea, this Olly was a keen student of mycology as it applies to food; he had learned much on walks with a retired botanist and local worthy called Gus, who portrays Olly as a man of great integrity. A man who on every one of their many walks showed signs of buckling under the pressure being applied by others."

Jolyon went on to say that Gus, this academic Doctor, believed that if this Olly had picked poisonous mushrooms, he would only have done so by mistake and as a result of unbearable stress. Gus had used a telling phrase – "Here was a man breaking into pieces in front of my eyes."

Olly knew that he could not stem the tears. When they came, Jolyon nonchalantly reached into a drawer and pulled out a nicely pressed mauve handkerchief.

"Here we are, Olly," he said. "So much better than those soggy paper things don't you think?"

After Olly had composed himself, he said: "I've just thought, Jolyon. What about the woman. Cat? Could she make things bad for me? She's vindictive enough. There was a bit of a threatening tone when she felt she was being rejected."

Jolyon smiled. He had anticipated that one.

"I mulled this over, and I wondered whether this woman, married to a platinum-plated husband (is it a Maserati or something he drives?) would want to stand up in court and say: 'I have an inadequate husband, and therefore couldn't contain my sexual desire, so I leapt on the chef at my favourite restaurant and pinned him to a bench."

He tittered to himself. Then he said: "As you know, Olly, correspondence – amounting to an exploratory howl of outrage – is already underway, on your behalf, and although the opposition has yet to blink, I sense that they'll already have a bit of a tic going in the eyelid.

"If it is decided that we go for them, and it gets to court, I want you to be reassured we'll have a couple of quite devastating grenades ready to lob..."

"One. The Pyggs. In their swinish desire for cash and to vent their malice (and malice is a juicy component in libel) the Pyggs told some... well, I was going to say *porkies*! And the thing about the Pyggs, not known to the newspaper, is that they have form."

He continued: "A couple of years ago the Pyggs defamed the bowls club treasurer. Gus, who was then chairman of the club, tells us he made them write a letter of apology which was displayed on the noticeboard of the village hall."

Jolyon added, with obvious delight: "Gus is quite willing to expose them as porky purveyors, malicious stirrers. They are known to be infamous and therefore should not have been trusted by the newspaper. It would only be fair if you sued them too, even took their sty from them. You will want to when you see copies of a couple of lie-filled emails they sent celebrating your downfall."

Jolyon pushed back his hair and began to laugh, his shoulders bobbing up and down. It was a chortly laugh, the kind that pranksters indulge in moments before teacher treads on the stink bomb.

"I love this bit..." Jolyon said, rubbing his hands.

"So, to grenade number two. The paper identifies Ella as the intended target of the noxious plot. Bad move. Why on earth would this Olly, who knew that Ella didn't really care for mushrooms, and who absolutely *hated* fried bread, serve both foods to her? No, quite reasonably he served them to Zac, a sweet gesture to his oldest friend?"

Jolyon didn't really need Olly's contribution or opinion because it was all as watertight, not merely as a duck's arse, but as watertight as the arses of an entire *flotilla* of ducks (a phrase he had recently taken to using when he knew that the opposition stood no chance).

"And all this has ruined you, Olly. Not really, of course, but for the purposes of this action, if it plays out, you are unemployable." He held up two cuttings from catering magazines.

"They've had the good sense not to repeat the libel but they've drawn attention to the scandal and said enough to inform your peers that, professionally, you're very bad news. Now wouldn't it be nice if the newspaper paid your wages in advance for the years ahead in order to say sorry...?"

Olly's consultation with Ella went less well than his talk with Jolyon. Ella wanted to see what the newspaper had written. On one occasion he said he had forgotten to bring it with him, and on another visit said that he had forgetfully left it in the car. He had run out of reasonable excuses.

He took in the newspaper but kept it folded on his lap at Ella's bedside until he had done groundwork to make his journey easier. The business with Cat had to be explained away.

"Oh yes – the paper," he said casually. Hurriedly added: "The barrister was brilliant yesterday. Says we can prove it's all a pack of lies. By the way, that woman who I'm supposed to have jumped on is that Cat, the one nobody likes. I think she's got a screw loose."

He looked inquiringly at Ella to see if she had swallowed the deceit but she was still chewing on it. "Oh," she said at last, taking the paper.

She read in silence, Olly watching.

"Well," she said at last. "I suppose that's *one* version of events."

Olly didn't like her tone. The phrase suggested that no objectively true version had been established. In other words, it was painfully, very painfully, obvious to him that she didn't know what to believe.

45

Ella rang Olly from the ward as soon as the doctor had moved on to the next patient. In a week she would be home. She would have some drugs and iron tablets for the anaemia they had discovered while monitoring her recovery.

The kidneys had healed nicely.

It seemed ungrateful to raise it but Ella wondered why she had been denied information about the level of improvement. She decided to find out.

The doctor who came to her, a young woman with shining hair, enormous glasses and a ready smile, said: "It's not untypical for patients who have this poisoning to go into remission for a few days, and then to regress rapidly. Go quickly downhill." She pointed to her feet to emphasise the point.

"It works in mysterious ways. It can lie undetected, quietly killing you inside. We daren't be too confident about our progress and so we had to keep you in the dark for while. But we were very watchful. We kept the good news to ourselves until we knew you really were on the way to recovery."

Olly had made a welcome home streamer. He had ensured the

flat was spotless and put a *boeuf bourguignon* in the oven an hour before he was due to pick Ella up.

Tilly had rung and squealed with joy when she heard from Olly that Ella was being discharged. As she was about to ring off she said: "Forgot to ask. How did it go with the dishy Jolyon?"

"Great. As you said, it's classic libel. He's written to them but he did ask, if they batted it back, whether I'd give it a go in court. He mentioned costs in the unlikely event that it went wrong but he was very bullish about the outcome."

"I've been thinking of that Ol. Costs. Risks. We'll talk soon. Hug Ella for me."

Then Zac rang. Olly didn't doubt for a minute that he was thrilled to know that Ella was well enough to come home but it didn't take him long to mention his plans for the *Zac's* building.

He had spoken to several agents letting business premises and taken a decision. They'd advised that *Zac's* might sell as a going concern; time would blur connection with the incident and allow a potential buyer to be found. But the way to quicker revenue was to turn the place into a shop or shops.

Zac had decided that a top-end outdoors shop and a high quality hot food outlet was the way forward; evidently there was plenty of Chinese money chasing choice sites for restaurants.

And then, he said to Olly – not pointedly but just by way of information – there would be the extra revenue from the flat.

"No hurry, of course Ol. Get Ella strong before you even think about your next step. And remember, I want to give a bit back somehow. You two have given me an asset."

"And how's Maurice?" Olly asked.

"Bad. He's just sacked his oncologist. Kicking the messenger I suppose."

"Oh dear," said Olly.

"Look, Ol," Zac said, "I'm going down for a meeting on Friday. Could divert to yours and say hello to Ella, drop some flowers in."

"Do that Zac. She'd love to see you."

46

In some contrary way, the arrival of the first hard winter frost seemed to warm Ella, to bring back the glow that had been dampened by illness.

Olly, ever watchful, believed that having had a close encounter with death she was finding exhilaration in the ordinary. The warmth she gave out had spread to him.

There had been a notable moment; she had laid her hand on his as they sat together, hearing the wind buffeting the window above the sound from some light and frivolous TV programme. He dare not respond but kept his hand still, grateful of the chance to make amends, rediscover normality.

They were to remember this phase of their lives as restorative. Ella had been steered through critical illness and was now looking for her mandolin, writing Christmas cards, being gentle with herself, immersing herself in books, challenging herself with ever bigger and more complex jigsaws.

It was another stage of Ella's healing, but it was doing wonders for Olly too. He had stopped hurrying; he cooked unadventurously but with care and love, waiting for Ella's approval at the first taste.

There would be her favourite baked aubergines tonight, and then pasta and crab. Ella had rediscovered wine, rolling it in her mouth as if she had taken the first sip of her life, her eyes closing in ecstasy.

They had luxuriated in the hours of time at their disposal. They were waiting for news of Jane's house sale and then they could start to plan knowing they had money behind them. There was some kind of a future.

Olly knew that Ella's vision for the future would include a baby but things were so good at the moment it was a subject they steered clear of. Strange, though, that she didn't talk about the possibility of suing the newspaper.

He believed that she didn't want to witness the public testing of the newspaper claims in case anything new and hurtful emerged. He knew that she had not removed the mental question mark she had placed over the incident involving Cat.

Olly rang Gus, whose pleasure in hearing Olly's voice – and his relief on hearing that Ella was now well – was palpable. They skimmed over events and Olly began to wonder how the conversation would ever end. Gus talked of his response to the lawyer's letters and how the village seemed to have turned against the Pyggs.

"Janice is *so* ashamed. You know they went off with a couple of reporters to a hotel? They're going to find life very uncomfortable."

He expressed disapproval of "that man Zac" who had shut the restaurant so peremptorily, who didn't seem to have any regard for the feelings of those who had created the place that bore his name. "Poor show," he said, "poor show."

It was Gus himself who did the signing off, although he wanted to talk and talk.

"Look" he said, "do take care dear boy. And every good wish to you both."

Olly tracked Ben down to a brasserie in the city and sent him a text.

He rang in his break and in seconds lifted a load from Olly's conscience, ridiculing the very idea that Olly should feel guilty about anything.

"One of those things, chef. Forget it. So Ella's OK? Can't tell you how that makes me feel inside. Tell her she's beautiful and that I'm still madly in love with her."

"Will do, Ben. How's the job? What's the next move?"

"Get Christmas over and then I'll have a look round," he said. "Got in touch with your friend Rafa. He phoned. From Spain, bless him. What a man! Absolutely *loves* you. He's still around Calella whatever-it-is."

"Calella de Palafrugell. Fantastic place. Out of the way. Sun. Fish. Kids jumping off rocks into the sea. Go if ever he asks you, Ben."

"He's got nothing to offer at the moment but he's marrying a local girl whose dad has a couple of restaurants, so you just never know..."

"He won't marry Ben. The bloke's been bobbing and weaving for years. Loves them and always leaves them. Tell you what, if Rafa *does* marry, I'll show my bare bum in your brasserie."

"I eagerly await developments, chef. Could you make it a Saturday when we're always packed out?" Ben didn't properly say goodbye, and Olly suspected that it was because he had been overcome by laughter, or had remembered something that was burning on the grill.

It's not a homosexual thing, Olly said to himself, but some men you *love*, absolutely *love*. Men like Ben. Men like Rafa. Men like Gus.

◇ ◇ ◇ ◇ ◇

When Olly went down to open up the main door, and Zac came in, he didn't look in any regretful way at the restaurant interior, as Olly always did when he passed through, and as Ella had done when she came back from hospital ("What a terrible waste," she had said, looking round, "and just look at my *poor* flowers").

Zac kept his eyes forward as we walked towards the stairs to the flat. This confirmed for Olly that already *Zac's* had been consigned to the company records as a stage in the expansion of the empire.

The talk was of Maurice's denial about his diagnosis, of the cold, of Christmas plans, but anything of any import was avoided. They sat round the kitchen table nibbling biscuits and drinking coffee.

The question of the free tenancy of the flat had not been mentioned since *Zac's* shut and it came as a surprise to Olly and Ella when Zac broached the matter. He did so by wrapping what he had to say within a compliment.

"Seeing that place down there (he hadn't looked) makes me feel proud of what we did. What you did. Me and Dad didn't have any of the sweat and the tears."

"Maybe we could have soldiered on. People forget. We had a really loyal customer base. They kept coming back."

"No, Ol, it would have been like starting from scratch again. It was best left." He licked a forefinger and swept it round his plate gathering biscuit crumbs.

"I know I owe you. So don't hurry to get out of the flat."

Olly took this to be an early warning that he'd like a rent-payer in quite soon. He explained that Jane was selling their house and that he should receive quite a bit of money so they would find somewhere else to rent.

"No real hurry. But any time-scale on that, Ol?"

Olly felt anger rising in him: "Zac. You've just said you owe us. Yet I've got a feeling you want us out of this place. I feel that you think we're a drain. Now if you really do owe us, let us stay until we get the cash from Jane and I see where we're going with this libel thing. That could mean risking big money but then, it could be the making of us."

"Simmer down, Ol. There's no rush. And the libel thing. Tilly's been in touch. Did she say? She's willing to set aside dosh just in case you lose and she wondered whether I could match what she's risking."

Ella looked at Zac and said: "No, we didn't know. That's just like Tilly. But we can't let her."

They looked at Zac. "I've said that it sounds like a really strong case and I'd think about it and be in touch. Of course I'd like to get behind you but there's a lot happening at the moment, then there'll be Dad's affairs to unscramble."

"So the answer is no, Zac?"

"I didn't say that. I'll get back to her."

Next evening, Olly rang Zac and asked whether he had given any thought to helping with the financial safety net; if the newspaper decided to defend any action there would have to be money set aside, just in case.

"I am *really* sorry Ol but I can't really risk anything at the moment. I'm really extending myself. I've been taking a lot on."

"That's no surprise. But you're a man who likes a deal. What about backing us and pocketing ten per cent if we win? Or twenty per cent?" He said this with a cold disdain. "Does that sound like a better deal?"

"Sorry...I couldn't Ol...even though the odds are with you."

"So you won't do it for money, will you do it for friendship?"

There was no reply. Olly pictured Zac writhing, imagined the self-disgust.

He thought of the mushrooms and wished he had not been so heavy on the garlic. He put the phone down. If Zac really wanted to help, to act like a friend, he would ring back.

He didn't, and never, ever, rang Olly again.

47

Josephina had found Olly's Yorkshire puddings a great disappointment. Now she wanted to taste a real, English pork pie.

Olly took this as a command rather than a request. He couldn't resist Josephina, especially when she made a baby face and purred. It was her way of getting what she wanted. No wonder Rafa was so smitten and kept giving her babies.

Today he would make Josephina a pork pie, and serve it the English way with a nice, simple, crisp salad, bit of pickle; nothing fancy, nothing Spanish.

Having no mincer, he would chop the pork and he'd wrap the water crust round a big jar, and make jelly by simmering pork bones. It was Ibérico pork. He was intrigued as to how it might taste. He would chill the pie, saving it for late evening when the sun was going down.

They'd manage with a few *pintxos* and some olives during the afternoon when – Olly knew full well – the wine would flow as they sat in the swing seats, chatted and watched the yachts, the divers' boat going out, and the fearless boys flopping off the rocks and into the shimmering sea. He'd also do a *tortilla*, with Ella in mind. She never seemed to tire of damned tortillas.

Calella de Palafrugell was such a far cry from home where right at that moment, as the sun got up and hit the rocky outcrops, Britons would be turning back the clocks, turning on the central heating, and rooting out scarves and gloves.

Olly and Ella had never regretted for a moment settling here, leaving the little pub-cum-restaurant in rural Yorkshire, getting a couple to manage it for them, especially as the couple in question were Ben and that lovely wife of his, Ashley, so they could sleep easy.

They had never for a second regretted putting the money from the libel case into what really was a little goldmine. And they would never forget Tilly's unbelievable support, putting her house on the line knowing the vagaries of the legal system.

Olly knew that he could just about afford not to work. But he couldn't live without cooking, spreading pleasure, getting approval for his *"Ingles tapas"* and his *pintxos*. He still did not know the real difference between these and didn't care. They were just delicious morsels. He had invented one, involving garlicky prawns and an aspic glaze.

This was the kind of languid place where you tended not to agonise over things but to enjoy instead, to look out to sea, to roll up another slice of dried ham and let the cold wine wash it down to cleanse your palate for another slice. He thought of it as a barefoot, tee shirt paradise.

One thing that had struck him recently was that although he loved food, his main pleasure was in seeing others eat it; Ella dipping her baguette into the baked aubergines she loved, breaking a bit off her tortilla and nibbling it.

The job, working for Rafa, or rather his father-in-law, was hardly work. There were busy lunchtimes, but the food was simple, much of it was cold, customers were in no hurry, and the local produce was superb.

The *apartamento* was a bit cramped but for the last couple of winters, when there were few tourists, Rafa had installed Olly and Ella in a spacious place overlooking the sea.

Sophie and Dylan had been over for a week last winter but he'd not seen much of them. They'd been out each night looking for clubs, and, learning that Calella was more a place of gentle promenading, they got worse for wear in bars, threw themselves about in one or other of the two night spots for the young, and slept most of the following day.

When Tilly visited, they had tried to treat her like a queen. In fact, she pleaded for simple peace and quiet, a chilled wine in the afternoon. She had loved the area, sitting for hours sketching and writing, reading and then dozing.

When Josephina and Rafa arrived, Ella went to them and carried in the two bottles of wine they had brought and urged Josephina to be careful on the uneven path to the *apartamento*. She was heavily pregnant and was carrying Mateo, who was sucking his thumb. Ana, the elder child, walked alongside, looking as if she would rather be somewhere else.

The afternoon drifted by. The children were undemanding, Ella sending them away to do drawings, and make masks. It was dream-like up above the shoreline, in sight of the beach and the rocks where little figures moved about like ants. Rafa told Spanish jokes and constantly squeezed Olly's forearm, laughing in his face, occasionally stopping to lean over and kiss Josephina.

Towards sunset, Olly offered the pork pie to Josephina, formally, on a board, and they all laughed as he got her to cut it as if it was a wedding cake. Once wedges had been plated up and the salad bowl had been passed round, she tasted the pie, grimaced and made a play of wanting to spit it out.

Then she laughed, spluttering and scattering crumbs, saying *"Lo siento, amigo!"* pronouncing it *delicioso*, claiming that the black pig made all the difference.

When Rafa and his family had gone, Ella and Olly sat side by side on the swinging seat.

"OK," Ella said "Who's putting him to bed?"

"Your turn," said Olly."

They looked fondly to where Jake sat, teasing the dog. The boy was tired from playing in the sun.

He was rolling on his back, listlessly.

"He's dead beat and bored now Ana's gone. I'll help getting him showered and tucked up." Although they spoke of getting Jake to bed as a chore, it was nothing of the sort. They both delighted in doing it, jointly, singing with him, wrapping him in a towel, settling him, kissing him goodnight.

Olly got up and said: "You know, he asked today why he had black hair and brown skin and why we were different. Funny, he's never ever asked before has he?

"I explained about adoption, and I told him about his Aunty Tilly, and how Dad had said: 'Can I be your daddy now?' How people can choose a child to love if they don't have one. I said that we had loved him straight away, as soon as we saw him. He was very accepting about it."

When Jake was asleep, they sat, as they often did, in the dying light on the creaky, makeshift veranda with cups of coffee. The evenings for much of the year were like July evenings at home, after a scorching hot day. For some reason, Olly began to think of Zac.

"You have to wonder, don't you, about what became of Zac..."

"Yes. I sometimes do. Maybe we – you – really should have responded to him when Biggus was killed. Letting bygones be bygones and all that. He was practically pleading for things to be OK again. Didn't he want to organise some sort of a wake in Richard's memory?"

"Yeah. Seemed a bit false. Bit contrived. I prefer to keep my own memories of Richard, and I think you do. Anyway, things could never have been OK. Ever. He sent a photo with the email of him with the woman who looked a bit like you..."

Ella chose not to answer.

"Darling Biggus. So sad. So very sad." She said wistfully. "Not so much for Vi, who's so durable, more for Vega. Vi said she was inconsolable. Vi never let us know whether the driver got jail – or did she?"

"Can't think. I'm sure the driver wasn't to blame. You know old Biggus, he'd have stepped into the road with a headful of calculations going on in his head."

Olly sounded thoughtful. "You know, he absolutely doted on you. But it's such a long time ago. There was a time when everything was so intense, wasn't there? Looking back, you were right, I was so bloody insecure all the time, so unreasonable..."

"Always wanting to police me, read my thoughts, check my past!" They laughed together.

"But it doesn't work. We're not perfect and we can never be answerable, Ol. Somehow we got there. *Here,*" she said lifting her arm pointing to the sea that was now dappled with silver from a big moon.

Then she said: "We must never go back there. You know, to all the angst and anger. But there was one thing I always wanted to ask about..."

"Ask away, El. I know that now we could talk about anything, absolutely anything. We're so strong. I'm strong in that way."

"What it was, Ol, was about Zac and what happened. A little moment that I never forget. I've re-lived it many times now. It was when I was writing out menus and you were going through invoices, and you turned to me and said, quite out of the blue: 'They say Emperor Claudius was killed by poison in webcaps.'"

"And?" Olly said.

"That was just *before*, in fact the *day* before, you brought back the mushrooms that you wanted Zac to try. I've always wondered why poison mushrooms were on your mind at that precise moment..."

Olly was silent.

"The other was that one minute you'd been seething with hate for Zac, exploding, and the next you were all sweetness and light. It was as if a weight was being lifted off your shoulders...

"And one more thing, Olly, about those times, before we absolutely, *absolutely* promise never to mention this sort of thing ever again, was that the Cat woman – you know, 'sex romp' Cat – rang me."

God, Olly said to himself, what's coming? What other stuff does Ella know?

"She rang *you*? You've never said..."

"Yes. She said that she wanted me to know that you had lured her to the garden and then undid her bra and that the washing up lady – that would be Esme Pygg – could confirm it."

Olly's mind raced, trying to assimilate memories and the order of events, and recall who knew what. It was so long ago. He hung on Ella's words...

"Some partners would have believed her, she sounded so credible. And she didn't seem to have any reason to lie. But I know you better than that."

Olly sat in the darkness. He lifted his cup of coffee but put it down without taking a sip. He was thinking hard.

"But what does it matter in the big scheme of things?" Ella said. "Everybody has secrets, Ol. You, me, everybody. We have imperfections. We tell white lies out of love, and the blackest of black lies, sometimes to hurt. What matters is love and devotion to each other. Our love. And that darling boy in there."

She took Olly's hand and they stepped through the darkness into the dimly lit *apartamento*, past Ella's huge seascape near the door, past the mandolin hanging on the wall, to the door of the bedroom where their son was sleeping.

Olly said nothing but he was thinking...admiring Ella's good sense... agreeing with every word.

Books by
NEIL PATRICK

When **The Healing Hut** came out it was hailed as one of the most inspirational books of the year. It is both funny and sad and takes readers into the world of a young man called Kyff who believes that he will never recover from the loss of his wife.

In fact he finds salvation by occupying his late father's allotment hut, and by letting a host of colourful, caring and hilarious characters into his life. His despair drops away as he takes heart and helps his new friends to fight to protect the allotments, threatened by development.

Just Dying To Tell takes readers on a journey (by tandem!) with a sick man called Sniffer whose final wish is to tour the Fens where he grew up.

With his supporters, he camps out, drinks, laughs, argues and reminisces, enjoying the great outdoors and the familiar places they call at.

But Sniffer is carrying a secret and it is weighing him down. Will he come clean and reveal what he is dying to tell, before his life ends?

Lightning Source UK Ltd.
Milton Keynes UK
UKOW02f0055040916

282124UK00004B/79/P